POSTCARDS FROM THE DEAD

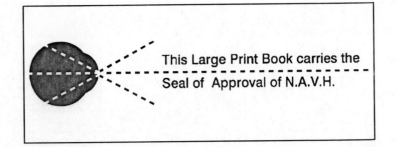

A SCRAPBOOKING MYSTERY

POSTCARDS FROM THE DEAD

LAURA CHILDS

KENNEBEC LARGE PRINT
A part of Gale, Cengage Learning

Detroit • New York • San Francisco • New Haven, Conn • Waterville, Maine • London

GALE
CENGAGE Learning·

LIBRARY OF CONGRESS CATALOGING-IN-PUBLICATION DATA

Childs, Laura.
    Postcards from the dead / by Laura Childs.
       pages ; cm. — (Kennebec Large Print superior collection) (A scrapbooking mystery)
    ISBN 978-1-4104-5284-9 (softcover) — ISBN 1-4104-5284-0 (softcover) 1. Bertrand, Carmela (Fictitious character)—Fiction. 2. Women detectives—Fiction. 3. Scrapbooking—Fiction. 4. New Orleans (La.)—Fiction. 5. Large type books. I. Title.
PS3603.H56P67 2012b
813'.6—dc23   2012028503

Published in 2012 by arrangement with The Berkley Publishing Group, a member of Penguin Group (USA) Inc.

Printed in the United States of America
2 3 4 5 6   17 16 15 14 13

POSTCARDS FROM THE DEAD

CHAPTER 1

A dazzling night filled with gigantic floats, silver beads, dizzying lights, fire-twirling flambeaus, and a crowd that was fueled by too much Dixie Beer and Southern Comfort. This Wednesday evening, the Loomis krewe's parade rolled through New Orleans's historic French Quarter, pumping out all the brazenness and utter abandon they could muster. And the city of New Orleans fairly sizzled, caught in the throes of another fantastical Mardi Gras celebration, beginning with the Epiphany and ending with that crazy-costumed, over-the-top super finale known as Fat Tuesday.

Smack-dab in the middle of it all, Kimber Breeze, the perky, Botoxed blond reporter from KBEZ-TV, stood on a delicate wrought-iron balcony outside the Hotel Tremain. Four floors above Royal Street, she chirped happily into her microphone and smiled broadly at the cameras as she interviewed various French Quarter denizens and broadcast parts of the parade spectacle live.

Inside, in the elegant but slightly frayed Bonaparte Suite, fifty costumed revelers sang and danced and whooped it up. Most were there for the free booze; only a few had been invited for actual interviews.

Carmela Bertrand, owner of the Memory Mine scrapbooking shop, was one of those waiting her turn on the balcony. Carmela wasn't a big fan of Kimber Breeze, but she knew a photo op when she saw one. And her business, still not fully recovered from that enormous hiccup known as Hurricane Katrina, could always use a punch of publicity.

"This is taking forever," Carmela drawled to her best friend, Ava, who had come along to keep her company. Having taught a morning class on stencils, then spent the afternoon unpacking boxes filled with new mulberry and banana leaf papers, Carmela wasn't in the mood for the zydeco music and the fever-pitch energy that pulsed through the room. Carmela would have preferred to be tucked snugly into her little French Quarter apartment, watching *Wheel of Fortune* and enjoying a calm, relaxing evening with her two dogs, Boo and Poobah.

"C'mon, *cher*, enjoy the party!" urged Ava. Ava was a party girl and former Southern beauty queen, while Carmela was clearly the laid-back cocooner. "Loosen up and live a little!"

Carmela smiled tolerantly and smoothed back a strand of honeyed blond hair from her short, choppy bob. Not quite thirty, Carmela was lithe and youthful-looking, with eyes the same flat blue-gray as the Gulf of Mexico, and lush lashes that tipped up slightly at the ends. Though her peaches-and-cream complexion rarely saw the need for makeup, she did enjoy the natural hydration properties of Louisiana's industrial-strength humidity. Carmela was also the one who favored more classic (okay, conservative) clothing in colors of navy, cream, and camel, while Ava, always willing to push the envelope as far as humanly possible, loved to dress in black leather pants and tight low-cut tops.

"Tonight's a school night," Carmela joked. She knew that tomorrow morning, come nine o'clock, she had to be primed and ready for the onslaught of customers that would pour into her shop. Most would be frantic to grab reams of paper, rubber stamps, and rolls of purple and green ribbon. All the better to create Mardi Gras menus, party place settings, and scrapbook pages.

"Oh my gosh!" Ava suddenly screeched, "I don't believe it! There's Sugar Joe!"

Carmela stood on tippy-toe and tried to peer over the heads of the costumed crazies. "Where?" Sugar Joe Panola was the best friend of her ex-husband, Shamus Meechum. But while Shamus was a rat fink of the first magnitude, Sugar Joe was actually a pretty decent guy.

"On the monitor, on the monitor!" cried Ava, pointing.

Carmela swiveled her head to where Raleigh, one of KBEZ-TV's camera guys, sat at a portable console. "Let's watch," she said. "See how it goes for him." *Maybe see what's in store for me.*

Over the years, Carmela hadn't enjoyed a particularly warm relationship with Kimber Breeze. Truth be told, whenever they'd had dealings with each other, Kimber had pretty much tried to sandbag her. But Carmela didn't hold with harboring old hurts and grudges. After all, what good did it do to hang on to them? Nothing, really. Unless, of course, it was a grudge involving an ex-husband. Then it was perfectly legitimate.

Threading their way through the rambunctious crowd, Carmela and Ava eased up to Raleigh and his equipment. Raleigh, who was middle-aged and favored khakis and T-shirts, seemed to have a perpetual hunch from lugging around battery packs, cables, and camera gear. And trailing after Kimber. And listening to her shrill, domineering voice.

"How come you're not out there with Kimber?" Carmela asked him.

"No room," said Raleigh, as his fingers worked the dials. "That balcony is a tight squeeze for even two people. So I've got one camera locked on Kimber, another one on the parade below, and one running in here." He waved a hand. "Which means besides being cameraman, I get to play floor director tonight."

"What does that mean exactly?" asked Carmela.

Raleigh shrugged. "Switching between cameras A, B, and C."

"And all this feeds directly back to the station?" asked Carmela, indicating the monitors. She found this technical part fascinating, akin to assembling a video scrapbook.

"That's right," said Raleigh. His brows beetled and he was suddenly on alert. "Oh hey, here we go."

Carmela and Ava watched the monitor as

Kimber interviewed Sugar Joe. Which, for the preening Kimber, pretty much turned into a flirt fest.

"Maybe she'll flirt with you," Ava said to Carmela, then giggled wickedly.

"Maybe she'll turn tail and walk away," said Carmela. She wasn't sure what Kimber's reaction would be to her. Stamp her foot and refuse to do the interview? Could happen.

On the monitor, Kimber gave Sugar Joe a warm hug. Then, a few seconds later, Sugar Joe came bounding in from the balcony. Sugar Joe was tall with buzz-cut blond hair and a broad, open face. When he saw Carmela and Ava he broke into a grin.

"Carmela!" Sugar Joe cried out. "And Ava!" He spread his arms wide open, the better to hug them. "You ladies look ravishing!" Sugar Joe told every woman within a two-mile radius that she looked ravishing. And he greeted each and every woman with, "Hello, beautiful!" Carmela decided Sugar Joe's boundless enthusiasm for the fairer sex wasn't the worst thing in the world.

"You looked mighty handsome on camera, Sugar Joe," cooed Ava. Ava had a way with the opposite sex, as well.

But Carmela was more interested in the broadcast. Raleigh had switched to the parade feed now, capturing an enormous pirate ship that was gliding by, illuminating the night with thousands of white twinkle lights.

"Now this feed's going to the station?" she asked Raleigh.

"It's going there, but not live," he told her. "It's being automatically archived for later."

"But a portion of this broadcast will be live?"

Raleigh glanced at his watch and seemed to tense up. "Oh yeah. In about eight seconds." He slouched forward and spoke into his microphone, "Okay, Kimber, time to cut in for station ID." He paused while he twiddled a dial on his console. "Kimber?" he said again. "Better be on your toes, girl, because I'm coming to you live in five." Raleigh stole another quick glance at his watch, then began his countdown: "Five, four, three, two . . ."

But when Kimber's monitor came on, no one was there.

"Crap!" whooped Raleigh. He frantically keyed her microphone. "Kimber," he hissed, "you're *on*!"

A blank screen. Still no Kimber.

Suddenly a blur of motion flashed across the screen, and then Kimber's face was pressed tightly against the camera's lens in a grotesque grimace.

"What?" cried Raleigh. He jerked back. "Oh man, now the lights went out! Jeez Louise, I gotta switch my feed!" His fingers quickly pushed buttons, cutting over to the parade that was lumbering by below them.

Was Kimber just goofing off? Carmela wondered. Was she being a pill and trying to rattle poor Raleigh?

But something didn't sit right with Carmela. From her perspective, Kimber had looked . . . terrified. "No, put the balcony feed up on the other monitor!" she cried to Raleigh. "Something's wrong!"

He shook his head. "Can't. The klieg's down. No light out there."

Carmela stood motionless for one more second, knowing it wasn't her place to interfere. Then she quickly reconsidered and pushed her way through the almost impervious, partying crowd and out onto the balcony.

Arriving slightly breathless on the little half-circle balcony that hung out over the street, Carmela stopped dead in her tracks. Bizarrely, Kimber was nowhere to be found.

Huh? Where on earth did she disappear to?

Carmela blinked and glanced around again.

Kidnapped by space aliens?

She saw only two cameras, locked in place, their dark lenses and all-seeing red eyes staring indifferently at her.

As Carmela fought to figure out what strange trick had just been played, shrill screams echoed from the street below. Startled now, she turned and glanced down. An enormous pink-and-gold dragon float was rolling by, the dragon's ten-foot-wide gaping mouth spewing smoke and shooting sparks, while an enormous tail wagged back and forth across the entire width of the street. Perched high atop the dragon's spiky back were at least forty white-robed krewe members tossing strands of silver beads to the screaming, deliriously happy crowd.

But still the screams persisted. And now the crowd wasn't just crying out for beads! Now, horrified faces were upturned.

Looking at me?

Puzzled, Carmela glanced down and saw a fat black cord snaked tightly over the balcony railing.

Leading to . . . ?

Her heart did a slow-motion flip-flop. Then, with a feeling of dread and a swirl of vertigo, Carmela leaned farther out over the narrow wrought-iron balcony and gazed straight down.

That was when Carmela saw Kimber's

lifeless body dangling ten feet below her and gasped in horror. Kimber's face was a massive purple clot. One slender high heel hung from her foot; the other foot was completely bare. Then a spotlight from the dragon float suddenly angled its bright light upward, revealing Kimber's twisting body. And Carmela's scream rose in a frantic plea, mingled with hysterical shrieks from the crowd below.

CHAPTER 2

Horrified, trying to get a grip on her initial shock and almost paralyzing wave of fear, Carmela jerked herself back upright. Was that really Kimber Breeze dangling from a black cord? Yes, it was. Oh, dear Lord, yes it was. With her face all purple and her body so limp it looked practically devoid of bones!

Hot gorge rose in the back of Carmela's throat and then receded. Gasping, she sucked in great gluts of air, fighting her overwhelming nausea and trying hard to clear her brain. She knew she had to summon help. Immediately. Squaring her shoulders, Carmela prepared to step back into the suite and sound the alarm. As she did, she glanced hastily right, then left. And saw that the nearby balconies practically kissed up against the very one she was standing on.

Could someone, presumably Kimber's killer, have escaped onto one of those rounded balconies? Of course they could have.

Tilting her head back, Carmela gazed upward and saw a metal fire escape, really just a rickety ladder, bolted to the exterior of the Hotel Tremain. It led, presumably, to the rooftop. Another escape route? It could be. Unless the killer had somehow slipped back into the suite, where the revelers continued to drink and dance and shout greetings to each other.

A nightmarish scene, Carmela decided. Almost akin to some sort of twisted, locked-room mystery.

Then the party screeched to a halt as two hotel security guards crashed into the suite at the exact moment Carmela stepped in from the balcony. And, like a black poison tide gliding in atop the waves, the shocking news of Kimber's demise suddenly spread throughout the room.

And that was when the worst possible thing that could ever happen happened. Panic struck and the crowd began to scatter! A costumed Punichello slipped out the door. A vampire and a skeleton slithered after him. Two Chinese opera characters followed in their wake. Then a stream of show-girls and top-hatted gents that included Sugar Joe!

"No!" Carmela cried. She pushed her way over to one of the security guards, an older man with a lined face, a cap of white hair, and a walrus mustache. "We've got to keep everyone here!" she told him, as people continued to dash past them. "These people are either witnesses or suspects!"

But it was an impossible task, like herding cats.

People pushed their way toward the double doors, then oozed their way down the various stairways and elevators even as the fire department arrived outside, red lights flashing and sirens blatting, to raise their ladder up to where poor Kimber still dangled.

And five minutes after that, when a contingent of police finally arrived in the Bonaparte Suite, only a handful of people were left.

"This is preposterous!" fumed Detective Bobby Gallant. "There were fifty people in this room and now there are six?" Gallant was relatively young for a detective, with a dark complexion and swirl of dark hair, dressed in a black leather jacket and chinos. He was usually cool and unflappable, but tonight he bristled with fury.

"We tried to keep them here," Carmela told him, "but it was impossible. Everyone

19

kind of panicked." She knew Gallant fairly well, knew that he was a credible, careful detective who had solved more than his share of homicides.

"What about you two?" Gallant barked at the security guards. "What were you guys doing?"

The hangdog expressions on the guards' faces pretty much said it all. They were rent-a-cops through and through. No street experience, no expertise in crowd control, and they'd certainly never dealt with a homicide. Not even close.

"They tried," said Carmela, coming to their defense, "they really did. But everyone got scared and bolted."

Gallant turned his attention to Raleigh, who sat crumpled and dejected before his monitors and console. "I sincerely hope you have a guest list," he said.

Raleigh looked sick. "Just a list of the people Kimber was supposed to interview."

Gallant shook his head, as if a swarm of angry bees were buzzing around him. "It's a start." He pointed a finger at one of the uniformed officers who had accompanied him. "Gary, you talk to everyone who's still here and try to get them to remember exactly who was present in the room."

"Everyone was in costume," said Ava.

"Some of them even wore masks." Even though Ava pretended to be indifferent, Carmela could tell she was shaken by Kimber's death.

"Peachy," sighed Gallant. "Makes our job that much harder."

"What about the cameras that were recording?" asked Carmela. "Maybe something there?"

Gallant lifted an eyebrow. "That might help."

"Raleigh?" said Carmela.

Raleigh nodded. "Sure. I guess." He moved woodenly, as if in a trance.

Gallant looked around the room, then back toward the balcony. "What kind of crazy crap was going on here, anyway?"

"Maybe a better question," said Carmela, "is who had it in for Kimber Breeze?"

Gallant focused on her. "Seriously? From what I understand, the woman was amazingly popular. Then again, TV personalities generally are."

"But Kimber had her detractors, too," said Carmela.

"You included?" said a rich baritone voice behind her.

Carmela whirled about swiftly and found Detective Edgar Babcock gazing at her. He was, of course, her sweetie and personal

21

cuddle bunny. Aside from that, Babcock was tall, lanky, and handsome. His ginger-colored hair was cropped short and neat and his blue eyes were constant pinpricks of intensity. Amazingly, he was always well dressed. A cop with a curious taste for designer duds.

"Detective!" Carmela cried out. She would have much rather flung her arms around Babcock's neck and delivered a huge kiss, but he had rushed here for a murder investigation. So . . . she had to show some decorum.

"What have we got?" Babcock asked Gallant.

"Victim hung over the balcony," said Gallant. "Rubber cord around her neck."

"Witnesses?" asked Babcock. Now he switched his gaze to Carmela.

"None," said Carmela. "At least I don't think so."

"None that we know of," said Gallant. "Yet."

Carmela and Gallant spent two minutes filling Babcock in. He listened, nodded, then stepped out onto the balcony. Carmela followed him.

"You shouldn't be out here," said Babcock.

Carmela glanced down to where two firemen were gently passing Kimber Breeze's lifeless body down to a pair of EMTs in blue jumpsuits. "Neither should she," she said. A white ambulance had pulled up onto the curb, its red light twirling lazily. No hurry now.

"Seriously," said Babcock. "Why were you here? You do, after all, have a somewhat checkered past when it comes to dealing with the notorious Miss Breeze."

Carmela shrugged. "The TV station was doing real-people commentaries and play-by-plays. As part of their Mardi Gras coverage. One of their producers called and asked me to participate, so I figured why not?"

"You didn't know Kimber was doing the interviews?"

"No, I did not. Not until I got here."

"But even when you saw it was her," said Babcock, "you decided to go ahead. Maybe gain a little extra publicity for your scrapbook shop?"

"Publicity never hurts," said Carmela. She glanced down again and saw that a shiny black medical examiner's van had pulled up. On the other hand, she thought, maybe this kind of publicity wasn't so great. Then she noticed that, ten feet away, the parade revelers had seemingly gotten bored with the Kimber Breeze incident and were now drinking from *geaux* cups and snatching beads out of the air. *Laissez les bon temps rouler.* Let the good times roll. Even in the presence of death.

Then again, Carmela told herself, people in New Orleans lived with a constant reminder of death. The aboveground cemeteries, or Cities of the Dead as they were famously called, loomed everywhere. A reminder that all good things must end.

"Lieutenant?" Bobby Gallant stood in the doorway looking out at them.

"Yeah?" said Babcock, turning.

"We've got some TV people who just showed up," said Gallant. "The owner of the station and a reporter. They want to do a live on-the-scene report. And maybe ask you a couple of questions."

"Okay," said Babcock. "Obviously we can't say much at this point, but I suppose we could get the public involved. There's a good chance somebody down below saw something." He hesitated, tossing around the pros and cons for a few moments, then made up his mind. "Maybe we can even get a description." He looked directly at Carmela. "Yeah, a TV interview is probably good exposure."

"So go expose yourself," said Carmela.

24

■ ■ ■ ■

The owner of KBEZ, dressed in a charcoal-gray three-piece suit and sporting a gold Rolex on his wrist, greeted Babcock with a somber expression. "Ed Banister," said the man, extending his hand. He was chubby and bespectacled with a fringed ring of gray hair, like an old-fashioned friar, around his shiny pink dome. "Anything we can do in the way of cooperation, just ask."

"I understand you want to do a live broadcast," said Babcock. He wasn't swayed by Banister's offer to help. Babcock knew darn well this was an opportunity for KBEZ to own the story and leapfrog the other TV stations and print media.

"Yes, a remote," said Banister. "Obviously we'd like to be first out with this story because she's one of ours. We'd also like to interview you, too, detective, and . . ." He glanced at Carmela. "Carmela? Is that your name? You were first on the scene?"

Carmela nodded. "I'm Carmela Bertrand. And, yes, I ran out onto the balcony and found Kimber."

"We might want to do a second interview with you," said Banister. He glanced over at Raleigh. "Seeing as how our equipment is

25

all set up and ready to go." Banister seemed to consider his words, then glanced at Babcock again. "That's if we have your permission, detective."

"Fine with me," said Babcock. "Truth of the matter is, your broadcast might help shake things loose for us."

"Exactly my thought," said Banister, nodding.

"So if you do your news story, then I say a few words, that should serve both our purposes," said Babcock. His brow furrowed. "Only, who's going to . . . ?"

"I am," said a young woman, elbowing her way to the front of the pack.

"This is Zoe Carmichael," said Banister. "She's a sort of apprentice at KBEZ-TV." He sounded just this side of nervous.

But Zoe wasn't.

"I can do it," she said. She waved in front of her face a small microphone that was attached via cable to a battery pack clipped to her belt. Petite, with a mass of reddish-blond hair, Zoe had a pert nose and cherubic smile.

"Raleigh?" said Ed Banister. "Kindly make this happen."

Zoe, looking both confident and eager, scurried over to confab with Raleigh. Two minutes later, he'd positioned her in front of the balcony door, aimed a key light at her, completed a sound check, and was back manning his equipment.

"You're going live?" asked Carmela. She'd watched and listened to the proceedings with great interest. It seemed incongruous to her that the TV station Kimber Breeze worked for would jump to capitalize on her death like this. On the other hand, it *was* a heck of a news story. *Pretty, sexy TV reporter murdered on balcony overlooking crazy Mardi Gras parade.* It had *ratings* written all over it.

"The control room will cut into our regular programming," explained Raleigh. "They'll put a news flash visual on the screen and then we'll go live." He was answering Carmela's question as well as explaining to the young reporter Zoe exactly how it was going to go down. He fiddled with the dials on his equipment, then moved behind a camera and focused his lens directly on Zoe. "Okay?"

Zoe did an exaggerated smile, wiggled her shoulders to shake loose any tension, then said, "Okay. I'm as ready as I'll ever be."

Raleigh pulled on a headset, listened to the instructions from the control room back at the station, then began his countdown.

"And five," said Raleigh, splaying out his

fingers. "Four, three . . ." He counted down silently until one finger pointed at Zoe.

"This is a KBEZ-TV news alert," said Zoe. "We're coming to you live from the Bonaparte Suite at the Hotel Tremain, where, just moments ago, a brutal murder took place on the balcony behind me. Sadly, the victim was our own reporter Kimber Breeze." Zoe allowed for a dramatic pause, then seemed to adopt an even more somber tone of voice. "While doing a broadcast from this fourth-floor balcony, Kimber Breeze was apparently strangled by an unknown assailant. With a makeshift noose wrapped around her neck, Miss Breeze plunged to her death." Zoe tilted her head, as if considering this. "Obviously, the police suspect foul play."

Raleigh gestured to Babcock, who stepped in next to Zoe. Raleigh pulled back on his camera lens and, suddenly, a two-shot appeared on the monitor.

Zoe asked a few quick questions, which Babcock handled effectively, and then Raleigh moved the camera back in for a close-up of Zoe. "We at KBEZ-TV are as stunned and shocked as you are," said Zoe. "If you know anything, anything at all, please contact our tip line at the bottom of the screen. And, rest assured, we'll continue to bring you up-to-the-minute news on any and all developments." She paused. "This is Zoe Carmichael coming to you live for KBEZ-TV."

"Good," said Banister, after a few seconds. "Excellent." His mood seemed to have improved.

Zoe beamed.

As Detectives Babcock and Gallant conferred with Banister once again, Carmela sidled over to Zoe. "You were very composed," she told her, "considering the circumstances."

"Thank you," said Zoe. She looked thrilled. And energized by her turn in front of the camera.

"You've been a reporter at KBEZ for how long?" asked Carmela.

"Actually, I've been Kimber's assistant for almost three years. Tonight was the first time I've ever been allowed to do a live report."

"This was your first?" said Carmela. She was surprised and impressed with Zoe's poise and composure. On the rare occasions she'd had to do public speaking, she usually downed a Xanax.

"I was working down the block when I got the call," said Zoe, "doing the odd bit of generic footage and commentary on the parade." She rolled her eyes. "As if they'd ever use it. Plus they put me with the C-team cameraman, a guy who seems to delight in cutting off the top of my head."

"Do you think you'll stay on this story?" Carmela asked, curious about this young go-getter.

"I hope so," said Zoe. "Of course, it's up to Mr. Banister, the station owner. "But if I do good . . ." She tilted her chin up and her eyes fairly sparkled.

"Then you'll be a regular on air," said Carmela.

"That's my dream," said Zoe. "That's always been my dream." She turned to Raleigh and said, "I want to interview her, too. Maybe the station can run it later." Zoe smiled at Carmela. "Okay with you?"

"I suppose," said Carmela, as Ava gave a thumbs-up.

So Raleigh adjusted the lights again and Zoe and Carmela stood facing the camera. When Zoe received the high sign, she smiled at Carmela and said, "We're talking to Carmela Bertrand, owner of Memory Mine scrapbook shop here in the French Quarter. I understand you were a witness?"

"No," said Carmela, "I was actually standing inside."

"Then how . . . ?" Zoe began and trailed off.

"I noticed some movement on the monitor," said Carmela, "and that's when I stepped out onto the balcony to see what was happening."

"And you found Kimber Breeze," said Zoe. "Hanged."

"Yes, apparently so," said Carmela.

"What happened next?" asked Zoe.

Carmela hesitated. Should she tell Zoe that she immediately checked out the adjacent balconies and fire escape? That she'd already inadvertently launched her own amateur brand of investigation? No, that probably wasn't a good idea.

"I immediately sounded the alarm," said Carmela. "I suppose I was in a mild state of shock. Or panic."

Zoe asked a couple more questions that Carmela neatly sidestepped, and then the interview concluded.

"Okay, thanks," said Zoe. She didn't sound particularly enthused. "There might be something we can pull out of that."

"Great," said Carmela. She took a deep breath.

Together, they wandered back out onto the balcony.

"So this is where it took place," said Zoe.

"I would have liked to shoot the police interview out here, but Mr. Banister cautioned me not to be too specific. I guess he's saving the actual locale stuff for our ten o'clock news." Zoe said it so casually, Carmela was a little taken aback. Then again, maybe if you were a newsperson covering a daily dose of murders, kidnappings, drownings, and robberies, you got a little impervious to it all. For your own self-protection and peace of mind. Or maybe they just became an endless litany of sad stories.

"Do you think —" began Carmela. The rest of her words were drowned out by high-pitched shouts. A man, angry and obviously in pain, was making a huge fuss at the door of the suite. Gallant rushed to meet him and a frantic scene suddenly developed out in the hallway.

"Let me through! Let me through!" cried a man. His face was blanched white and he was waving his arms furiously as the security guards sought to restrain him.

"What on earth?" said Carmela, peering inside. Then she saw him determinedly force his way past the security guard, even as he brushed at his tears.

"Oh my gosh," said Zoe, in a hushed tone.

"Do you know who that is?" asked Carmela.

"That's Davis Durrell," said Zoe.

"The hotshot money manager?" said Carmela. She'd heard of Durrell. Who hadn't? Durrell had been touted as some kind of financial wunderkind. And, over the last several months, he had racked up serious press in the business section of the *Times-Picayune.*

Zoe nodded. "He's also Kimber's boyfriend."

CHAPTER 3

"What happened?" cried Durrell. His jacket and tie were askew, his eyes were darting and frantic, and he looked shaken to the core. "Where is she?"

Babcock crossed the room with two long strides. Carmela heard him do a rather professional introduction. Then he put a hand on Durrell's shoulder and spoke in hushed tones. Durrell listened with an unbelieving look on his face. He said, "No, no, no," three times, then snapped his mouth shut, looking drained. Babcock spoke some more, and then Durrell shook his head in utter confusion and clenched his jaw, as if trying to nullify Kimber's death through sheer force of will. Trembling, still listening to Babcock, Durrell finally dropped his head into his hands. Anger, denial, acceptance.

Babcock stood there looking uncomfortable. His role as a homicide detective was not to comfort the bereaved, but to pursue the killer. But Babcock was a gentleman and, as Carmela well knew, possessed a good deal of sensitivity.

A few minutes later, Durrell seemed to pull it together. He ground the heels of his palms in his eyes to brusquely wipe away tears, then growled out a couple of more questions. Carmela couldn't hear Durrell's words, but she surmised they concerned the circumstances of Kimber's death. Then Babcock turned and nodded in Carmela's direction.

Carmela gave a start. *What? Me? What can I possibly add to the conversation?*

But Durrell had already pulled himself away from Babcock and was bearing down on her with a determined look.

"I'm so very sorry," Carmela told him, after they hastily introduced themselves and shook hands. "My sincere sympathies."

"Detective Babcock told me you were here the entire time," said Durrell. "He said you were the one who found her." Durrell fairly quivered with intensity. His dark eyes flashed and color was returning to his cheeks now, giving his handsome face with its full lips and aquiline nose an intense, eager appearance.

Carmela nodded. "I was here in the suite,

yes. Along with a lot of other people who were hanging out. Before and after their interviews."

"But they all left," said Durrell. "Fled like rats," he snapped.

"I'm afraid so."

"When it happened, you weren't actually out . . . ?" Durrell's voice cracked as he turned to stare at the open doors that led to the balcony.

"No," said Carmela. "I wasn't on the balcony with her. No one was."

"Someone was," said Durrell.

Carmela swallowed hard. "Well . . . yes. I suppose that's true."

"But you were the one who found her," Durrell pressed. "You sounded the alarm. At least, that's what Detective Babcock seemed to imply."

"I ran out there," said Carmela, "when I saw that something was . . . amiss."

"Amiss," repeated Durrell. Tremendous pain shone in his eyes.

Carmela bit her lip. *Amiss* seemed like a horrible choice of words. Far too lightweight considering the terrible scene she'd just witnessed.

"Do you think . . . ?" began Durrell. He licked his lips and fought to keep from falling apart. "Do you think she suffered?" His voice was an anguished whisper.

Carmela thought about Kimber's purple puffed face, her body twisting helplessly, the lifeless pose, the dangling shoe. And did what she thought was best. Lied through her teeth. "No, I don't think she suffered."

Twenty minutes later the crime-scene investigators arrived with cameras and lights and gear stowed in black leather cases. And Carmela and Ava were pretty much hustled out of the suite.

But not before Babcock asked Carmela a few more questions. "Do you know him?" Babcock inclined his head toward Kimber's boyfriend. "Durrell?"

"I've never met him before," said Carmela. "Why?"

"You just seemed . . . friendly toward him."

"No," she said, "that was compassion. Sympathy. The same as I'd show to anyone who'd just suffered a traumatic loss." Carmela thought for a moment. His question seemed strange. "Why do you ask?" Was Babcock jealous, she wondered? Was there a little green monster perched on his shoulder? Or did he see Durrell as a suspect?

"No reason," said Babcock. His eyes slid over to Durrell again.

"But you know him," said Carmela. "Don't you? This isn't your first meeting." Something was going on, only she didn't know what.

"I know him only by reputation," said Babcock. He stepped away as Ava shuffled up, clutching a drink in her hand.

"That poor man," said Ava, indicating Durrell. "You can just feel his pain. It's *visceral*."

"What a mess," said Carmela. She meant it as a blanket comment, referring to Kimber's murder, the mob that had fled, the bombshell broadcast, and any evidence the police were left to sort through.

Ava nudged Carmela with her shoulder. "C'mon, *cher*, let's blow this pop stand. Let's head over to Mumbo Gumbo and get something to eat. Maybe a nice stiff drink, too. Do us both a world of good."

"I don't think I could swallow a single bite," said Carmela. Still fresh in her memory was the image of Kimber's purple face.

"Then you can have a little chuglet of wine," urged Ava. "As for me, I can always manage to choke something down. Especially when it's shrimp jambalaya or crab étouffée."

"You do have the ability to eat through

any crisis," said Carmela. "But what I can't figure out is how you stay so skinny."

"Nerves," said Ava. "I'm just a bundle of frazzled nerves."

"You seem pretty relaxed to me."

"I hide it well," said Ava, grabbing Carmela's hand and giving a tug.

But just as Carmela and Ava stepped out into the hallway, Raleigh came charging after them.

"Hang on," said Raleigh. He gave a furtive glance to make sure nobody was watching. "I want to give you something." He pulled a small black square out of his pocket and slipped it into Carmela's hand.

"What's this?" Carmela asked. It looked like a cartridge of some kind.

"A CF card," said Raleigh. "Compact flash. You know, a memory card. It's the digital recording I made of all the people milling around. Before . . . you know . . . the murder."

"You don't by any chance have a recording of what happened on the balcony, do you?" asked Ava.

Raleigh shook his head. "Afraid not." He still looked shaken as he turned his attention back to Carmela. "I don't know if I captured anything important or not, but I wanted you to have a copy. Just in case."

"Why me?" asked Carmela.

Raleigh pursed his lips. "Because you're good at what you do."

"Scrapbooking?" said Ava, puzzled.

Raleigh lasered his eyes on Carmela. "No, investigating." He drew a deep breath, then said, "This may come as a surprise to you, but Kimber admired you, in a grudging sort of way."

"What are you talking about?" said Carmela.

"Kimber didn't *like* you," Raleigh continued. "Not in the conventional sense. But she thought you were plenty smart."

"Really," said Carmela. His words pretty much dumbfounded her. Kimber had always projected an attitude of disdain. And now Raleigh was telling her that, underneath it all, there'd been grudging admiration? This was almost too much to absorb. Something did not compute.

"The video," said Raleigh, pointing at the digital card. "I'd appreciate it if you take a look at it."

"The police have a copy?" said Carmela.

"They haven't asked for one yet," said Raleigh.

"Then why give one to me?" asked Carmela.

"Like I said, because you're good at

investigating," said Raleigh. "I know you've helped Babcock crack a couple of cases."

"I got lucky," said Carmela.

"No, you got good," said Raleigh. "Remember, I work in a newsroom, so I get the inside poop on what goes down in this town. I know how you helped with that murder at the church." He paused. "Just look at it, will you? As a favor to me. See if you can spot anything or anyone that's out of place. Something you think looks a little hinky."

"I can't play this," said Carmela, turning the card over. "I don't have your kind of equipment."

"Then come by the station tomorrow," said Raleigh. "I'll transfer it to a DVD."

Carmela thought for a long moment. "Okay, I guess I can do that."

Mumbo Gumbo was a cozy little restaurant located in the old Westminster Gallery space. Crumbling brick crept halfway up the interior walls, and then the ensuing smooth walls were painted a cream-and-gold harlequin pattern. A large bar, the color of a ripe eggplant, dominated a side wall. Above the bar, glass shelves displayed hundreds of sparkling bottles. Heavy wooden tables with black leather club chairs were snugged next to antique oak barrels that held glass and brass lamps. Large bumper-car booths were arranged in the back. Potted palms and slowly spinning wicker ceiling fans added to the slightly exotic atmosphere of the place.

The music tonight was blaring zydeco interspersed with haunting Cajun ballads, while about fifty people seemed to be jostling at the hostess stand, trying to get a table. But Carmela had an in. She'd once dated Quigg Brevard, the owner. Not seriously, but not frivolously either. They'd had a couple of fun dates, though nothing had sparked. Only now that she was involved with Babcock, Quigg seemed to think she was primo dating material again. So when Quigg spotted Carmela across the proverbial crowded room, he hurried over.

All broad shoulders in a sleekly tailored Italian suit, Quigg was dangerous looking with his olive complexion, dark eyes, and sensuous mouth. And with his big-cat way of moving, he could almost take a girl's breath away. Almost.

"Hello, sweetheart," Quigg growled at Carmela. He kissed her on the cheek, but landed only a half inch from her mouth.

"Hey, sugar," said Ava.

Quigg's eyes never left Carmela. "Hello,

Ava." Then he snapped his fingers and, like a magician's attentive assistant, the hostess quickly appeared at his elbow.

"Booth six," said Quigg.

The hostess, a tall dark-haired woman in a sleek black jumpsuit, looked suddenly discombobulated. "The Duvall party's been waiting over an hour for that booth!"

"They'll have to wait a little longer," said Quigg.

Carmela, Ava, Quigg, and the unhappy hostess caravanned to the booth, where menus were produced and a bottle of wine was brought out.

"This is new from my vineyard," said Quigg. "Something I call Ruby Revelry." He filled gigantic Riedel glasses with the lush red wine, then squeezed into the booth alongside them. Quigg was your basic obsessive-compulsive oenophile, dying to know what they thought of his new St. Tammany vintage.

Ava immediately took a gulp and pronounced it superb. Carmela took a demure sip and smiled.

Appeased, confident in the quality of his new wine, Quigg leaned back and said, "What trouble have you two been in tonight?"

Carmela sighed and said, "Oh, not much.

We just witnessed a murder."

Quigg's dark brows arched. "Seriously. Who? Where?"

"Remember Kimber Breeze?" said Ava. "From KBEZ-TV?"

"The hot blonde?" said Quigg.

"Bingo," said Ava.

"She's dead?" said Quigg. He looked surprised.

Carmela and Ava quickly filled him in.

"Ah, man," said Quigg, when they'd finished their tale. He looked shaken and genuinely shocked. "She comes in here all the time."

"Came," said Ava. "Kimber's in the past tense now."

Quigg shook his head in disbelief and squinted at them. "I think she might have been in here earlier tonight."

"Really?" said Carmela, her ears perking up.

"Seriously?" said Ava. "Wow, that's some crazy coincidence."

"Can you pin that down for sure?" asked Carmela.

"I can try," said Quigg. He jumped up from the booth and loped over toward the hostess stand. He was back a minute later with one of his servers in tow, a young blond woman with a pert pixie cut named Misty.

Quigg made hasty introductions, then said, "Misty says she waited on Kimber earlier. Around . . . what do you think? Five o'clock?"

"That's right," said Misty, nodding.

"You're positive it was her?" asked Carmela.

"The lady from the TV station?" said Misty. "Oh sure, it was her."

"Do you still have the credit card slip?" Carmela asked. She wanted actual confirmation.

"They paid cash," said Misty. "But I'm one hundred percent positive it was her." Misty was nervous and fidgeting now, as if she'd been called to the school principal's office. "You want to know what she ate?" Misty asked.

"Actually," said Carmela, "I want to know if she was with anyone."

"Um . . . yeah she was," said Misty. "A guy."

"What kind of guy?" asked Carmela.

"He was decent looking," said Misty, giving up a little smile. "But his clothes were a little shabby."

"Do you think it could have been the guy we saw tonight?" Carmela asked Ava. "Her boyfriend, Durrell?"

Ava shook her head. "No way. Durrell had

45

that fat cat look. Nothin' shabby about him."

"What does a fat cat look like?" asked Quigg. He was slightly bemused.

"Like you," said Ava. "Zegna suit, big honkin' Rolex. Lots of snap and attitude. Like . . . rich."

"I'm not rich," said Quigg.

Ava snorted. Quigg owned two restaurants and a winery. That amounted to a significant net worth.

"So," said Carmela, interested now, "it doesn't sound like the same guy at all."

"Maybe Kimber had another boyfriend." Ava smirked. "Maybe she liked to go slumming once in a while. I wouldn't put it past her."

Misty shrugged. "Maybe."

"Did you by any chance catch the dinner companion's name?" asked Carmela.

"She called him *something*," said Misty. "As I recall, it was kind of an unusual name."

"Try to remember," urged Carmela. "It would be very helpful."

"It's important," said Quigg, trying to add emphasis, "because Kimber Breeze was murdered tonight."

"Murdered!" Misty was suddenly shocked. She clapped a hand to her chest as if her heart had just constricted with pain. "That's awful! How was she . . . ?"

"Hanged," said Ava, casually taking a sip of wine. "Off the roof of the Hotel Tremain."

"Dear Lord," said Misty. Now she looked like she was on the verge of tears. "That's bizarre!"

"Yeah," said Ava. "Bizarre that it would happen right during Mardi Gras in one of the murder capitals of the world."

"The name?" said Carmela, trying to get back to the question at hand. "If you could possibly remember her companion's name?"

Misty cocked her head as she thought for a few moments, then said, "She called him something . . . like Dusty or Duncan. That's not quite right, but it was like that."

"You're sure it wasn't Durrell?" Carmela asked. "Davis Durrell?"

Misty shook her head. "Nope. It was something a little more unusual."

"Does that help?" asked Quigg.

"Maybe," said Carmela. "I think so."

"Have some food," said Quigg. "It's on me. Order whatever you want." He handed them two multipage accordion menus that Carmela had designed for him a couple of years ago. Back when they'd been dating . . . or not dating.

Ava didn't waste any time in perusing the menu. "I still can't believe all the gumbo variations!" she exclaimed.

"Quigg's got a thing for gumbo," agreed Carmela. Indeed, the menu listed chicken andouille gumbo, seafood okra gumbo, crab and oyster gumbo, and even lobster gumbo. Of course, there were also traditional New Orleans dishes such as crawfish pie, red beans and rice, alligator piquant, and chicken jambalaya.

Ava ordered seafood okra gumbo, while Carmela opted for a crab étouffée. And when the food arrived, along with a complimentary stuffed artichoke appetizer, Carmela found that she was, indeed, hungry.

"See?" said Ava, as she gobbled her gumbo, "I knew you could eat a little something."

"I think I could eat a lot of something."

"Good for you," said Ava, patting Carmela's hand. "Here, have some more wine." Ava topped off Carmela's glass as well as her own. Then she said, "Are you gonna stop by the TV station tomorrow and pick up that DVD?"

"I suppose," said Carmela. She knew Babcock would hate it if she got involved. Then again, that line had already been blurred. Like it or not, she'd been pulled into the murder by dint of just *being* there.

"We'll take a look," Ava said, giving a wink, "and see what we can see."

"Even though we don't know what we're looking for," said Carmela.

"You'll figure something out," Ava said, knowingly. "You always do."

CHAPTER 4

A rosy dawn peeped through the gauze curtains in Carmela's bedroom as she stretched languidly and rolled over to try to catch another ten minutes of sleep.

Then the memory of Kimber's murder flooded back to her and she sat bolt upright in bed.

Kimber. Was she really killed last night? Was I really there?

"Yes," Carmela said out loud. "Kimber's dead."

Boo, her wrinkly little fawn-colored Shar-Pei, who'd abandoned her cushy dog bed for Carmela's cushy people bed, let loose a wet, rumbly snore.

"What are you doing up here, sweetie?" asked Carmela.

Boo, who was lying with her back to Carmela, pretended not to hear.

"I know you can hear me," said Carmela.

Boo's tiny triangle-shaped ears twitched

and her eyelashes fluttered lightly.

"Get down, Boo Boo," said Carmela. "You know you're not supposed to be up here."

Now Poobah, her other dog, a spotted mongrel that had been rescued from the streets, was staring at her with rapt attention. He rested his muzzle on the edge of the bed and rolled his eyes as if to say, *Can anyone join this pajama party?*

"No, you little stinker," Carmela cautioned him. "You stay off the bed. There's a reason you guys have your own special overpriced dog beds." Carmela swung around and slid her legs out from under the covers, then brushed the soles of her bare feet across the white flokati rug. "You guys are incorrigible," she said. "Always pushing the envelope." She knew darned well that once they'd eaten breakfast, had their morning constitutional, and watched her latch the door and leave for work, they'd jump right back on her bed for a doggy slumber party. And sometimes even a pillow fight.

But what could she do? Lay down one of those nail grids the police used for stopping car chases? Huh, a lot of good that would do. Boo and Poobah were so smart they'd probably figure a way around it.

"Coffee," said Carmela. She pulled on a white terry cloth robe and shucked her feet into a pair of furry slippers. Then, her mind slipping back to the disastrous events of last night, she walked out into the living room of her cozy little apartment. "And not just any coffee. This morning I feel the need for French roast."

She stumbled past her dining room table and over to her small galley kitchen. Once, back when she was married to Shamus Meechum, of the Crescent City Bank Meechums, Carmela had lived in an enormous mansion in the Garden District. Once she'd had a housekeeper who set out bone china cups for her. Once she'd owned a six-hundred-dollar DeLonghi Lattissima coffee maker from Italy that had steamed, frothed, and au laited like a personal barista. But that was then and this was now. Her unsuccessful marriage had finally been dissolved and Carmela was infinitely happier, her soul delightfully at peace. And now her Mr. Coffee and dollar ninety-nine ceramic mugs were more than adequate. In fact, they were just dandy.

After measuring out a nice strong ration of coffee, she set it to brewing and plodded to the front door to get the morning paper.

What kind of front-page article would there be about Kimber's death? Carmela wondered.

Something lurid? No, that was more KBEZ's style. That and . . .

Carmela nudged open her front door and bent down to grab the paper. And noticed that a postcard, what people used to refer to as a penny postcard, was centered on top of this morning's *Times-Picayune*.

She snatched up both, assuming the postcard was some sort of advertising gimmick, and went back to the kitchen. A few years ago, just before she'd opened Memory Mine, Carmela had worked for a small design firm where she'd created print ads and newspaper inserts for Splendide Baked Goods and before that, package labels for Bayou Bob's Chunked-Up Chili. So she was more than familiar with the constant churn of advertising clutter.

Slapping everything on the counter, Carmela reached for her coffee mug. And suddenly stopped dead. Because a glance at the postcard revealed that it wasn't an advertising postcard at all. It was a picture postcard of a cemetery.

Huh?

She blinked in disbelief, picked the card up, and stared at it. It was sepia-toned with delicately scalloped edges, like something from an earlier era. The photograph — she was pretty sure it was a photo — depicted whitewashed tombstones against a tangle of black wrought-iron fence.

Turning it over, Carmela felt her heart do a sickening flip-flop. Because there was writing, too. A scrawl of black ink that looked like it had been written today, just this morning. It read *Why didn't you help me?*

And it was signed *Kimber.*

Five seconds later, Carmela was on the phone to Ava. "This isn't your idea of a joke, is it?" she asked. Ava lived directly across the courtyard in a funky second-floor studio apartment, directly above her Juju Voodoo shop.

Ava yawned into the phone. "What are you talking about?" Another yawn followed. "Uh, jeez, it feels like I've got the entire Gobi Desert stuck in my eyes. Awful. How many glasses of wine did I have last night? Do you remember? 'Cause I sure don't."

Carmela's voice carried no trace of sleepiness anymore. "I just found a very creepy postcard stuck to my morning paper."

"Um . . . what?" Clearly, Ava had just rolled out of bed.

"And the postcard is signed *Kimber Breeze,*" said Carmela. "Well, actually just *Kimber.*"

There was dead air for a few seconds, and

then Ava said, "Seriously? Give me a minute, I'm coming over."

Two minutes later, Ava came flouncing across the courtyard wearing a full-length red peignoir trimmed in purple marabou.

"You look like a refugee from Madame Kitty's old-time bordello," said Carmela. She had to smile in spite of herself. In spite of the ugly postcard that had left her feeling more than a little shaken.

"Can I help it if I'm a gal with a taste for the exotic and the louche?" said Ava. She grabbed the matching marabou stole that dangled down the front of her filmy robe and flung it over her shoulder. "Now . . . let me see that postcard."

Carmela handed it to her.

Ava took it, turned a speculative gaze on the photo, then flipped the postcard over and read the message. "Well, kiss my adorable sweet booty," she said in a quiet drawl, "somebody's sure got a sick sense of humor."

"Don't they?"

"Who would do a crappy thing like this?" wondered Ava.

"I don't know," said Carmela, "but I'd sure like to find out."

Ava looked askance at Carmela, as if she were studying her. "This isn't some kind of stupid-pet-trick joke, is it? Designed to freak out the upstairs neighbor?"

"I wouldn't do that to you," said Carmela. She smiled. "Not like this anyway."

"And I know I didn't fall fast asleep for six weeks and wake up on April Fool's Day." Ava lifted a hand to scratch her mass of dark curly hair. "Well, jeez. This is just plain weird."

"Yes, it is."

"I hate to think that somebody's been creepy-crawling around our courtyard," said Ava, glancing over her shoulder. Water pattered in the three-tiered fountain, and colorful bougainvillea spilled from giant terracotta pots. But the courtyard's essence seemed to have been disrupted. Somehow, it didn't feel quite so cozy and safe anymore.

"But someone slipped in," said Carmela.

"And the dogs didn't hear anything?"

"There was nary a bark, grunt, or growl all night."

Ava handed the card back to Carmela, gingerly, like she was disposing of a dead mouse. "I gotta hustle my bustle and get ready for work," said Ava, " 'cause Mardi Gras's my second-busiest season next to Halloween. But let's try to put our heads together tonight. See if we can figure this shit out. See if anything . . . relates."

"Come over for dinner," said Carmela. "We'll take a look at that DVD I'm supposed to pick up from Raleigh."

Ava cocked an index finger at her. "There's a plan."

By the time Carmela walked in the front door of Memory Mine, she was ready to blow off the whole postcard mystery. The sun was shining, any number of Mardi Gras parties would be in full swing this weekend, and she knew she was quite possibly the luckiest girl in the world. The fact that she owned her own scrapbook shop made it possible for her to be amazingly inventive with paper, photos, and other fun crafty items, as well as hang out with other crafty women. In other words, Carmela earned her living doing what she loved most. And, really, how many people could genuinely claim that?

Those warm, fuzzy feelings lasted for about thirty seconds. Until she stepped inside her shop and was stopped by the worried face of Gabby Mercer-Morris, her assistant.

"You saw the news," said Carmela. It was a statement, not a question.

"Yes, I did," said Gabby, making nervous gestures with her hands. Gabby possessed a sincere, caring manner and an open, demure face with guileless eyes. She reminded Carmela of a sweet-natured sorority sister. In fact, Gabby also dressed in twinsets and today wore a peppermint-green cashmere sweater set teamed with a soft dove-gray wool skirt. Gabby's dark hair was shoulder length and she continued to brush it back nervously, still not wanting to believe the news about Kimber Breeze.

"The whole thing was pretty awful," said Carmela. Now she felt guilty for feeling so upbeat just a few moments earlier.

"I can't believe you were there," said Gabby. "I mean, you show up to do an innocent little interview and find yourself smack-dab in the thick of things."

"Luck of the draw," said Carmela.

"I'd call it bad luck," said Gabby, shaking her head with regret. "Why does something like that have to happen right in the middle of Mardi Gras? Lord knows, New Orleans gets enough negative press for all the drinking and carousing that goes on here." Gabby was suddenly fired up and rolling. "And let's not forget the immodest women who shake their beads and everything else up there on those second-floor balconies."

"You realize," said Carmela, "that last year's Mardi Gras brought more than three hundred fifty million dollars into the city."

"True," Gabby admitted. "It does contribute to our economy."

"And lots of visitors find their way to us," Carmela pointed out.

"I understand that," said Gabby. "And I'm sure we'll be crazy busy over the next few days. In fact, I'm *thankful* we'll be busy."

"Me, too," said Carmela. "A good spurt of business could really fluff this month's bottom line." Business could always be better. But that was pretty much the story all over New Orleans.

"But have you seen the paper?" asked Gabby. She waved a copy of the *Times-Picayune* in front of Carmela. "I mean . . . it isn't good."

A sick feeling lodged in the pit of Carmela's stomach. "Uh . . . no. I didn't get around to actually reading it yet."

"Your name is mentioned."

"Oops," said Carmela. Her ex-husband, Shamus Meechum, was sure to spot it and call to register his disapproval. She could always count on Shamus for a negative vote or sarcastic comment. Except where his own drinking, free spending, and carousing were concerned. Then the blinders went on big-time.

"But you were mentioned only in passing," said Gabby. "As a kind of witness." She glanced at the paper and furrowed her brow. "But it also says there'd been something like forty different witnesses and that most of them ducked out before they could be questioned." She glanced up. "Is that true?"

"They fled like rats from a sinking ship," said Carmela.

"That's terrible," said Gabby. She picked up a spool of purple gossamer ribbon and fiddled with it. "I hope you called Detective Babcock?" Gabby was a big booster of Edgar Babcock. In fact, she had her fingers crossed that Carmela and Babcock would get married someday. She even prayed to St. Valentine, the patron saint of love, and had purchased a few ubiquitous saint candles from Ava's shop to hopefully spur things along. Her good intentions hadn't paid off thus far, but Gabby had faith.

"First Bobby Gallant showed up and then Babcock," Carmela explained. "So we have two intrepid homicide detectives working the case."

"That's good," said Gabby. "Two heads are always better than one."

"Just like us," said Carmela.

But Gabby wasn't finished discussing the murder. "Even though Kimber was a real pill," said Gabby, "her death is a genuine tragedy."

Carmela grabbed a pack of silk flowers and slit it open with her thumbnail. "I guess," she said.

Carmela got to work then. Hanging batches of teacup stickers on a rack, experimenting with some new rub-on tape, and arranging a new collection of card stock frames. Since Memory Mine was located in an old brick building in the French Quarter, the shop itself boasted tons of charm. Longer than it was wide, the shop featured high ceilings, planked wooden floors, lovely arched front windows, and brick walls.

On the longest brick wall, Carmela had placed wire paper racks that held thousands of sheets of paper. Because, no secret here, Carmela was a paper addict. She loved mulberry paper with its infusion of fibers, as well as linenlike Egyptian papyrus and the botanical vellums that were embedded with real flower petals.

Once Carmela lined up scissors, punches, and rulers on the large back table, the one they'd dubbed Craft Central, she glanced around and smiled to herself. This was what it was all about, of course. Owning your own business so you could be supreme allied commander in charge of your own destiny. Like lots of women, Carmela didn't aspire to be the crazed CEO of a Fortune 500 company, giving orders, hiring and firing, dashing about the country and eating airline food. But she did relish being an entrepreneur. She found it exciting and challenging to build, grow, and nurture her own business. And if financial rewards blossomed along the way, then so much the better!

"Carmela!" called Gabby. "Telephone. It's Babcock."

Carmela dashed into her little office at the back of the shop and snatched up the receiver. "What?" she said.

"And a warm hello to you, too," said Babcock.

"Oh, sorry," said Carmela. "I thought maybe you were calling with news." She eased herself into her purple leather chair and spun slowly from side to side.

"Even if I did have news," said Babcock, "I wouldn't be confiding in you."

"You see," said Carmela, "that's so not right. Especially when I have some inside information for you."

"What are you talking about?"

"Here's the thing," said Carmela. "Last night Kimber had dinner with some guy.

Probably not her regular boyfriend, from what I can tell. In fact, he was described as someone who's a little rough around the edges. A guy possibly named Dusty or Duncan."

Silence spun out for a few moments, and then Babcock said, sounding not at all pleased, "Please tell me how you know that."

CHAPTER 5

Carmela took a deep gulp of air, then said, "Okay. The thing is, Ava and I had dinner at Mumbo Gumbo last night and found out about this from Quigg. You know, the owner?"

Babcock made a rude sound into the phone. He was well aware that Carmela had dated Quigg a couple of times.

"Anyway," said Carmela, "Ava and I just happened to speak with Quigg as well as the waitress who served Kimber Breeze and her dinner companion."

"Excuse me, you just *happened* to find this out?" said Babcock. He didn't sound pleased. "It sounds more like you were investigating."

"I wouldn't do that."

"Of course you would," said Babcock. "You realize, Carmela, just because someone is hanged, stabbed, or bludgeoned to death in New Orleans, it isn't necessary for you to drop whatever you're doing and try to solve the crime."

"I don't do that."

"Maybe it just *feels* like you do," said Babcock." He made a blowing noise that sounded like the exhalation of a baby whale. "Okay, sorry. It's just that I'm being yanked in a million different directions right now. Plus there's a floater we just pulled from the Mississippi that's possibly connected to a drug cartel. And now this Kimber Breeze thing has been dropped in my lap."

"Kimber's murder made serious headlines, huh?" said Carmela. "The *Times-Picayune* had it front page, *above* the fold."

"National headlines, too," said Babcock. "But why wouldn't it go big? Her own TV station released part of the tape! It's blurry and hard to tell what's going on, but the idea that they'd do something like that is really quite . . . depressing."

"You realize," said Carmela, "for them it's about her murder *and* the ratings."

"Understood," said Babcock. "But now the mayor has taken a personal interest in getting this case resolved as fast as possible. At least that's what has been made very clear to me."

"Because this is a high-profile case?"

"That and because Ed Banister, the station owner, is a major contributor to the mayor's campaign."

"Ouch," said Carmela. "Politics rears its ugly head."

"It usually does," said Babcock. "And, by the way, how well do you know Joe Panola?"

"Sugar Joe?" said Carmela.

"That's right. He was there last night, though he scrammed with the rest of the lowlifes."

"He's a good guy," said Carmela.

"I have two witnesses who place him at the murder scene."

"There were forty people at the murder scene!" Carmela exclaimed.

"But apparently this Sugar Joe character was the last person to see Kimber Breeze alive."

"Sugar Joe's not a killer," said Carmela. "He's a . . . I don't know, he's like an heir to a big sugar plantation."

"The Evangeline Sugar Corporation based in Lafayette," said Babcock. It sounded like he was reading from his notes. "Joe Panola is also a friend of your ex-husband."

"So what?"

"That would give you a strong reason to come to Mr. Panola's defense, wouldn't it?"

"Absolutely not," said Carmela, getting a little hot. "And, by the way, have you checked out the Hotel Tremain yet? Do you know who rented the rooms on either side of the Bonaparte Suite? Does that fire escape lead to the roof? And is there an easy exit onto another building?"

"You're too much," said Babcock.

"These are just normal questions," said Carmela. "Really just observations."

"Normal for you, maybe."

"So you did check to see if these could be exit points?"

Everything's been looked into," said Babcock.

"And?"

"That's confidential information."

"Tell me *something*," said Carmela.

"The fire escape does, in fact, lead to the roof of the building."

"So there are probably several easy means of escape," said Carmela. "Like jumping down to a neighboring building."

"Unfortunately . . . yes."

"And the rooms on either side?" Carmela pressed.

"Unoccupied," said Babcock.

"Somebody could have been in one of them," mused Carmela. "I mean, that's probably how the murderer got away so fast." She paused. "Don't you think?"

"What I think doesn't matter," said Babcock. "I need to rely on empirical evidence."

"Which is . . . ?"

"Not a lot. Yet."

"Huh," said Carmela. It wasn't the answer she wanted to hear. She sat there tapping her foot, wondering if she should tell Babcock about the postcard she'd received. And decided not to. It would make him all bonkers and bring out his protective male instincts. Which was the last thing she wanted right now.

"Okay," said Carmela, "what about Kimber's boyfriend, Davis Durrell? Have you done an in-depth interview with him yet?" Carmela figured Durrell might be able to offer some ideas about Kimber's murder. Or at least he could speculate.

"I'm on my way to talk to him now," said Babcock.

"Will you call me afterward?" Something had just popped into Carmela's head.

"Probably not."

"Because I was just wondering," said Carmela, trying not to rush her words, "how Durrell happened to arrive at the murder scene so quickly."

Five minutes later, the clock struck nine the front door was unlatched, and Baby Fontaine and Tandy Bliss, two of Carmela's

68

scrapbooking regulars, came charging in.

"What the heck, Carmela!" yelped Tandy. She was short and skinny to the point of being emaciated, and she had a tight crop of hennaed curls ringing her bony face. "*Now* what did you get yourself involved in?"

Baby, her companion, was fifty-something and still gorgeous, a Garden District socialite who sported Chanel jackets teamed with perfect white blouses and blue jeans. Her pixie-cut blond hair was always perfectly coiffed and her face was amazingly unlined. In direct contrast to Tandy, Baby's nature was far more gracious and tactful.

"Carmela's not involved," said Baby, in a soothing tone. "She just happened to be there."

"Thank you, Baby," said Carmela.

But Tandy peered across the tops of her red half-glasses and said, "Phoo. If Carmela was there, then she's already spinning murder theories." She tilted her head in an appraising gesture. "Am I right?"

Carmela hesitated. Fact was, she *was* noodling a few theories. There was Kimber's mysterious dinner companion, of course. And the boyfriend who had seemed, dare she say it, over-the-top hysterical?

"If Kimber was killed on purpose," Tandy

continued, "it would be more like a crime of passion. I mean, maybe Kimber was involved in an illicit affair. Or even something illegal, like drugs or organized crime." She said this casually as she dug into her scrapbook tote and pulled out a Tupperware container filled with homemade peanut butter bars. She ripped off the plastic top and held the container out to Gabby. "Care for a bar, honey?"

"Sure," said Gabby, taking one.

"Hanging someone from a fourth-floor balcony doesn't sound like passion to me," said Baby. "It sounds extremely premeditated. Also, I'd venture to guess that Kimber knew her killer. That's how they were able to get so close to her."

"Never can tell," said Tandy, who seemed to thrive on imagining worst-case scenarios. "It could have been a random stalker."

"You think?" said Gabby.

"Sure," said Tandy. "Think about it. Kimber was a pretty TV reporter in a high-visibility job. Somebody saw her on TV, became intrigued, and then got it in their sick little head that they were in love. Or in hate. Or whatever."

"That's not a bad theory," said Gabby.

Tandy continued. "You know how much things have changed down here. Lots of new people moving in to snap up abandoned properties and try to make a fast buck in real estate." She snorted. "Lots of people from not here." *From not here* was New Orleans slang for someone who wasn't born and bred there.

Gabby took a bite of peanut butter bar and gazed at Carmela with questioning brown eyes. "What do you think, Carmela? You're always so good at constructing theories and figuring out motives."

Baby nodded. "She's the best. Silly us, we came stampeding in like a herd of cattle and never gave Carmela a chance to talk." She flashed Carmela an encouraging smile. "What do *you* think? You can always pull random threads together and make a logical connection. What do you think about Kimber's murder?"

All eyes were suddenly turned on Carmela, as the women spread out around the table.

Carmela almost didn't show them the postcard. Then, at the last second, she changed her mind. After all, what could it hurt? And it did seem related to the murder, in some strange, sick way. So she pulled the cemetery postcard from the pocket of her suede jacket and slowly placed it in the middle of the table.

"Take a look at what turned up on my doorstep this morning," she said.

Tandy's mouth opened and closed in a gasp, like a fish hauled out of water. Then, in a loud bray, she exclaimed "Holy shih-tzu, Carmela!" Snatching up the postcard, Tandy pored over it like a fiend. She flipped it back and forth a dozen times, then looked up, wrinkled her nose, and declared, "It's a crank. Has to be."

"Of course it is," said Baby, who'd been hunched over Tandy's shoulder, studying the strange postcard. "But what a terrible nasty joke. If that's what you can even call it!"

"You found this on your doorstep?" said Gabby. She just looked stunned.

Carmela nodded. "Uh-huh. This morning, with my newspaper."

"Who would do something like that?" asked Gabby. She hugged herself, arms crossed in front of her, as if she had a sudden chill. "A crazy person?"

"It's a joke," Tandy repeated. "A bad joke, but a harmless one."

"What if it's not?" said Gabby. "What if it's not harmless at all?"

"What do you mean?" asked Baby.

"It could be a warning," said Gabby, her

eyes going big. "What if somebody thinks Carmela is some sort of star witness and they're telling her to back off and shut up?"

That gave them all pause.

"But I wasn't a witness," Carmela said, finally. "I was there, yes, but I didn't actually see anything. Just the . . ." She gulped. "The aftermath."

"Maybe somebody *thinks* you know more than you do," said Gabby.

"That's a very interesting theory," said Tandy. She was starting to buy into Gabby's argument.

"It's ridiculous," said Carmela, grabbing the postcard back. She suddenly wished she'd never shown them the darned thing. "I was hoping we'd get a good laugh out of it."

Gabby peered at her. "Did you really?"

"Sure," said Carmela. But deep down, she knew that wasn't the absolute honest truth. So what had she really wanted? To be assured by her friends that the postcard meant nothing? To elicit their opinions on whether she might be in serious doo-doo? Perhaps. But now that she'd shown the postcard to Gabby and Baby and Tandy, it felt like it really should be heeded as a warning. Except, if it was a warning, wouldn't the writing have said *Back off* or something equally strident?

Why did the scrawled message say *Why didn't you help me*? And why had this sick someone signed Kimber's name? Carmela shivered. And for the first time, she felt an inexplicable creepy sensation, like somebody had just walked across her grave.

"Did you tell Babcock about the post-card?" asked Gabby.

"No, I did not," said Carmela. "And I don't want you to, either. It's probably nothing and he's got enough to worry about right now."

Luckily, Baby stepped in to lighten the tension that hung in the air like sticky strands of Spanish moss. "I guess we're all looking forward to Carmela's class on cigar box purses tomorrow afternoon, aren't we?"

"Wouldn't miss it," declared Tandy, "since I've got a couple of designs in mind." Tandy was a dedicated scrapbooker and crafter and never missed any class or daylong seminar that Carmela taught. Paper moon, lettering, memory boxes, Paperclay classes — she attended them all and worked painstakingly on each and every project.

"I think," said Carmela, also striving to break the tension, "what we need right now is a nice, fun project."

"A quickie project," said Tandy.

"We can make that happen," said Gabby. She glanced across the table at Carmela, as if looking for confirmation.

"I just happen to have some wonderful photocopied angel images," said Carmela, "to paste on the front of a small booklet and make an angel notebook."

"What?" yelped Tandy, "I *love* angels."

"Who doesn't?" said Baby, "they're so sweet and . . . angelic."

"How do we start?" asked Tandy.

Carmela grabbed three small paper notebooks, loosely bound with stitching, and placed them on the table. Then she rifled through one of her flat file drawers and pulled out two dozen or so angel images.

"First you need to choose your angel," Carmela told them. ·

There was a mad scramble as Gabby, Baby, and Tandy pawed through the images and each selected one.

"My angel looks like Gabriel," said Tandy.

"I think mine looks like the angel Michael," said Baby. "I think he's my favorite. He leads the Lord's armies against the devil."

"So what now?" asked Tandy.

"Take your angel image," said Carmela, "and scout around the shop for some paper that picks up the same colors. Most of the angels are sort of ethereal looking, so I suggest you look at our pink and mauve mulberry papers as well as our purple and gold lokta paper from Nepal."

"Then what?" said Baby.

"Add a little paint?" asked Gabby.

Carmela nodded. "Yes, but first you're going to cut your angel image into a circle and back it with a slightly larger circle, using card stock in gold or black to really make it pop. Once that's done, you want to select a little gold charm or embellishment to go at the top and bottom of your image."

"We have some wonderful new floral embellishments," said Gabby. "Lilies and vases and vines."

"Those would work perfectly," said Carmela. "Okay, so you glue mulberry paper onto your cover, add your circular angel image with charms, then do a little enhancing with paint."

"Enhancing how?" asked Baby.

"Drizzle on some strands of gold paint," said Carmela, "sort of Jackson Pollock-style. Or use a sponge and just dab some paint on and smear it gently, so the effect is slightly cloudlike."

"Love it," said Tandy. She was suddenly up and out of her chair, scouting for paper.

"And we're off and running," grinned

Carmela.

"Aren't you going to make one, too?" asked Baby.

"I'm going to hide in my office and try to finish my own project," said Carmela.

"What if we get stuck?" asked Baby.

"Gabby will keep an eye out, or you can holler for me," said Carmela. She smiled at Baby. "Really, you'll be fine."

Two minutes later, tucked into her office at the back of the shop, Carmela turned on her computer and brought up an image of an ad layout she'd been working on. She was ready (finally and for sure!) to put her Garden District home on the market. She knew Shamus would blow a gasket, to say nothing of his nasty big sister Glory, but the home was hers fair and square. It had been part of her divorce settlement and now it was hers to do with as she wanted. Rip it down, turn it into a bawdy burlesque house, or sell it.

Selling seemed like the best option.

The layout she'd blocked out so far was good. Her headline said *Garden District Greek Revival*. And farther down the page she'd put a short bulleted list of the home's features: grand facade with double galleries, magnificent gardens, eight bedrooms, five bathrooms, two parlors, white elephant. She

77

smiled, then carefully deleted that last point. She really did want to sell the place, after all.

She'd also left room in her layout for three good photos. One exterior shot for sure and probably two interior shots. Carmela had already scheduled her ad to appear in the next issue of *New Orleans Home*. Now all she had to do was schedule a photo shoot. Her good friend Jekyl Hardy had already recommended a top-notch interior photographer, so that was settled.

Now if Jekyl would show up to help art-direct the shoot, all would be right with the world.

Grabbing her phone, Carmela punched in Jekyl's number. She listened for a couple of seconds, and then it went to voice mail.

"Call me," she said, "about the shots of the house. Thanks. Oh, it's Carmela."

She stretched an arm up and grabbed a sample cigar box purse off a shelf. The sides were covered in a peach-colored paper, then collaged with images of hearts, flowers, and butterflies. As a focal point, she'd glued an inexpensive cameo on one side. The bamboo handles had been painted with gold paint and wrapped with peach chiffon. She'd carried it once to a chamber orchestra concert, and at least a dozen people had asked where she'd bought it. So . . . a grand success.

Carmela knew her customers were going to have a ball using their imaginations to make their own cigar box purses. The purses were a fun amalgamation of scrapping, collage, and graphic design. She thought about how to kick off her upcoming class, decided she pretty much had it figured out, then leaned back in her chair and let her mind wander.

Back to the murder, of course. Which got her wondering if there was anything worth seeing on the DVD that Raleigh so urgently wanted her to look at.

And she thought about the man, Dusty or Duncan or whoever, that Kimber had eaten dinner with last evening. Might Kimber's assistant know who he was? Hmm. Maybe. What was the assistant's name again?

"Zoe," Carmela murmured to herself. "Her name was Zoe."

CHAPTER 6

Carmela pushed her way through the double glass doors into the lobby of KBEZ-TV. It was sleek, done mostly in white laminates, and super contemporary in design, like the deck of the starship *Enterprise*. In contrast, a slate-gray receptionist desk loomed like a twenty-first-century Stonehenge. Hung on the wall behind the desk was an enormous piece of contemporary art. Done in moody blues and purples, the oil painting depicted two slavering dogs amid some sort of wreckage. To Carmela, it looked like two unlucky creatures who'd barely survived a nuclear holocaust.

"You have some very interesting art," Carmela said to the dark-haired young lady who sat behind the desk and was dressed, interestingly enough, in black and white. "Who's the artist?"

"Sullivan Finch," said the receptionist. "He's very hot right now. *Art Now* magazine hailed him as the new Damien Hirst."

"What would you call a piece like that?" asked Carmela, gesturing to the dog painting. *Besides depressing?*

The receptionist assumed a serious look. "According to his brochure, Mr. Finch specializes in postapocalyptic and dystopian subject matter."

Now there's a line of mumbo jumbo.

"No kidding," said Carmela. "And he's from here?"

"He hails from Slidell, but has a studio in the Faubourg Marigny." The Faubourg Marigny was an up-and-coming bohemian neighborhood filled with rehabbed buildings and directly adjacent to the French Quarter. In recent years it had become a mecca for new restaurants, bars, and galleries.

"Cool," said Carmela. She didn't know what else to say; the Finch painting was so dreary.

The receptionist smiled, revealing a bit of coral lipstick on her teeth. "I have a brochure if you'd like. In fact, Mr. Finch has an upcoming opening."

Carmela accepted the brochure out of pure politeness.

"And whom may I buzz for you?" asked the receptionist.

"Um . . . Raleigh," said Carmela.

"He's expecting you?" asked the receptionist.

"Should be," said Carmela. "I'm Carmela Bertrand. I did an interview last night with him and Zoe."

"Oh my gosh!" exclaimed the receptionist. "You were . . ."

"I was there," said Carmela. "At the Hotel Tremain."

"Must have been awful," said the woman, giving a little shudder.

"Trust me," said Carmela, "it wasn't good."

The receptionist pushed a couple of buttons and spoke into her headset. "Carmela Bertrand to . . . yes, all right." She looked up with a somber expression, as if she were having a difficult time processing Kimber's death. "Raleigh will be right out."

Two minutes later, Raleigh appeared in the lobby. He crooked an index finger and said, "Glad you could make it. C'mon back."

Carmela followed Raleigh down a white corridor hung with more strange paintings. Then they took a hard left and she suddenly found herself in a dark room filled with an acre of consoles festooned with blipping lights and dials, and an overhead green screen.

"This is your office?" Carmela asked. "This is where you put it all together?"

"Editing suite," said Raleigh. "I don't have an office. Only the bigwigs have offices."

"So where do you hang out?"

"There's a kind of bullpen for camera guys and reporters. Think shared desks, burned coffee, and stale air."

"I always figured this business was glamorous," said Carmela, realizing that TV, like so many other industries, existed behind a thin veneer of bewitchery. "So . . . you made a DVD?"

Raleigh grabbed a silver disk and handed it to her.

"Thanks." Carmela smiled warmly at him, since he looked like he was still in a blue funk.

"I appreciate your doing this," said Raleigh.

"I haven't done anything yet," said Carmela.

Raleigh made a grimace. "I know lots of folks thought Kimber was a real pain, but we always got along just fine."

Carmela wanted to say, *That's because you were one of her minions and followed her every move with a camera. Because you always made her look good.* But she didn't say it. Raleigh was feeling bad enough. There was no reason to take a cheap shot and make matters worse.

"I'm sorry for your loss," said Carmela. Raleigh seemed to be taking Kimber's death exceedingly hard.

"Thanks. You coming to the funeral? I hear it's planned for Saturday."

"Well . . . maybe," said Carmela.

"It's gonna be a big deal," said Raleigh. "Mr. Banister is personally supervising all the details."

"Kind of him," said Carmela. *Perhaps because he's afraid of a wrongful-death lawsuit?* Carmela turned to leave, then said, "I'd like to have a quick word with Zoe. Do you know, is she here right now?"

"Zoe's probably in Kimber's office," said Raleigh. "Trying to . . . I don't know . . . pick up the pieces?"

They walked down another corridor and stopped in front of an office with a bright red door. The Plexiglas sign to the left of the door read *Kimber Breeze*. Raleigh gave a perfunctory knock and pushed the door open.

Zoe was standing next to a credenza, sorting through a stack of papers. The office was spacious and open, with a large blond-colored wooden desk, potted bamboo plants, colorful posters on the wall, and a bunch of photos that all prominently featured Kimber.

"Oh, hey," said Zoe, when she recognized Carmela. "What are you doing here?"

Carmela made a vague gesture. "Just finishing up a spot of business." She turned to Raleigh and said, "Thanks so much; I'll be sure to let you know." Raleigh gave a sad nod and loped back down the corridor.

"Got a minute?" Carmela asked as she slipped into the office.

"Sure," said Zoe. "You were meeting with Raleigh?"

"I was," said Carmela. And that was all she was going to reveal.

"I suppose there's lots going on with the investigation," said Zoe. The girl looked bright, chipper, and ready to conquer the world.

Carmela nodded. "I'm afraid there is."

"You seemed like you were pretty close to that detective last night." Zoe tilted her head. "The cute one who seemed to be in charge. Are you two dating?" Zoe had a way of turning an impertinent question into chatty banter. Carmela figured that was probably the sign of a good reporter.

"Lieutenant Babcock," said Carmela.

"And we are dating. Have been for a while."

"That's great," said Zoe. "Because then you'll have an inside track on the investigation, won't you?" She smiled and gestured toward a coffeepot that sat on a window ledge. "Can I offer you a cup of coffee?"

"Actually," said Carmela, "I was wondering if I could ask you a couple of questions."

"Sure," said Zoe. She walked around Kimber's desk and settled into her chair.

"Do you know anyone named Dusty or Duncan? He would have been quite close to Kimber." Carmela slid into the chair across from her.

Zoe peered at her. "Are you sure you don't mean Durrell? Kimber's boyfriend?"

"No," said Carmela. "I think there was someone else in Kimber's life who had a name similar to that. Someone she had dinner with last night, just before she went to the Hotel Tremain."

Zoe stared at her, then her face clouded. "Oh, man!"

"What?" said Carmela, instantly on alert.

"Could it have been Dingus?"

Carmela frowned. "Maybe. Why? Who's Dingus?"

"He's her kid brother."

"Kimber has a brother?" This was news to Carmela. Then again, she didn't know all that much about Kimber Breeze. Other than the fact that Kimber had been mean-spirited and always seemed to be jostling for a news scoop.

"Well, I guess Dingus is just his nickname. His real name is Billy. He lives somewhere southwest of here. I think maybe near Theriot." Zoe lowered her voice "Nobody knows this, and Kimber kept it under extremely tight wraps, but she actually came from very humble beginnings. I'm guessing now, but I think she grew up dirt poor, even though she always put on airs like crazy."

"So how do you know about her brother?"

"Through bits and snatches of stuff I picked up over the last couple of years. Plus, he called here a few days ago. I didn't hear the whole conversation because Kimber was forever shooing me away. But from the way things sounded, I think he was asking her for money."

"Really," said Carmela. This was a new development. A ne'er-do-well brother asking his wildly successful sister to float a loan?

"From what I could gather," said Zoe, "Kimber's brother was fairly desperate. He was afraid his farm might be foreclosed on."

"Do you know," said Carmela, "did Kimber help him?"

Zoe shrugged. "I have no idea. But the

idea of Kimber bailing somebody out? Definitely not her style."

"Even her own brother?"

Zoe shrugged.

"Do you have any idea how I might contact this brother? Like I said, Kimber had dinner with a young man last night and . . ." Carmela hesitated as Zoe's eyes got big.

"She was with him?"

Carmela nodded. "It looks that way."

Zoe made a wild leap to the notion that was starting to percolate in Carmela's brain. "Do you think her brother might have had something to do with Kimber's death?"

"Doubtful," said Carmela, with far more conviction than she actually felt. "But I'd sure like to talk to him."

Zoe picked up a pen and scratched a quick note to herself. "I bet the police would, too."

"I know they would," said Carmela.

The wheels continued to turn in Zoe's brain for a few moments. Then she said, "Actually, I think Mr. Banister, the station owner, already contacted her brother. I guess he was pretty upset."

"Who was upset?" asked Carmela. "The station owner or the brother?"

"Both," said Zoe.

"You know," said Carmela, "I think I'd like that coffee after all."

Zoe slid open a desk drawer, grabbed a clean mug, and went over to the coffeepot. She poured out a cup of coffee for Carmela, then refilled her own mug and brought them back to the desk.

"There was something else going on, too," said Zoe. "That might relate to all this."

Carmela took a sip of coffee and winced. It was hot and strong. "What's that?"

The corners of Zoe's mouth twitched. "Kimber had a stalker."

"Seriously?" Carmela almost spilled her coffee.

"Oh yeah," said Zoe. "Of course, there were lots of guys who saw Kimber on TV and wanted to date her. She was forever receiving fan letters and e-mails. Some guys even fantasized they were in love with her." Zoe paused. "But there was one guy in particular who *really* scared the poop out of her."

"How so?" asked Carmela. "Did he threaten her?"

Zoe wrinkled her nose. "Not in so many words, but he did ugly things."

"Like what?"

"Think dead animals on your doorstep or blood spattered all over your car."

"He found out where she lived?" said Carmela. That would have been terrifying.

Zoe nodded.

"Were the police informed?"

"I believe so," said Zoe. "And I think there were a few untraceable phone calls in the middle of the night."

Carmela took a deep breath. "Did Kimber ever receive any weird postcards?"

"Postcards?" said Zoe.

"Specifically of cemeteries," said Carmela.

Zoe looked confused. "I don't think so. Why?"

Carmela quickly told Zoe about the postcard she'd received.

Zoe's reaction was one of surprise and horror. "Whoa . . . that's crazy!" She shook her head, definitely looking a little freaked. "Do you think Kimber's stalker is . . . um . . . that now he's targeting you?"

"Please don't say that," said Carmela. "I'm sure it was just a prank."

"Maybe," said Zoe, but she didn't look convinced.

They sat there for a few moments, each lost in thought.

Then Carmela glanced around Kimber's office and said, "What's going to happen now? Who's going to take her place?"

"I am," said Zoe.

Carmela gazed at Zoe with renewed interest. "I thought you were Kimber's assistant."

"Assistant, understudy, backup, call it whatever you like," said Zoe. "The truth of the matter is, I've been shadowing her and learning the ropes. So, when the time comes, I can go on air."

"And be a reporter? Like you were last night?"

"That's always been the job description, yes," said Zoe. She gave an unhappy grimace. "I thought landing a job as Kimber's assistant would be my ticket to a big TV career. Except Kimber turned out to be a greedy camera hog. She wanted to do every single report, feature story, station ID, and promo piece herself." Zoe looked nonplussed. "There wasn't much room for me, except for serving as her gofer. You know, go fer coffee, go fer her dry cleaning, that sort of crap."

"That must have been extremely disappointing," said Carmela.

"It was," said Zoe. "The only saving grace was that Kimber wanted to quit doing fluff pieces, like cat shows and ribbon cuttings at malls, and move into hard-edged investigative reporting. In fact, she was already working on a couple of things."

"So who was going to do the fluff pieces? You?"

"That was the plan. That *is* the plan."

"So working for Kimber wasn't exactly a bed of roses," said Carmela.

Zoe shook her head. "She tried to cut me out of everything."

"How did that make you feel?" asked Carmela.

"Awful," said Zoe. "Like a second-class citizen."

Carmela thought for a moment. "And now?"

"Truthfully?" A grin split Zoe's face. "I'm on top of the world."

CHAPTER 7

Back at Memory Mine, afternoon business was brisk. Gabby was showing off their new line of leather-bound albums to a couple of customers, three women were happily browsing the floor-to-ceiling paper racks, two were oohing and aahing over their selection of silk and gossamer ribbon. But one woman, an older lady with a Snooki-type beehive, looked distinctly perturbed as she wandered about muttering to herself.

"Can I help you?" Carmela asked the perturbed-looking woman.

"I want to decorate some tags to use as place cards for a Mardi Gras dinner party I'm having, but I'm just not finding a single thing that works," said the woman.

"Actually," said Carmela, "we have some rather nice precut tags."

"You do?" said the woman. Her penciled eyebrows rose in twin arcs.

Carmela grabbed a packet of tags to show

her. "Let's see . . . these tags come in gold, cream, and green."

"I do like that Mardi Gras green," allowed the woman. "But then what? What do I do with them?"

Sensing this woman needed some serious hand-holding, Carmela said, "What about using a deckle-edged scissors to trim the edges and make them a little more interesting? Then you can print your guests' names on purple paper, cut that out, and center it on the tags."

"Okay." The woman still looked hesitant.

"You could also add a few frills," said Carmela. "To really punch things up. For example, maybe use gold ink and rubber-stamp a fleur-de-lis motif? Then stamp on a double image using silver ink."

"I hear what you're saying," said the woman, "and I'm liking it." Her good humor was beginning to shine through.

"You could also take some gossamer ribbon and thread it through the hole in the tag," said Carmela.

"Sold," said the woman. "I'll take all of the items you just mentioned."

Carmela grabbed the tags, colored paper, rubber stamp, ink pads, and ribbon, and put it all in a brown kraft bag, then added her crack-and-peel sticker. "If you need more ideas," she told the woman, "stop by any time."

Since Baby and Tandy had long since departed, Carmela hustled back to straighten up the craft table. She wondered how their angel notebooks had turned out, then figured they'd for sure show her tomorrow when they came back to make cigar box purses.

The ribbon rolls also needed organizing, and then her FedEx guy came clumping in to deliver a huge box of rubber stamps. Carmela lovingly unwrapped her new goods, marveling over the designs — some wonderful ballet and music images — and calculated just how she could incorporate the images into upcoming craft projects.

And all the while Carmela's hands were working, she was also noodling around ideas. Or, to get real about it, she was noodling around suspects.

She wondered if Zoe could be considered a legitimate suspect? After all, the girl had been coveting Kimber's job for a couple of years. Perhaps the frustration and pressure had gotten to be too much?

And what about Kimber's mysterious stalker? Carmela certainly wanted to quiz Babcock about him. There had to be police reports on file, right?

Then there was Kimber's brother, Billy. Where exactly did he figure in all of this? Had Kimber lent him money or had she turned him down cold? If she'd turned him down and the brother had been angry and upset, had he hung around? Or did he hotfoot it back to . . . where was he from? Somewhere out near Theriot.

And what about Davis Durrell? Was he a suspect or just a sad bystander? As a financial manager, could he have somehow mishandled Kimber's funds and then been stuck with trying to get rid of a furious client/girlfriend?

Carmela was fairly quivering with ideas when she called Babcock's cell phone.

"Carmela," he said, by way of a greeting.

"Hey," she said, trying to be upbeat and cheery without sounding wheedling, "I'm just checking in."

"You're calling because I interviewed Durrell this morning," said Babcock. He was no fool. He had her number, for sure.

"Well . . . yes. I wondered how that went."

"Durrell seemed subdued. Emotionally exhausted. Pretty much what you'd expect."

"Not upset?" asked Carmela.

"I'd say he was that, too."

"Did Durrell offer any ideas?"

"Nothing in particular," said Babcock.

"He talked about Kimber being a high-profile celebrity, which he thought placed an inevitable target on her back."

"Kimber was a celebrity?" Carmela found that moniker a little preposterous.

Babcock heard the skepticism in her voice. "A minor celebrity, okay?"

Carmela thought back to her conversation with Zoe and decided to mention the stalker.

"Were you aware Kimber had a stalker?"

"How would you know that?" Babcock sounded on edge.

"Uh . . . I think somebody from the TV station mentioned it. Anyway, you knew about this?"

"Of course," said Babcock, "I'm not without substantial resources."

"What does that mean, exactly?" asked Carmela.

"It means I walked down the hall and asked someone in records if there were any arrests or reports concerning Kimber Breeze."

"And that's when the stalker thing came up?"

"Yes. Obviously."

"Well . . . ?"

"Well nothing," said Babcock. "The last stalker report was something like eighteen months ago. There hasn't been an incident since."

Carmela thought about that. "I wonder why not?"

"Could be anything," said Babcock, sounding unconcerned. "The stalker might be obsessed with someone else, he might have conquered his compulsivity with medication, or he could even be incarcerated."

"Jeez," said Carmela. "Everything you just mentioned, it all sounds very . . . creepy."

"The nature of police work," said Babcock, "is to deal with unsettling people and situations. You realize, my dear, a homicide investigation isn't about exciting car chases, flashing lights, TV interviews, and receiving the thanks of a grateful city."

"I know that," said Carmela. "It's just . . ." She stopped midsentence. "Do you know . . . was Durrell's relationship with Kimber purely girlfriend-boyfriend? Or did he manage her money, too?"

"I asked him about that," said Babcock. "He said they were a couple only."

"So she wasn't his client?"

"Not unless he's lying. And I have no reason to believe that he is."

"What about Kimber's brother?" said Carmela. "Billy . . ."

"Laforge," said Babcock. "Billy Laforge."

"Have you found out anything about him?"

"Gallant drove out to his farm this morning, but the brother wasn't at home. When Gallant spoke with a neighbor, a guy who worked as a kind of occasional hired hand, the man said he hadn't seen Billy for a few days."

"You think the brother is on the run?"

"No, because I know Ed Banister at KBEZ talked to him about funeral arrangements. We just haven't connected yet. But we will."

Carmela digested all that Babcock had told her. It seemed like the investigation was going nowhere fast.

"Okay," she said, "what about Zoe? That young TV reporter you talked to last night?"

Now Babcock sounded tired. "What about her?"

"She's been waiting in the wings for a long time."

"Waiting for what?" asked Babcock.

"Do we have a bad connection?" asked Carmela, "or are you just being obtuse?"

"*Excuse* me?"

"Zoe Carmichael's been waiting to step into Kimber's job," Carmela said in a rush. "Waiting to jump into her four-inch stilettos and leap onto the TV screen. Zoe's been counting the hours."

"How would you know that?" asked Babcock.

"Because I just talked to her."

"Carmela! You *are* meddling!"

Carmela played dumb. "Can I help it if I just find things out?"

"You're going above and beyond just finding things out. You're on the hunt."

And it's exciting!

She was bursting to say that, but didn't.

Instead, Carmela said, "Apologies. I'll pull back. I promise."

"Why do I not believe you," said Babcock, as the connection went dead.

Carmela spun her chair around in a lazy circle, thinking about Kimber's murder. And her list of sort-of suspects. And wondered who she could talk to next.

The person I really want to talk to is Durrell. But that's not going to happen.

She spun around again, catching quick images of a Jasper Johns print, the Eiffel Tower, ballet dancers, and old maps that were tacked on her office wall. All there to hopefully inspire a megawatt brainstorm.

Why can't I talk to Durrell?

Because I would need a very good excuse or reason.

Carmela was enjoying this little conversation with herself.

So make one up.

Two minutes later, Carmela had an appointment with Davis Durrell for first thing tomorrow morning. She'd told his secretary, a nice older-sounding woman named Mavis, that she wanted to drop by for a couple of minutes to personally offer her condolences. Mavis, trusting soul, had bought it.

Happy now, Carmela sauntered out into her shop.

"Need some help?" she asked Gabby, who was standing at the cash register ringing up a customer.

Gabby shook her head. All seemed under control. In fact, they were edging toward closing time. So there probably wouldn't be . . .

Another customer?

The front door opened and a waft of cool air whooshed in, shepherding in a tall man in a long, dark coat. He was lantern-jawed with a long horsy face and piercing eyes that peered out from beneath bushy gray eyebrows. The man glanced around with what felt like a hint of merriment, spotted Carmela staring at him, and immediately stuck out a bony hand. "Marcus Joubert," he said, smiling and revealing large, almost pointed teeth. "Your new neighbor."

"Oh, my gosh," said Carmela, shaking off a strange feeling of unease and stepping forward to shake his hand. "You opened the new shop next door, you're the proprietor of . . ."

"Oddities," said Joubert.

"It's nice to finally meet you," said Carmela. "I'm sorry I haven't been over to formally welcome you to the neighborhood. It's been so crazy here and I . . ."

Joubert flapped a hand to dispel her concern. "Don't be silly. Of course you're busy, it's Mardi Gras." He gave a wolfish grin. "But I think when you find time to visit, you'll find I've orchestrated a rather unusual shop."

"I've heard rumbles to that effect," said Carmela. "Hence the name Oddities."

Joubert nodded. "But I understand, Ms. Bertrand, that you sometimes deal in strange things, too."

Carmela wasn't following him. "Excuse me?"

"This morning's *Times-Picayune* said you witnessed a rather gruesome murder." Joubert seemed to take a strange satisfaction in mentioning Kimber's murder.

Carmela thought it a little odd but reminded herself there were lots of crime groupies. Babcock had told her all about it.

102

There were people who were forensics freaks as well as cop wannabes who followed all the action on police scanners and radios.

"I wasn't really a witness," she told him. "I was just sort of *there*. Along with a quite a few other people."

"Still," said Joubert, "the French Quarter has a well-deserved reputation for strange goings-on. Where else does one find voodoo shops, strip clubs, absinthe bars, haunted hotels, and shops filled with priceless antiques nestled shoulder to shoulder?"

"Point well taken," said Carmela. "I guess we're just a patchwork of craziness."

Joubert reached into his coat pocket and pulled out a small black envelope. "An invitation to my open house," he told her. "This Saturday evening."

"Thank you," said Carmela, accepting the envelope.

Joubert gave a thin smile, then lifted his hat and tipped it at Carmela. "I'd love it if you could come." He glanced over at Gabby. "You, too, ma'am."

"We'll certainly try," said Carmela, following him to the door and then waving good-bye.

When the door had closed behind him, Gabby said, in a low voice, "He makes me nervous."

"Seriously?" said Carmela, even though she'd felt a little tickle, too. "I think he's just an odd duck who forgot to mail his invitations."

"Have you seen what's on display in his front window?"

"I haven't really had time to look," Carmela admitted.

"Well, when you do," said Gabby, "I'd love to hear your reaction."

Carmela spent ten more minutes straightening up Memory Mine. Then she turned off her computer, latched the back door, and bid good night to Gabby, who waved a hurried good-bye as she slipped out the front door. Alone now, Carmela moved to the front counter, enjoying the peace and quiet that came with the close of day. Grabbing a pen, she quickly scrawled out a grocery list. Ava was coming over tonight for dinner and she wanted to fix a nice pot of shrimp and tomato stew. And if she could find fresh pecans at Mason's Market, she might even whip up a tin of her strawberry pecan biscuits.

And what else? Oh, wine. Except she had plenty of that, compliments of Quigg, who had gifted her with two full cases.

The streetlights in the French Quarter

were just coming on, spilling little puddles of light onto the sidewalk, as Carmela exited her shop. Across the street, Glisande's Courtyard Restaurant looked cozy and enticing with small white lights twinkling in the palmetto trees that fronted the restaurant. Upstairs, through the black wrought-iron grillwork, Carmela could see a tuxedo-clad waiter setting up for what was probably a private dinner party. Probably a pre–Mardi Gras gala.

As she turned and cruised past Oddities, Carmela slowed, then stopped to stare in the front window. The shop, she decided, was aptly named. Because what she saw struck her as very odd indeed. There was a strange arrangement that featured a stuffed capuchin monkey, antique medical devices of indeterminate usage, old black-and-white photos of conjoined twins, an apparatus that looked suspiciously like a thumbscrew, and any number of bleached white animal skulls and bones.

Carmela stood in the fading light and wondered, *Is there even a market for items this bizarre?*

Then she let her mind wander even further afield. *Would a man who sells animal bones and thumbscrews be the same type of person who was interested in local murders? And who might even leave dead animals on someone's doorstep? Hmm.*

CHAPTER 8

Shrimp, tomatoes, brown sugar, and cream bubbled enticingly in a large pot, and a tin of muffins baked in Carmela's oven, all exuding rich smells and promises. Carmela pulled dishes from her cupboard while Ava lounged at the dining room table, firmly ensconced with a glass of wine. Boo and Poobah lay at her feet, seemingly fascinated with their dear aunt Ava.

"When are you gonna get these saggy bottom chairs recaned, *cher*?" Ava asked. "I feel like I'm gettin' pulled down into a sinkhole."

"I know," said Carmela, "I never seem to get around to that." She had picked up a wonderful pecan dining room set in the scratch-and-dent room of a Royal Street antique shop. Only problem was, the chair seats sagged like old army hammocks. Probably, she decided, the end result of all the rich étouffée, soft-shell crab, stuffed artichokes, and other New Orleans butter- and cream-rich delicacies that had been consumed by the chairs' previous owners.

"Still," said Ava, "I gotta hand it to you. Your apartment looks fantastic."

Carmela's one-bedroom garden apartment was a tour de force. Posh and elegant from dozens of forays through French Quarter antique shops, the living room was furnished with a brocade fainting couch, marble coffee table, and squishy leather chaise with ottoman. An ornate gilded mirror hung on one wall, while lengths of handmade wrought iron that had once graced an antebellum mansion hung on the opposite redbrick wall. The wrought iron made a perfect shelf for her bronze dog statues and collection of antique children's books.

"Is that painting new?" asked Ava. She pointed to a moody oil painting of a redbrick Creole cottage.

"Got it last week," said Carmela. "At Dulcimer Antiques."

"You do have impeccable taste," said Ava.

"Which you always call white-bread Republican." Carmela laughed, as she ladled her stew into yellow Fiestaware bowls.

"It's just that your style's decidedly classic," said Ava, "what with all the Aubusson carpets, oil paintings, and antiquey stuff. While my personal preference veers toward fringe, feathers, and froufrou." Ava's apartment over Juju Voodoo always looked like a novelty shop had exploded. The walls were painted a lush peach, her window trim edged with gilt paint, and her chairs and sofas covered with furry leopard and zebra throws. Her lampshades were trimmed with feathers and her idea of artwork included leftover voodoo masks from her shop. The effect was basically Marilyn Monroe meets Marilyn Manson.

Carmela carried their bowls to the table and set them on woven rattan placemats she'd laid out earlier. "I'll tell you, I felt like an oldie but goodie this afternoon when I talked to that reporter Zoe. She's, like, twenty-four years old, but she's got the business savvy of someone who's forty-four."

"She seemed like a real go-getter," said Ava. She spooned up a helping of shrimp and tomato stew and blew softly on it.

"She's a sharpie," said Carmela. "Talking to her was like watching an updated version of that old black-and-white movie *All About Eve*."

"Heard of it," said Ava, "but never seen it."

"Oh, you'd like it," said Carmela. "Bette

Davis plays an aging Broadway star while her mousy little assistant, played by Anne Baxter, plots to take over her life and starring roles. And then it actually happens! The mousy little girl elbows Bette Davis into oblivion and ends up a big star!"

"Huh," said Ava. "That does sound kind of creepy." She swallowed another spoonful of stew and said, "Dang, this is good! And just the right amount of garlic!"

"What really gave me goose bumps," Carmela continued, "was the look on Zoe's face when she talked about being on top of the world now that Kimber was gone and she was going to take her place."

Ava glanced up sharply. "You think Zoe might have wanted Kimber out of the way?"

"I know she did," said Carmela. "It was her heart's desire."

"Yeah, but did Zoe literally *push* Kimber out of the way?" said Ava. "Like off that balcony?"

"With a cord wound around her neck," said Carmela.

"Can't forget the cord," agreed Ava.

Carmela hesitated. "I hate to point a finger at Zoe, because there isn't a single shred of evidence. On the other hand, the girl certainly had motive."

"Still . . ." said Ava. "She's just a kid."

"But think about it," said Carmela, "you're the underpaid, underappreciated assistant who's constantly lurking in the wings, waiting for your big shot."

"And you think Zoe maybe took that shot?"

Carmela's shoulders slumped. "I'm not sure what to think. Although Zoe didn't exactly seem heartbroken over Kimber's death. In fact, it was pretty much the last thing on her mind."

"Maybe Zoe just has a reporter's focus," said Ava. "I think they have to train themselves to block out emotions." She grinned. "Kind of like I do when it comes to old boyfriends."

"Anyway," said Carmela, "for a newbie she certainly did a masterful job with that live segment last night. Handled it like a real pro."

Ava grabbed a strawberry pecan muffin and spread a generous amount of butter on it. "What did you find out about Kimber's boyfriend? What was his name? Durdle?"

"Durrell," said Carmela. "I have a hunch he might know more than he's let on so far. Particularly since I found out from Zoe that Kimber had a stalker."

"A stalker?" Ava shivered. "That's creepy." She grabbed another muffin, broke off a couple of pieces, and fed them to Boo and Poobah.

"Yes, it is," said Carmela.

"You think Kimber might have confided in Durdle? About who she thought the stalker might be?"

"Durrell," said Carmela. "Maybe. Since they were going together it would seem logical."

"But Kimber wasn't logical," said Ava. "She was . . . how can I put this delicately? Kapow crazy!"

"Babcock would spit a rat if he knew," said Carmela, "but I'm going to meet with Durrell tomorrow morning."

"Good for you. On what trumped-up pretext?"

"Sympathy?"

"Works for me," said Ava. "As long as you're able to keep a straight face."

Carmela poured out another two fingers of wine for each of them. "What do you know about Oddities, that little shop that's opening next door to me? The owner dropped by this afternoon to say hi and give me some sort of invitation." She'd been so busy, she hadn't even had time to look at it yet.

"Ooh," said Ava, "I got an invitation, too. For their open house." Ava grinned. "They probably think I'm a kindred spirit, owning a voodoo shop and all. Anyway, the Oddities open house is this Saturday evening. Want to go?"

"Why not?" said Carmela. "Who wouldn't want to attend a party at a creepy little shop that has a stuffed monkey in the window?"

The phone jingled from across the room.

"Telemarketers," said Ava. "Or maybe you lucked out and won a million bucks!"

Carmela jumped up to grab it. "Hello? Publishers Clearing House? Am I the lucky winner?"

"Carmela, darling," came a smooth male voice, "I see you and your partner in crime were involved in a juicy little murder over at the Hotel Tremain. Or should I call it the Hotel Travail?"

"Jekyl," said Carmela. Jekyl Hardy was one of New Orleans's premier Mardi Gras float designers and an art appraiser by trade. He was also a dear friend of Carmela's and had helped her cofound the Children's Art Association.

"You okay, lovey?" he asked.

"Doing okay," said Carmela. "Though Kimber Breeze did get herself hanged from the balcony. You probably read about it in the paper. Or saw the news."

"Or got the full poop on Twitter," called Ava.

"Are you a suspect?" Jekyl asked.

Carmela was taken aback. "No!"

"Well, you should be," chuckled Jekyl. "There was never a shred of love lost between the two of you. Whenever you and Kimber were in the same vicinity you acted like a couple of hissing wombats."

"You forget I'm not the murdering type," said Carmela. "I'm a pussycat."

"She is!" Ava yelled at the phone. "You're the wacko in the group!"

"Tell Ava she's the light of my life," said Jekyl.

Carmela dropped the phone. "Jekyl says you're a crazy bee-yatch."

Ava flapped a hand. "Yeah, yeah."

"So I got your message," said Jekyl, "and the photographer *is* available Saturday morning. Shall I go ahead and set it up?"

Carmela thought for a minute. Kimber's funeral was also scheduled for Saturday morning. "Just a minute. I gotta confab with Ava." She dropped the phone again and asked, "Are we going to Kimber's funeral?"

Ava nodded. "Oh, yeah. We gotta do that. We have to complete the circle of life and death." She frowned. "Or would that be death and death?"

"Could we move the photo shoot to Sunday?" asked Carmela.

"Might work," said Jekyl. "I'll check with the photographer and get back to you."

"Great."

"You two divas are coming to the big party at the Pluvius float den Sunday night, aren't you?" As head float designer for the Pluvius krewe, Jekyl was accorded access to any and all Mardi Gras parties.

"Is this a formal invitation?" said Carmela.

"You may consider it that," replied Jekyl, "even though it's not engraved in gold and printed on industrial-strength parchment."

"Mmm," said Carmela, "the Pluvius den." Shamus was a member of the Pluvius krewe. "That means Shamus will be there." Knowing her goofball ex-husband would be lurking about made the party somewhat less appealing.

Jekyl let loose a wicked, high-pitched cackle. "Just adorn your body in something super slinky with a plunging neckline and make him positively drool!"

"He probably won't even notice," said Carmela. In recent months Shamus had developed an eye for much younger women with cascades of blond hair. And even though Carmela hadn't yet hit thirty, she felt practically decrepit next to Shamus's current stable of bubble-headed kewpie dolls.

"Oh, Shamus will notice," said Jekyl. There was a long pause and then he added, "Because he's still in love with you."

Carmela wandered back into the dining room and plopped down at the table. "Two things. Jekyl says Shamus is still in love with me."

"That's not so far-fetched," said Ava. "Shamus does get a stupid, moony look on his face whenever he sees you. On the other hand, it could be garden-variety gas pain. Or the deevorce blues."

"The other thing," said Carmela. "Jekyl says I should be a suspect."

"Agh, he's way off base on that," said Ava. "Because you're the *investigator*."

"Babcock would have a cow if he heard you say that."

"Let him," said Ava. She scrunched her brows together. "Face it, Carmela, you're good at this stuff. You're the Nancy Drew of New Orleans." She cocked her head and thought for a few moments. "Or are you Trixie Belden? I can never remember which one was my favorite girl detective."

"Speaking of detecting," said Carmela,

"we were going to take a look at Raleigh's DVD."

"Then let's do it," said Ava.

They moved over to the leather couch and Carmela popped the DVD into her player.

"Will there be coming attractions?" asked Ava.

"No, but I have kettle corn," said Carmela, as they waited for the video to cue up. She always had kettle corn.

"Pass," said Ava, rubbing her tummy. "I'm way too fat as it is."

"You're a size six," said Carmela.

"In Beverly Hills," said Ava, "a size six is considered an extra large!"

Then the video was running, a grainy color image that was slightly out of focus but did seem to reveal most of last night's action in the Bonaparte Suite.

"This must have been shot with a wide-angle lens," said Carmela. "See how things look a little distorted?"

"I thought it was because everybody was drinking," said Ava. She held up her wine-glass. "Because I'm drinking."

"Shh," said Carmela. Even though there wasn't any sound, she wanted to concentrate.

They watched as people came and went, jostled and smiled, kissed and hugged, drank and hung out.

After forty minutes of watching with not much happening, Ava said, "Nothing's going on. In fact, it's pretty much a total yawn."

"But look," said Carmela, pointing at the screen, "there's Devon Dowling coming in from the balcony." Dowling was a local antique dealer. "So the murder hasn't taken place yet."

"Okaaaay," said Ava, "then it's about to take place, right?"

"I think so," said Carmela, leaning forward.

The picture suddenly shook, as if someone had jostled the camera, and then there was a shot of Sugar Joe stepping in from the balcony.

"There!" said Carmela. "Right after Sugar Joe came in, Raleigh was talking into his headset, trying to cue Kimber for a live break. That's when it must have happened. Somewhere . . . in the next minute or so."

They continued to stare at the screen.

"But nobody went out onto the balcony," said Ava. She leaned back. "Holy bazookas, you don't think Sugar Joe . . ."

"I don't think so," said Carmela. Sugar Joe had always seemed fairly even-keeled to her. At least compared to Shamus's other friends.

"Still," said Ava.

Carmela reached out and pushed the Stop button. She rewound for a couple of seconds and hit Play.

"What?" said Ava. "Did you see something I didn't?"

"Watch the upper left-hand corner of the screen," said Carmela. "You see that man dressed in a white clown costume?"

"Okay," said Ava.

"You see where he's standing? He's right near the entrance to the balcony. And then, after those two vampires go by, he's not there anymore."

Ava stared harder. "Uh-huh."

"It's just possible," said Carmela, "that guy could be the killer."

Ava looked shocked. "You're telling me the goofball clown did it?"

Carmela sat back. "I don't know. It all happened so fast."

They replayed it again, then Carmela put it on slo-mo.

"The clown is standing there and then he's not," said Carmela. "That has to mean something."

"Maybe it means he stepped out to take a whiz," said Ava.

"At any rate," said Carmela, "it would be interesting to know who was wearing a white clown costume last night."

"Send in the clowns," said Ava, taking another sip of wine.

Later that night, after Ava had left, after Boo and Poobah had been walked, Shamus called.

"What?" said Carmela. She'd brushed her teeth and was tired and ready for a good night's sleep. Now Shamus's unwelcome hysteria had suddenly invaded her quiet space.

"It's about the murder last night!" said Shamus. "First I find out that Sugar Joe, my best friend in the entire world, is a suspect! Then I find out you were actually there!"

Carmela yawned. "Tell me about it."

"This is crazy town!" he screeched.

"Of course it is," said Carmela, taking a deep breath and trying to remain calm. "And now, if you don't mind, I'm going to turn out the light and . . ."

"You've got to help make this right!" implored Shamus. "Talk to that Dudley Do-Right boyfriend of yours and tell him he's looking at the wrong guy!"

"I can't do that."

"Sure you can," said Shamus. "Just *tell* him. Just vouch for old Sugar Joe. *You* know he's a good guy and *I* know he's a good guy; what more proof do you need?"

"Shamus," said Carmela, "just let this play out. I'm sure . . ."

"No!" cried Shamus. "You've got to intercede! You've got to tell that crazy Babcock to *back off*!"

Carmela leaned over and snapped off the light. "Good night, Shamus."

CHAPTER 9

Friday morning dawned cool and crisp. Shards of gray clouds hovered above the lazy curl of Mississippi River but didn't look particularly substantive. A gentle breeze, a pop of sun, and they'd be gone, swooshed away in a moment. Which meant another great Mardi Gras day.

Gabby beat Carmela to work by ten minutes, but only because Carmela stopped at Café du Monde to grab two café au laits. She juggled the two grandes in their green cups as she pushed through the front door. Then Gabby was there, greeting her and thanking her for bringing a caffeine lift.

"It's going to be a great day," said Gabby. "There's going to be a huge influx of customers, we've got the cigar box purse class . . ."

"Ava and I watched a video of the murder," Carmela told her.

Gabby looked suddenly jittery, and it

wasn't because of the strong coffee. "The actual murder? It's on video?"

"Well, no," said Carmela. "What we watched was a recording of the party in the Bonaparte Suite."

Gabby frowned and drew a sharp breath. "Did you see anything strange? Any . . . suspects?"

"There was one possibility," said Carmela. "A guy in a clown costume. Kind of like . . . you know, from that opera? Pagla . . ."

"You mean *Pagliacci*?" said Gabby. "The Canio character?" She and her husband, Stuart, were devoted opera fans.

"That's it!" said Carmela, kicking herself that she hadn't been able to dredge up the correct name. Why was she so well versed in pop culture instead? Probably because she watched way too much TV. "Anyway, one minute the Canio character was standing by the door that led to the balcony and the next minute he was gone. Poof."

"Is this speculation?" asked Gabby. "Or actual evidence?"

Carmela considered Gabby's question. "Um . . . I think mostly speculation on my part."

Gabby took another sip of coffee. "I hate to ask, but do the police have a copy of this same video?"

"I think Raleigh gave them a copy. No, I'm pretty sure he did."

"You better make darned sure," said Gabby. "Because if the police don't have it, and that video holds key information that could lead to a possible arrest . . ."

"Then I'd be withholding evidence," said Carmela. "Yeah, I know. I thought about that."

"So you need to be absolutely clear with Babcock," said Gabby.

Carmela wrinkled her nose. "I will. I promise." She gazed at the front counter, anxious to change the subject. "Anything? Any messages?"

Gabby handed her three pink message slips. "Just customers who left messages on the answering machine. Nothing earth-shattering. The most pressing is a woman who needs a Prussian blue ink pad."

"Okay, I'm gonna go in my office and get my head together for a few minutes." Carmela was meeting with Durrell in twenty-five minutes and she wanted to get clear in her mind exactly what questions to ask. She knew once she'd offered her cooked-up sympathies, Durrell would probably give her the bum's rush out the door.

"I've got our cigar boxes all lined up and ready to go for this afternoon," said Gabby.

"But I know you're going to want to pull some fun papers and decals and things."

"I have to pop out for a meeting in a couple of minutes," said Carmela, "but when I get back we'll pull papers and decals and things together, okay?" Carmela walked slowly back to her office, perusing the message slips, sipping coffee, and tossing around a few more ideas for her class today, which she was really beginning to look forward to.

In the shower this morning, she'd come up with an idea for a Parisian-themed purse and was anxious to sketch out her design. She was going to affix dark-blue paper with tiny pink dots on the outside of her cigar box. And then she was going to add an Eiffel Tower stamp that . . .

Carmela stepped inside her office, then stopped in her tracks so fast a tiny blurp of coffee sloshed from her cup onto the floor. Because sitting smack-dab in the middle of her desk, the one she'd tidied so fastidiously last night, was a sepia-toned postcard.

Postcard? Another postcard? Where did it . . .?

Carmela took a deep breath and carefully set her things on an adjacent credenza. Then she picked up the postcard and studied it. This one was a photograph of St. Louis Cemetery No. 3, circa 1902.

Dreading what she might find on the other side, Carmela slowly turned the postcard over.

Yes, another message had been scrawled there.

It read, *Carmela, I'm still waiting!* And it was signed *Kimber.*

Carmela reeled back, feeling gobsmacked. She blinked and read the message again as a sick, acidic feeling seeped into her stomach.

Who wrote this? she wondered. And, on the heels of that thought, *Oh crap, how did it get on my desk?*

Gasping, Carmela lurched from her office toward the heavy metal door that led out to the loading dock and alley. It was rarely used, except when she was expecting a large delivery or was trying to slip out of the shop discreetly. *Please tell me this door is locked tight.*

But like a twisted image in a bad dream, it wasn't. The door was shut, but it wasn't locked. The deadbolt wasn't engaged.

"Gabby, get back here!" Carmela shrieked.

Startled, Gabby snapped her head forward and dropped the packets of colored beads she was sorting. Then she was scurrying toward the back door, her skirt billowing out around her and her kitten heels sounding like castanets on the sagging wooden floor. "What's wrong?"

"Look at this." Carmela pointed at the brass lock on the door. "See the scratches?"

Gabby squinted as she moved in close. "Yes, I do." Then reality hit home. "Oh no, did somebody try to jimmy the lock?"

"I think so," said Carmela. She hesitated. No, she couldn't keep this a secret. She had to tell Gabby the truth; it was only right. "Actually, I know so. Wait a minute, there's something I have to show you." Carmela slipped back into her office, grabbed the postcard, and handed it to Gabby.

Gabby's face went slack. "You got another one."

"It was right here, sitting on my desk. Waiting for me."

Gabby jerked spasmodically. "You mean somebody broke into Memory Mine last night?"

"I think so."

"Just . . . just to leave this postcard?" Gabby was both frightened and confused. "But what . . . ?" She sucked in a gulp of air. "But they didn't *rob* us?"

"Doesn't look like it," said Carmela. "Have you checked the cash register today?"

"I peered in a few minutes ago and everything was fine."

"There you go," said Carmela. "The break-in was for scare purposes only."

"Somebody broke in just to leave a post-card?" Gabby repeated. In a city where robberies and muggings were commonplace, she couldn't seem to get past that. "Who would do something like this? I mean, it's terrifying, but it's stupid and nonsensical, too."

"I don't have a clue as to who's behind this," said Carmela, biting off her words sharply. "But come hell or high water, I intend to find out!"

But Gabby was suddenly thinking more rationally. "You have to call Babcock."

Carmela balked. "I really don't want to do that."

"We're talking about breaking and entering," Gabby pointed out. "I think that's technically a felony. It has to be reported."

"Yeah, but . . ."

"Listen," said Gabby, "whoever left this postcard, it could be the same person who murdered Kimber! That person might be . . . baiting you!"

"I suppose it's possible," said Carmela. *Actually, it's quite probable.*

"Or else . . ." Gabby glanced furtively at the postcard, and her voice took on a whispery edge. "It's like Kimber's reaching out to you from the grave."

"Trust me," said Carmela, "she's not. There's nothing magical or paranormal about this. There's a reasonable explanation."

Gabby put a hand on her hip. "You think so? Because breaking and entering to leave a wacked-out postcard on somebody's desk seems very *un*reasonable to me."

Five minutes later, with Gabby calmed down and a technician from A-Plus Locks on his way over, Carmela walked briskly down Burgundy Street to the Gallier Building. It was an old yellow brick building that had been built around the turn of the century. Not this century — the previous century. It had started as a sugar factory, morphed into a warehouse, then, in the early eighties, when rehabbing buildings became fashionable, turned into office space.

Now a sleek, modern elevator whooshed Carmela up to the fifth floor, the top floor, and disgorged her in the posh lobby of Gold Star Investments. Though the old yellow brick walls remained, Carmela wondered why every interior designer felt compelled to modernize old buildings. Why couldn't they just work with the good bones of these places? But no, chrome and glass fixtures had to be installed, and all sorts of modern touches added.

After introducing herself, Carmela was led by a tall, willowy receptionist in a navy blue skirt suit back to Durrell's office. Mavis, the secretary, who was indeed plump and motherly, sprang up to greet her. Then she rapped on Davis Durrell's door to announce Carmela.

The wood-paneled door swung open and Carmela stepped into an ultraplush office. A large executive desk anchored the center of the room. Two black leather Eames chairs faced it. Underfoot, the wine-colored carpet had two gold interlocking *D*s cut into it. Custom made for the ego-driven.

Carmela strode across the *D*s to greet Durrell. "I know we spoke briefly on Wednesday night, but I wanted to offer my condolences in a more personal way."

"Thank you," said Durrell. "I appreciate your concern." He looked subdued and a little haggard. Maybe because he was still in shock, maybe because he hadn't gotten much sleep. Or maybe because he was a little spooked that the police had drilled him with so many questions.

"I'm sure this is a trying time for you,"

said Carmela.

Durrell offered a thin smile and indicated that Carmela should take a seat. Once she'd settled in, he sat down behind his desk and faced her.

"You have no idea," said Durrell. "It's been ghastly."

Carmela decided that Durrell didn't look like a financial guru. Rather, he gave the outward appearance of an indolent Southern rich guy who sat around drinking Sazerac and trying to impress women by quoting verses from Proust. Which, for some reason, reminded her of Shamus, whose picture should definitely be in *Webster's Dictionary* under the word *lazy*.

But Durrell possessed the requisite three computer screens crawling with columns of red and green numbers; two iPhones, one at the ready and one plugged into a charger; an acre of mahogany desk; and photos of himself with his arm casually slung around the shoulders of a dozen or so minor celebrities — if you considered lawyers, real estate moguls, and a New Orleans Saints nose tackle minor celebrities.

"Anyway," said Carmela, touching a hand to her chest, "my heart goes out to you. If there's anything I can do . . ."

Durrell nodded. "You're very kind. Your

words come as a great comfort."

"Good to know," said Carmela, trying to muster a sincere smile that wasn't too smiley.

Durrell gazed across his desk at her, as if waiting for Carmela to continue.

"So," she said, "I understand you're a money manager?"

"That's correct," said Durrell. "I work with a select group of rather well-heeled clients." He offered a thin smile. "Are you an investor yourself? I understand you're recently divorced . . . from Shamus Meechum?"

"That's right," said Carmela.

Durrell leaned forward, rested his elbows on his desk, and steepled his fingers. "Forgive me, but newly divorced women often find themselves with generous settlements, yet they don't always possess the . . ."

"Financial savvy?" said Carmela. "The wherewithal to handle their own money?" Warning bells were suddenly clanging in her head. Granted, she'd come here under false pretenses. But now Durrell had suddenly spun the tables on her and was giving her a soft-sell pitch!

Durrell gave a helpless shrug, as if acknowledging the fact that not all women were financial geniuses.

"I'm managing just fine," Carmela said, deciding the man was pretty much pond scum. "In fact, I very much enjoy business."

"Do you now?" Durrell sounded just this side of disappointed.

"Running my own retail operation can sometimes be a challenge, but for the most part I'm loving it. As far as following the whims of Wall Street and directing my own investments . . . I'd say it's a constant learning experience."

"I'm sure Shamus must have been a great help," said Durrell.

"You know what?" said Carmela, "Shamus was no help at all. His family may own Crescent City Bank, but Shamus doesn't exactly have a degree in high finance from Wharton." Fact was, Shamus could barely balance his own checkbook and had made it through Tulane by the seat of his pants and lots of help from his frat rat buddies.

"Oh dear," said Durrell, feigning interest, "it sounds like you and Shamus have a somewhat hostile relationship."

"Not really," said Carmela. "Now that we're out of each other's hair, we get along better than ever." *Yeah, right. Sure we do.*

Durrell let loose a throaty chuckle. "Relationships . . ."

Which gave Carmela the conversational

entrée she'd been hoping for.

"How long had you and Kimber been dating?" she asked.

Durrell leaned back in his chair, as if he had to think about that. "Oh, maybe six months."

"I take it you were planning to get married?"

Durrell gave a far-off smile. "We talked around it. So, yes, I suppose our relationship would have eventually progressed to that point."

To Carmela his answer sounded more like lawyer-speak than the words of a lover. On the other hand, neither of them seemed like till-death-do-us-part commitment types, but how did she know what true feelings were hidden deep within someone's heart?

"Do you know how the police investigation is going?" asked Carmela.

"Progressing, I'm told."

"But such strange circumstances," said Carmela. She decided it was time to lob a hardball question at Durrell. "Can you think of any reason why someone would have targeted Kimber?"

"No idea," said Durrell. "Although my own theory is that someone had her in their sights because she was such a big deal here."

"You think?"

"Absolutely," said Durrell. "She had men swooning over her and women wanting to look like her. As you know, Kimber was extremely high profile. She was constantly being invited to walk in fashion shows, judge talent contests, and offer her personal opinion on just about everything."

"She was a big fish in a small pond," said Carmela. She wondered if that was the reason Durrell had dated Kimber. Had it given him access to people with money? Or had the two of them enjoyed a genuine relationship?

"She is greatly missed," said Durrell. He composed his face into a sad expression, though Carmela thought he looked slightly more watchful than sad.

"What about the investigative reporting Kimber was doing for the station?" asked Carmela. "Do you think she could have uncovered something that led to her being targeted?" In other words, had she poked her nose into a hornet's nest and gotten stung?

A flicker of surprise showed on Durrell's face. As if Carmela had caught him off guard. "Kimber liked to throw herself into every project one hundred and fifty percent."

"But as far as this investigative reporting,"

Carmela continued, "do you know what she was working on?"

Durrell reached out, touched his index finger to a fat Montblanc pen that sat on his desk, and carefully aligned it with a red leather notebook. "No idea."

CHAPTER 10

Juju Voodoo boasted a high-gloss red front door where fat, bouncy black letters spelled out Juju Voodoo. A multi-paned front window held a neon sign that glowed bright red and cool blue, illustrating an open palm with its basic head, heart, and life lines. A wooden shake roof, slightly reminiscent of a Hansel and Gretel cottage, dipped down in front.

"Ava?" Carmela called, as she pushed her way into the dark interior and was immediately greeted by flickering red votive candles and the fragrant aromas of sandalwood and patchouli oil.

Juju Voodoo was, of course, the premier voodoo shop in New Orleans. If you had your heart set on a life-size (death-size?) jangling skeleton, Ava could hook you up. Same went for voodoo dolls, evil eye necklaces, love charms wrapped in netting and lace, saint candles, incense, shrunken heads, and necklaces hung with carved teeth and bones. Inventory was key here, and Ava prided herself on having the perfect juju magic for whatever ailed you. Of course, most of the love charms were really herbs and spices, and the rest were fun tourist souvenirs.

But Ava did a land-office business and even offered a reading room in back, where, should you wish to commune with spirits from the great beyond, you could enjoy a tarot card reading, the *I Ching*, an astrology chart, or any other popular form of divination.

"*Cher*," said Ava, popping out from behind a colorful display of Indonesian masks. "I had no idea you were going to drop by. Hang on." She aimed her phone at one of the masks and snapped a photo, probably so she could send it to one of her customers. Since Ava had begun sending out photos of her merchandise, not only had she increased her customer base, but sales had nearly doubled.

"I was running around the neighborhood," said Carmela, "and thought I'd drop in."

Ava touched a finger to the side of her head. "Oh, right. You had your meeting with Durdle this morning."

"Durrell," said Carmela.

"Whatever," said Ava. She reached out and brushed aside an errant strand of gray goat hair that decorated a second mask. "How did that meeting go?"

"Pretty much the way I thought it would. Like pulling teeth to get any concrete information."

"Was he dodging your questions, or is the guy just a numbskull?" asked Ava.

"I think he's scared and nervous," said Carmela.

Ava's brows shot up. "Nervous over what? You think he killed Kimber?"

"It's possible," said Carmela. "But there was another vibe, too."

"Like what?"

"Hard to put my finger on it," said Carmela. "But it just *felt* like something else was going on."

"Huh." Ava turned to watch as Miguel, her assistant, pulled out a Day of the Dead Ferris wheel and did his spiel for a customer.

"Also," said Carmela, touching a hand to her hobo bag, "I have something weird to show you."

Ava, smart cookie that she was, seemed to instinctively know what little goodie Carmela had brought. "Don't tell me," she groaned. "You got another one?"

"Another postcard," said Carmela. "Yes." She pulled it out and handed it to Ava. "I found it on my desk first thing this morning."

Ava accepted it with some trepidation. "Are you telling me somebody broke into your shop and left this?"

Carmela grimaced. "We're having new locks installed even as we speak."

"Oh wow," said Ava. "Wow, wow, wow."

Carmela wasn't sure if Ava was bothered by the break-in or by the fact that a second postcard had turned up. Or both. She tried to dispel her friend's fear by turning flippant. "Isn't that a great little item to bring to show-and-tell?"

"Not really," said Ava. She set the postcard on the counter and stared at the offending object as if it carried traces of the bubonic plague. "Are you going to tell Babcock?"

"I don't know. The jury's still out." Carmela really didn't want to tell him. She knew he'd go ballistic.

"Let's pretend I'm foreman of the jury," said Ava.

"Okay," said Carmela.

"I vote you definitely show this miserable thing to Babcock. After all, he's a good guy, a smart guy. And, most importantly, he'll have your safety at heart."

"That's what I'm afraid of," said Carmela. "I'm afraid he'll want to . . . oh, I don't know . . . lock me in a glass cage or something."

"Which wouldn't be half bad if it were filled with bouquets of red roses and a case of fine champagne."

They stared at the postcard as if it were some strange talisman, dredged up from antiquity. Finally, Ava stretched a hand out and tapped it with a shellacked red fingernail. "Another graveyard scene. Do you think these cards are supposed to be clues for something?"

"Clues for what? Death? Eternity? A warning?"

"I don't know," said Ava, shaking her head. "That's the tricky thing about clues; you have to figure them out."

There was a faint tinkle of bells and a suck of cool air. Overhead, a white wooden skeleton moved in a slow click-clacking jig.

"Huh?" said Carmela, jerking her head toward the back of Ava's shop.

Then footsteps sounded and Madame Eldora Blavatsky, whose real name was Ellie Black, came walking in. She was Ava's resident fortune-teller and psychic.

"Hey, Ellie," called Ava.

Madame Blavatsky stopped abruptly and gave a little wave. "Hello, ladies." Then she said to Ava, "I'm a little early; hope you don't mind." She was dressed in a floor-length purple skirt, red blouse with puffy sleeves, and a paisley shawl draped around her shoulders. Beads hung around her neck and large agate and opal rings flashed on her fingers. Standard fortune-teller garb.

"No problem," said Ava. She made meaningful eye contact with Carmela and said, in a low voice, "*Cher*, are you thinking what I'm thinking?"

Carmela shrugged. "Why not? What would be the harm?" Carmela wasn't a huge believer in tarot cards, astrology, or even the *I Ching*. But when you had a genuine psychic in the house, who wouldn't want to see if you could tap the keg, so to speak?

"Do you have a minute?" Ava called to Madame Blavatsky. "We'd like you to look at something that we think is kind of creepy. Maybe get your read on it."

"Of course," said Madame Blavatsky. She walked slowly toward them.

Carmela handed her postcard number one, then postcard number two.

Madame Blavatsky studied the postcards, then gazed directly at Carmela. "These came to you."

"Yes," said Carmela.

"After you witnessed the hanging." Ava had obviously filled her in on Kimber's murder.

"I didn't actually witness it," said Carmela. "I found Kimber Breeze after the fact."

"But she was still hanging there," said Madame Blavatsky. "Her body had not yet been recovered."

"I'm afraid that's true," said Carmela, recalling the horror of the scene, the utter helplessness she'd felt.

Ava spoke up. "We thought perhaps you could try to glean some sort of essence or aura from the postcards. Help us figure out who sent them and why. You know, pierce the membrane into the unknown."

Madame Blavatsky nodded. "I can give it a try."

They all trooped toward the back of Ava's shop and into the small octagonal-shaped reading room. The room was cool and dark and swagged with dark-green velvet draperies. Backlit by two small lights were a pair of stained-glass windows that had been salvaged from an old orphanage that had been torn down in the late forties. They depicted two angels, each carrying a small lamb, and Ava had discovered them in the back room of an antique store. Ava found them meaningful and loved them. Carmela had reserved judgment. She thought they came from an unhappy place and might exude a touch of bad karma.

Carmela and Madame Blavatsky sat down at a round table covered with a purple paisley shawl, while Ava dimmed the lights.

"I think the spirits prefer it dim," Ava whispered to Carmela.

"Couldn't hurt," said Madame Blavatsky, as Carmela placed the two postcards in the middle of the table.

They sat for a few minutes, Madame Blavatsky with her eyes closed, and Carmela and Ava eyeing Madame Blavatsky, who seemed to be either focusing intensely or grabbing a quick catnap. Then her eyes suddenly flew open and she spat out one word. "Trickery."

"Pardon?" said Carmela. Had she heard the woman correctly?

"You mean someone's playing a trick on Carmela?" said Ava. "Well, we kind of knew . . ."

"No," said Madame Blavatsky. "It's not that simple. I'm picking up another energy field. Something that's black and amorphous, probably because it deals with deceit, deception, or illusion."

Now Ava's eyes widened and she grabbed

Carmela's hand. "Well *that* doesn't sound good."

"Do you know who's doing the deceiving?" asked Carmela, feeling a prickle of unease. "Can you see anything more?"

"I'm sorry," said Madame Blavatsky, "but that part is rather unclear. You see . . ."

Carmela and Ava leaned forward.

Madame Blavatsky drew a decisive breath. "There are *multiple* deceptions."

"Can you elaborate?" Ava asked.

Madame Blavatsky focused on Carmela. "I'm also getting strange images concerning the murder the other night."

"Really," said Carmela. "Do you get any feeling about the crime scene itself? The balcony?"

Madame Blavatsky's eyes closed again. "Small, a very tight space."

"That's it!" said Ava.

"But I'm seeing an image from a different vantage point," said Madame Blavatsky.

"Are you looking up?" asked Carmela. "From where the parade was happening below?"

Madame Blavatsky shook her head. "No, it seems to be a more . . . level perspective."

Maybe those adjoining balconies? Carmela wondered. And on the heels of that, *Doggone, maybe I should stop by the Hotel Trem-*

ain and take another look.

Madame Blavatsky's eyes popped open and she let loose a long sigh. "Did that help? Any of it?"

"You know," said Carmela, "I think it might."

On her way down Dauphine Street, Carmella pulled out her cell phone and called Raleigh.

"Hey," she said, when she finally got him on the line. "I took a look at that DVD you gave me."

"Yeah?" said Raleigh. "What did you think?"

"The only thing that really jumped out at me," said Carmela, "was the clown."

"Huh," said Raleigh. "That struck me as strange, too."

"He's there one second," said Carmela, "then gone the next. Anyway, I found it a little creepy."

"You think I should give a copy of that video to the police?"

"I think you pretty much have to," said Carmela.

"Okay," said Raleigh. "Thanks."

"Listen," said Carmela, "were you always teamed with Kimber? As her cameraman?"

"The last few months, anyway."

"Including those investigative reports she'd just started working on?"

"That's right," said Raleigh.

"Without betraying any confidences, can you tell me a little about those reports?"

"We hadn't shot much footage yet," said Raleigh. "Maybe, like, five minutes of B-roll."

"What's B-roll?"

"Ah, just crap you stick in to pad a story. Location shots, stuff that helps to establish where you are or what you're talking about."

"So you're saying that Kimber was still basically in the research stage?"

There was a full ten seconds of dead air and then Raleigh said, "I can tell you a little about what I know, which isn't all that much. One investigation centered on a big-shot real estate developer named Whitney Geiger. Kimber had stumbled on some evidence that he might be running some kind of mortgage fraud scam."

"Well, shoot," said Carmela, sounding a little disappointed, "everybody and his brother is doing that these days. Was there anything else?"

"Yeah," said Raleigh. "The other thing Kimber was working on had something to do with a drug dealer. Kimber was moving a little more cautiously on that one."

"What kind of drugs?"

"Um . . . cocaine, I think."

"Dangerous," said Carmela. "Do you know who she was talking to?" In other words, did Raleigh know who the drug dealer was? If Kimber had actually made contact?

"I have no idea."

"So you don't know if Kimber made any inroads?"

"Not that I know of," said Raleigh. He cleared his throat and said, "Wait a minute, are you thinking Kimber might have been murdered by a drug dealer?"

"I don't know what to think," said Carmela. "But I suppose it's possible."

"Possible or probable?" asked Raleigh.

"Again," said Carmela, frustration welling up inside, "I don't really know."

It was a snap getting back into the Bonaparte Suite. Carmela just told the harried desk clerk at the Hotel Tremain that she was with KBEZ-TV and needed to double-check to ensure that none of their equipment had been left behind. The desk clerk, who was in the middle of checking two couples in, just nodded and slid the key across the counter to her.

Once Carmela entered the suite, she

looked around cautiously. It was an over-sized hospitality suite, done in a sort of thirties style in colors of celadon green and faded plum. The first room, a very large sitting room, consisted of two sofas, six matching easy chairs, a dining room table and chairs that could easily accommodate sixteen people, plus a long oak credenza that had doubled as a bar when she was here two nights ago.

Walking across an acre of carpet, Carmela stepped into the adjacent bedroom. It, too, was large, comfortable, and plush, done in the same green and plum shades, with a bathroom en suite. The entire place had obviously been carefully cleaned and straightened, since a collection of hotel placards was now scattered about. Room service menus, instructions for ordering in-room movies, ads for limousine services. Like that.

Walking back into the sitting room, Carmela glanced at the filmy draperies. She knew what lay beyond them. The balcony.

Drawing a deep breath, she pushed the draperies aside, cranked the door open, and stepped outside.

Sunshine sparkled down and a cool breeze whispered gently. From this fourth-floor perch, the bird's-eye view of the French

Quarter was dazzling. Blocks spread out below filled with green and blue Creole cottages, yellow brick buildings, rooftops of gray slate, and narrow cobblestone streets. Carmela was also afforded a peek into a dozen or so lush interior courtyards that were walled and completely hidden to passersby on the street.

As she stepped to her left, the wrought-iron balcony suddenly shuddered and let loose a low metallic groan.

Carmela's heart skipped a beat. Was this thing secure? Was it steady? How the heck old was it anyway?

But Carmela didn't retreat. She stood her ground, grasped the railing, and quickly inspected the balconies to either side. Yes, they were in rather close proximity. Yes, someone relatively agile could climb from one to the other.

She gazed down, wondering if it was possible to clamber up from the balcony below. Possible, but not probable, she decided. That would take a killer with gazelle-like moves.

Carmela was about to step inside when Madame Blavatsky's words pinged inside her brain. What had she said? Something about a different perspective? A different point of view? So . . . had the killer climbed down from the roof? Possibly, although that seemed awfully tricky. She knew, from the little bit of rock climbing she'd done, that the descent was always more difficult than the ascent.

So then what?

Carmela narrowed her eyes as she gazed across the street. A tall, narrow building stood directly opposite the Hotel Tremain. The Magnolia Travel Agency occupied the first floor, while the second floor appeared to be occupied by Durand's Antique Coins and Maps. But the third-floor window was framed with floral curtains.

An apartment? Someone living there? Was that the perspective Madame Blavatsky had somehow seen? Because if it was, then maybe there had been a witness!

CHAPTER 11

It was a simple matter of returning the key, hustling across the street, and climbing two flights of stairs. There appeared to be two apartments. One that fronted the street, and one that faced the alley.

Carmela knocked on the door of the street-side apartment and held her breath. Seconds ticked by. She knocked again, this time a little more insistently. Then she heard a woman's voice. She seemed to be saying, "I'm coming, I'm coming."

A latch rattled, then the door opened. A woman's face appeared in the three-inch space where a chain stretched across.

"Yes?" said the woman. She was in her forties, with white-blond hair piled atop her head like a show pony. A red silk kimono was wrapped around her.

"Excuse me," said Carmela, "I don't mean to bother you, but I was wondering if I could ask you a couple of questions?"

The woman gave a slow blink. "About what?"

Carmela took a deep breath. "A friend of mine was killed two nights ago. On the balcony across the way."

Concern flickered on the woman's face and she said, "A tragedy. I . . . I saw some of it."

"Then you were here the other night?" Carmela was excited. Maybe this woman really was a witness!

"I was here and I already talked to the police," said the woman.

Carmela's heart sank. Probably nothing here if the police had already questioned her.

The woman reached up and unhooked the chain. "Come in. I'm sorry about your friend."

Carmela walked into an apartment that was painted Pepto-Bismol pink and had a matching Pepto-pink rug and sofa pillows, as well as a hyperactive Jack Russell terrier.

"That yappy little furball is Jacques," said the woman. "I'm Tabitha. Tabby."

"Nice to meet you, Tabby," said Carmela. "I'm Carmela Bertrand." She made a vague gesture. "I own the Memory Mine scrapbook store, a couple of blocks over on Governor Nicholls Street."

"Oh, sure," said Tabby. "I've seen your place."

"So the New Orleans police have already interviewed you," said Carmela.

"Not really interviewed," said Tabby, "but they stopped by. That night, in fact. I think they were canvassing the entire neighborhood."

"Hard to do with the parade rolling by."

"Almost impossible," said Tabby. "But I think since I live directly across from the hotel . . . well, they thought I might have seen the murder."

"Did you?"

"No, like I told them, I was watching the parade."

"So you saw nothing that happened on the balcony?" asked Carmela.

"I saw the lights," said Tabby. "They were there all night. But as far as seeing that anchorwoman strangled . . . no. I saw nothing like that."

"Maybe you didn't see anyone," said Carmela, "I mean, not an actual person. But, at any time, did you have a strange feeling? Or get a sense that something might be wrong?"

Tabby's brows pressed together, then she waved a hand. "Maybe. But you're going to think it's really stupid."

"No, I won't," said Carmela. "Tell me, please, what you thought you might have seen"

"Not really *seen*," said Tabby. "It was more . . . I suppose you'd call it a fleeting impression."

"Yes?"

"It didn't even occur to me until the next morning, after I'd talked to the police."

Carmela ducked her head, as if offering encouragement. "Your impression?"

The woman gave a wry grin. "You're really going to think I'm seriously strange."

"No, I won't," said Carmela. "I promise I won't."

"Just before the police and fire trucks roared up, I glanced across the street and, for some reason, thought about a soul or spirit." She looked thoughtful for a minute, then added, "You know, like a ghost."

"Why a ghost?" asked Carmela.

"Because the one thing that stuck in my memory, of *whatever* I caught sight of," said Tabby, "is that it was white and silky."

Just like a clown costume, Carmela thought to herself as she dashed down the street. Just like the clown costume she and Ava had seen on that video. The question was, how could she follow up? How do you go out and track down a clown?

Gabby looked more than a little frantic by the time Carmela lurched into Memory Mine. Her normally pale complexion was flushed bright pink and she was dashing about the shop, pulling albums off the shelf and digging through a basket of stencils.

"Oh good gracious," Gabby exclaimed, when she saw Carmela. "I was afraid you wouldn't make it back in time."

Carmela glanced at her watch. "We've got an hour and a half before the class starts. That's plenty of time."

Gabby exhaled slowly. "I guess." She still looked unsure. As if she couldn't just shut off her nervous energy like she was turning off a back burner. "The shop's been super busy and then two more people called to ask if they could join this afternoon's class . . ."

"I hope you told them yes."

"Of course I did," said Gabby. "I figure we can always use the business."

"We'll take it any way we can get it," said Carmela. "Classes, sales of paper, rubber stamps, and beads, or working after hours to design custom scrapbooks. But right now, why don't I man the front counter while you hustle over to the deli and grab us a couple of po'boys?"

Gabby gave a slow blink. "You want lunch?"

"Sure. Don't you? We need to fortify ourselves. It's going to be a hectic afternoon."

"Well, okay, if you think we've got time."

"There's time," said Carmela. "There's always time."

While Gabby dashed out, Carmela quickly pulled things together for her afternoon class. She grabbed a stack of paper, a bunch of ribbon, a few packages of charms, and some decals, and stacked it all in the middle of the craft table. Then she waited on a couple of people who needed green and purple paper, helped a woman find some butterfly paper as well as butterfly motifs, and took a phone order from a good customer who lived up in Natchitoches, a picturesque little town where the movie *Steel Magnolias* had been filmed.

And by the time Gabby came back with the po'boys, Carmela had worked up an appetite by helping yet another half-dozen customers.

"We're really jumping today," said Gabby, as she handed Carmela her sandwich.

"Works for me," said Carmela. "You want to take your lunch break first?" Her sandwich felt squishy, and she figured it was about to start leaking mayonnaise in a matter of seconds, but Gabby seemed the most in need of a relaxing lunch.

Gabby shook her head. "You go first. I'm too keyed up to eat right now."

"Okey-doke."

Carmela ducked into her office and unwrapped her po'boy. Gabby had gotten her favorite, of course. Deep-fried oysters smothered with cole slaw and mayonnaise on toasted French bread. It was decadent, goopy, and totally delicious. But she would have enjoyed it a lot more if images of white clown costumes weren't swirling in her brain.

Twenty minutes later, Baby swooped in, looking all preppy and cute in a navy blazer and winter-white wool slacks.

"You're early," said Carmela. She'd just pulled a few more sheets of paper and some stickers.

"I've been buzzing around the French Quarter all morning," said Baby, looking flushed and happy, "so I was already in the neighborhood."

"Getting ready for your big party Monday night?" Baby always threw an elegant catered party right before Fat Tuesday and this year was no exception.

Baby nodded happily. "Just finalizing the

158

flower arrangements with Cora Lou over at the French Bouquet. She's doing huge bouquets of purple delphiniums, golden roses, and green zinnias. Well, they're really chartreuse, but we're calling them green."

"Gotta have the traditional Mardi Gras colors," said Carmela. Purple for justice, gold for power, and green for faith.

"And I'm using that new caterer, Troubadour," said Baby. She rolled her eyes. "You're not going to believe the fantastic menu they came up with!"

"I can't wait," said Carmela. Baby's parties were always over the top and super luxe.

"Oh, and I talked to Ava about hiring her psychic. It's a go."

"Madame Blavatsky," said Carmela, recalling her earlier meeting with her. "She'll for sure keep your guests entertained."

"So much better than a magician, don't you think?"

"Or a mime," Carmela agreed. "Can't stand mimes."

"What is it about mimes," asked Baby, "that makes them so creepy?"

"Who's creepy?" demanded Tandy. She'd kind of sneaked up behind them and was looking decidedly interested.

"Mimes," said Baby. She waved her hand in front of her face. "You know, pasty white face, all that pantomiming."

Tandy scowled. "They're the worst. Plus they always have this superior attitude. Like you're *supposed* to find them witty and amusing." She shook her head. "I don't like entertainment that's so demanding."

"Baby was just telling me about her flowers and her new caterer," said Carmela.

"Yum," said Tandy. Even though she looked like she never ate a bite, Tandy could chow down like a long-haul trucker.

Baby nodded eagerly. "We're serving shrimp rémoulade and trout amandine and . . ."

Tandy held up a scrawny paw, like she was trying to ward off an alien attack. "Stop! Don't tell me. I want it to be a huge surprise!"

"Oh, it will be," Baby promised.

Ten minutes later, the rest of the crafters showed up and Carmela got seriously busy. Baby, Tandy, and seven other women crowded around the craft table, anxious to get started. Sitting in front of each of them was a natural birchwood cigar box with brass fittings and a bamboo handle.

"These are so cute," said Baby, caressing the unfinished wood.

"Adorable," said one of the women.

"They're almost too pretty to touch."

"But we're going to make them even more gorgeous," Carmela told her group. "In fact, we're going to give them a real Parisian flair."

"Sounds very Coco Chanel," said Tandy, peering over her half-glasses.

"They can be," said Carmela. "But first we start with a little paint job."

Gabby set four jars of aqua-blue paint on the table along with foam brushes.

"We're going to paint the outside edges," said Carmela. "Then, once your paint dries, we're going to glue on some paper." She held up a sheet of dark blue paper covered with pink polka dots.

"Cute," said Baby.

"Our purses are going to be polka dots?" asked one of the women.

"Just the background," Carmela explained. "Once we glue paper on the boxes, we're going to decorate them." She held up a decal of the Eiffel Tower. "And here's where it gets fun. "You choose the decals or rubber stamps or ephemera that you like best."

"Give us an example," said Tandy.

"Sure," said Carmela. She took the Eiffel Tower decal and stuck it on a small piece of foam core. "I'm adhering this decal to the foam core to give it some dimension. Now all I have to do is cut it out and paste it on my purse." She held it up to show them. "Then I'm going to add a few more fun designs. For example, I have some French postage stamps, a rubber stamp of some French poetry verses, and a piece of toile."

"I love it!" said Baby. "So we can kind of freestyle it. Do whatever we want?"

"Exactly," said Carmela. "Some of you might want to use a piece of French music, floral paper, a visual of a perfume bottle, or even a couture drawing." She glanced around the group, saw nods and under-standing in their eyes. "It's up to you, whatever you prefer."

Gabby edged closer to the table. "And remember, whatever you choose in the shop today is included in your class fee. And we do have some wonderful things."

"What about those fancy papers you have?" asked Tandy. "I saw some rice paper and some banana leaf paper."

"Go for it," said Carmela. "And if you want to pull a few items and do a kind of layout before you start gluing, that's fine, too. In fact, it's a really good idea." She reached up on a shelf and pulled down the cigar box purse she'd completed earlier. "As you can see, I used a piece of lace, added an image of the Arc de Triomphe, then stamped on some French postal cancellations."

"It's gorgeous," breathed Baby. "I just love all your details."

"Thank you," said Carmela. "But I'm sure all of your cigar box purses will be equally lovely."

A few of the women started painting then, while others wandered through the shop pulling out different design elements. Gabby scampered back to the front corner to wait on some new customers who'd wandered in, and Carmela went through her ephemera drawer to see if she could find any French maps, Metro tickets, or other fun Gallic items.

An hour later, with projects well under way, Carmela served mugs of Mariage Frères tea while Gabby set out a plate of colorful French macarons, along with the ubiquitous Mardi Gras king cake.

They were all relaxing, chatting, and getting to know each other when, suddenly, the front door swung open. It slammed against a shelf of leather-bound albums, causing some of them to teeter and everyone to stop what they were doing and look around.

That was when Edgar Babcock came

striding in. His face carried a solemn, purposeful look, and Carmela knew this wasn't a social call. No way had Babcock just idly dropped in to invite her to a candlelight dinner. The man definitely had something on his mind.

Babcock threaded his way to the craft table and said, in a forceful voice as he hovered above Carmela, "I need a word with you."

Activity ceased. Those who recognized Babcock as a homicide detective figured something was up. Those who didn't were still suspicious.

Gabby, who'd followed him back, glanced about the table nervously. "What you want to do now," she said, "is start applying your decals."

Carmela slipped into her office with Babcock hot on her heels. Once there, he didn't waste time with kisses, hugs, or even basic pleasantries.

"I want to see those postcards," he demanded.

"What?" Carmela was stunned. "Who told you about the postcards?" Which one of her friends was texting or tweeting when they shouldn't be? Shoot, was it Ava?

"Gabby told me," said Babcock.

"She shouldn't have done that," said

Carmela. *Now it's really gonna hit the fan!*

"Oh yes, she should have," said Babcock. "In fact, *you* should have told me. You receive strange anonymous messages on the heels of a murder? I'd say that's rather serious."

Carmela tried to defuse his anger. "It's just a crank."

"Perhaps you should let me be the judge of that," said Babcock.

"If I show you the postcards, are you going to confiscate them?"

Babcock's face slowly relaxed. He didn't quite manage a smile, but it wasn't the stolid Easter Island face he'd walked in with. "No, but I'd like to stash them somewhere safe."

"Like in your evidence room or fingerprint lab?"

"Those are a couple of places that come to mind," said Babcock.

"Well . . ." Carmela was still reluctant.

"I could confiscate the postcards on the grounds they're part of an ongoing homicide investigation." When Babcock saw the look on Carmela's face, he added, "Or you could just hand them over to me and demonstrate a little trust." Now he was the one doing the defusing.

Carmela did a quick calculation and

decided he probably deserved her trust. And she knew he did have her safety in mind. So she dug into her desk drawer and pulled out the postcards.

"Just slide them into an envelope," Babcock told her. "We don't want to have to wade through numerous sets of prints."

"Okay," said Carmela, putting them into a shiny black envelope. She knew Ava and Madame Blavatsky had already handled the postcards, but what could she do? Nothing, really. She hadn't conceived they'd ever be used as any sort of evidence.

"That's good," said Babcock, the corners of his mouth finally managing an uptick.

"Since we're on the subject of murder," said Carmela, "how are things proceeding with the investigation?" She didn't want to reveal her clown clue just yet. Her theory still seemed a little half-baked.

"Things are ticking along," said Babcock.

"What's up with Kimber's brother?"

"You mean did we arrest him?"

"Well, yes."

"We did not," said Babcock. "Since there was a decided lack of evidence."

"But you questioned him."

"Obviously. In fact, Gallant and I spoke to him just this morning."

"And?"

"The brother does indeed own a farm," said Babcock. "An alligator farm, to be specific."

Carmela wasn't surprised at this. In the state of Louisiana there were something like two hundred licensed alligator farms. Breeders raised them for hides and meat. Some of the larger alligator farms were also tourist attractions and put on shows. Though the idea of going into a pen with a twelve-foot alligator, then tapping its nose and feeding it a whole chicken, seemed incredibly foolhardy, it went on just the same.

"That's it?" said Carmela. "You just talked?"

Babcock nodded.

"How long did you talk to him?"

"Long enough," said Babcock.

"I know you said the brother wasn't a prime suspect, but could you detect any underlying motive?" asked Carmela. "Anything that *might* make him a suspect?" She wanted to cut to the chase.

Babcock looked like he wasn't going to reveal anything more, and then he said, "His farm is being foreclosed on."

"Ah," said Carmela. "So he *was* desperate for money. Is desperate."

Babcock's brows knit together as he gazed at her. "Would you care to venture a guess as to which bank is foreclosing on him?"

There was something in Babcock's voice. A wary tone . . .

"Oh crap." Carmela gulped. "Don't tell me it's Crescent City Bank. Shamus's bank!"

CHAPTER 12

Babcock gave an affirmative shrug. "Give that lady a plush pink teddy bear."

"Is there any way he can get an extension?" Carmela didn't even know Billy Laforge, had pretty much pegged the guy as a suspect, but now, in the blink of an eye, she was rooting for him. The little guy against the big bad bank. Carmela knew it was a little wacky, but it had always been in her nature to side with the underdog.

"I have no idea what his financial situation is," said Babcock. "That's not my area of interest or expertise. I'm far more concerned with questioning possible suspects and determining motive." He hesitated. "Basically, chasing down the bad guys."

"Gotcha," said Carmela, as her mind leaped into overdrive and she thought, *Maybe I can find something out from Shamus.*

"So I'm going to be busy tonight," said Babcock, moving a step closer to her, finally sending out the sexy vibes. "But maybe we could meet for a drink?"

Carmela was still a little distracted. "Sure. Where?"

"Across the street? Glisande's?"

"All right," said Carmela. "I should meet you there . . . what? Around five?"

Babcock leaned forward and kissed the top of Carmela's head. "Perfect. I'll see you there."

But before Carmela turned her attention back to her crafters, she had a phone call to deal with. A rather strange call from Ed Banister at KBEZ-TV.

"Carmela!" said Ed, greeting her with over-the-top exuberance. "I want to put you on TV!"

That pretty much caught her off-guard. "Seriously?"

"I'm dead serious," said Banister.

"Um . . . why?" asked Carmela. She didn't think her good looks, charm, and sparkling wit would exactly make for a kick-butt reality show. Or even warrant another interview.

"It's about the postcards," said Banister.

"Oh crap! Did Gabby . . . ?"

Banister hastened to fill her in. "No, no, your friend Ava told me all about them. We're still shooting our Mardi Gras documentary, and her shop was on our shot list. Tourists are fascinated by our local voodoo shops. You know how it is . . ."

"And while you were interviewing Ava she just blurted it out to you," said Carmela. "About the postcards." *Jeez, does everybody know about these stupid postcards?*

"Ava and I were discussing Kimber's murder — how could we not?" said Banister. "And then the postcard thing just naturally came up."

Naturally. Right. "I see," said Carmela, sounding a little grumbly.

"So what I'd really love to do," said Banister, "is put you on TV and do a feature story."

"Creepy postcards are fodder for a story?" asked Carmela. Somehow, she didn't quite see it that way. They were certainly a curiosity, but an actual story?

"No, no, they're a fantastic story!" Banister countered. "Linked to the Kimber Breeze murder, it suddenly gives us an added dimension of danger and mystery."

"Interesting," said Carmela, even though she still wasn't feeling it.

"Plus," said Banister, his voice intensifying, "it's possible a story on TV might even lure in the killer!" There was a moment of silence as they both chewed on this idea.

Then Banister added, "Maybe we could even offer a reward!"

"I don't know," said Carmela, "it sounds a little dangerous." *Dangerous for me.*

"But think of the ratings!" Banister rhapsodized. "Plus, you'd be an instant celebrity. Everybody and his brother-in-law wants to be a celebrity these days. Everybody thinks their life would make for great television viewing. And . . . and . . ." Banister was totally whipped up. "You could even, heh heh, outshine your ex-husband! Show up that crazy Meechum family."

"So there *would* be a bright spot in all of this," said Carmela.

"All I'm asking," said Banister, "is that you think about it. Will you do that? Think about it?"

"I'll think about it," Carmela promised. *For about three seconds.*

When Carmela finally made it back to the craft table, she was thrilled at how terrific the cigar box purses looked. Tandy had opted for a French menu design, while another crafter had woven strands of raffia into a bird nest, then affixed it to the side of her bag and added a tiny, feathered bluebird.

"You didn't need me." Carmela laughed.

"Are you kidding?" said Baby. "You were the inspiration for this entire class."

"The springboard," added Tandy.

"No," said Carmela, "you guys just let your imaginations rip. And that's what it's all about. So . . . good work." Pleased, Carmela wandered up to the front counter, where Gabby was tallying the day's receipts. "You told Babcock," she said, but not in an accusatory manner. "About the postcards."

"I'm sorry," said Gabby, looking nervous, "but I was terrified for you. I had this horrible vision in my head that the same maniac who hung Kimber Breeze from that balcony would come after you." She touched a hand to the side of her face. "And it was too awful to even contemplate." She hesitated. "Are you furious with me?"

"No," said Carmela. "It turns out Ava blabbed, too."

"Did she really? About the postcards?"

"Yup. She mentioned them to Ed Banister at KBEZ and now he's all whipped up and wants to do a feature story about them. Correction, about me receiving the postcards."

Gabby looked shocked. "You can't do that! The *police* need to deal with this, not a bunch of television goofballs."

"Well," said Carmela, "the television goofballs are all over this, like a rat terrier on a chew bone."

"And they want you to go on TV?" said Gabby, shaking her head. "What did you tell them? A big fat no, I hope."

"That was my gut reaction," said Carmela.

"Good," said Gabby.

"But now that I think about it . . ." said Carmela. "I mean, what if a story about the postcards *did* shake something loose? What if it helped flush out the killer?"

Gabby gazed at her with flashing eyes. "What if it got you killed? What about that!"

"I'm not saying I'm going to do it," said Carmela, "but if I did, it would have to be with some serious police protection."

"It still sounds too risky."

"Just the same, I'm going to run it past Babcock."

"And he's going to say no," said Gabby. "He's going to despise the idea!"

"You think?"

"I know he will," said Gabby. She leaned across the counter toward Carmela and lowered her voice to a whisper. "Carmela, whoever murdered Kimber is a *maniac*. Believe me, you don't want a guy like that turning his attention on you."

"The thing is," Carmela said with a grimace, "if the killer and the postcard guy are

174

one and the same, then I already have a target on my back."

Carmela was helping the last couple of crafters apply a tricky stencil design when Shamus called. As Gabby made meaningful hand signals, indicating it was Shamus the rat, Carmela sighed deeply and slipped into her office to take his call.

"Hey," she said to Shamus, taking care not to convey too much warmth or excitement. Lest he read something into it. Like getting back together for an extracurricular tryst.

But Shamus was syrupy sweet. "Carmela!" he said. "Babe!"

With a greeting that warm and friendly, Carmela knew he was up to something. "What do you want?"

"Can't I just phone my ex-wife to say hello?" said Shamus.

Carmela considered his words. "No. Because there's always a hidden agenda. Whenever you call me, it's to ask for a favor or some sort of . . . I don't know . . . concession. So. What do you want?" Carmela could imagine Shamus sitting at his desk, nervously jiggling a foot. Tall, good-looking, a swipe of brown hair across his broad, handsome face, and an easy grin that could turn into a smirk at a moment's notice. He'd been born into money and pretty much figured the world was his pearl-producing oyster.

"Did you get a chance to talk to your police detective friend?" Shamus asked.

"Not really."

"But you're going to, right?" said Shamus. "I mean, Sugar Joe is awfully unnerved. Him being a prime suspect and all."

"Somehow I don't really think he's a legitimate suspect," said Carmela.

"Oh no?" Shamus sounded surprised but pleased.

"I don't think the police will try to pin this on him. Sugar Joe was just sort of . . . tossed into the mix. Doesn't mean too much."

"Heh heh," said Shamus. "So you *did* work on your cop lover boy. Good for you, babe."

"Whatever," said Carmela.

"There's something else I need to talk to you about," said Shamus.

"What's that?"

"I want to invite you to a special art opening at the Click! Gallery." The Click! Gallery was an established French Quarter gallery. In fact, Shamus had once had an exhibit of wildlife photography there.

"Yeah?" said Carmela. "When's the opening?"

"Tonight," said Shamus.

This was typical Shamus, Carmela decided. Always leaving things to the last minute. "Excuse me, but this is awfully late notice."

"You're a spontaneous person," Shamus urged. "So be a sport and come." He paused. "I'll be there."

"Shamus," said Carmela, "we're no longer married and you're no longer large and in charge. Besides, what if I happen to have plans for tonight?"

"I bet you don't," said Shamus. "And I'm being real nice and polite because I'm asking such a big favor. Aren't I being polite? Aren't I being sweet?"

"Riddle me this, riddle me that, Shamus. What *are* you talking about?"

"Here's the deal," said Shamus. "Crescent City Bank is sponsoring this art exhibition, and part of the profits from the sale of the artwork will be donated to charity."

"So you're asking me to come as a ringer," said Carmela.

"Well . . ." said Shamus.

"You want me to help make the crowd look bigger so you get media coverage. Which is kind of like . . . I don't know . . .

177

stuffing the ballot box."

"You make my motives sound so duplicitous," said Shamus. "When all I want is for you to show up and have fun."

"Doubtful," said Carmela. She let loose an exasperated huff, then said, "What charity?"

"I don't know. Something to do with orphan animals, I guess."

"You're not just saying that to pluck at my heartstrings, are you?"

"I wouldn't do that," said Shamus.

"Of course you would," said Carmela. "Crap, it's probably to raise money so rich kids can take polo lessons."

"Please," Shamus wheedled. "You could drop by for, like, twenty minutes. It wouldn't kill you. And it would mean everything to me."

"I was going to do something with Ava."

"That's perfect," said Shamus. "Bring her along. The more the merrier."

"Mmm . . . maybe I could drop by if you shared a little information with me."

Shamus was instantly on alert. "What are you talking about?"

"There's an alligator farm over near Theriot that Crescent City Bank is about to foreclose on . . ."

"I don't work in mortgages or foreclosures," snapped Shamus. "I'm in private banking. Basically, it's up to me to maintain smooth customer relationships with our major account holders."

"Your role at the bank is to schmooze fat cats," said Carmela. "Take 'em to lunch and pay for drinks. Play a round of golf with them and slip them football tickets once in a while. I'm sure the job's a pressure cooker."

"It is," said Shamus, with all seriousness.

"But maybe you could check on this one little thing for me?"

Shamus made a rude sound.

"How about this," said Carmela. "Straight-ahead quid pro quo. Any information you can dig up in exchange for my personal appearance tonight."

"I suppose." The reluctance in Shamus's voice made him sound like a stubborn five-year-old who was finally agreeing to lie down and take his nap.

"And one more question," said Carmela. "Are you familiar with a real estate developer by the name of Whitney Geiger?" Geiger was one of the stories Kimber Breeze had been working on. Carmela knew it was tenuous, but she was looking at all possible connections to the murder.

"Why are you asking?" said Shamus.

"Geiger's name came up in conversation and I'm curious about him," said Carmela. She was pleased that she'd answered Shamus's question without giving a legit answer. *I should have Shamus's job.*

"I don't know him well," said Shamus, "but Geiger's in the Pluvius krewe with me and Sugar Joe."

"Seriously?" *So he'll probably be at the float party Sunday night.*

"Yeah, of course I'm serious."

"So what do you know about him?" Carmela asked.

Shamus hemmed and hawed for a few moments, and then Carmela said, "I really will make this worth your while."

"So you'll really come to the art show tonight?"

"I'll be there with bells on. And Ava on my arm. Two cute chicks for the price of one."

"Okay," said Shamus. "You drive a hard deal, but we do have a deal."

"So tell me," said Carmela.

"Whit Geiger owns a company called Royale Real Estate. He was a mortgage banker for a while, but now he's building a slug of mega mansions over near the Lake Vista area."

"Anything else you know about him?"

"Not that I can think of at the moment," said Shamus.

"I'm going to need you to find out a little more. Could you ask somebody at the bank? Someone who deals in real estate?

"Mmm . . . maybe."

"It would mean a lot to me," said Carmela.

"And you're really coming to the Click! show?"

"Yes, a promise is a promise." *Even though you never kept yours. Particularly your marriage vows.*

"Excellent," said Shamus. "See you tonight!"

Once Carmela had called Ava and put her on red alert for the Click! Gallery show, she hustled her buns across the street to meet Babcock.

Glisande's Courtyard Restaurant was already full, its dining room decorated in a lovely French country style, its bar a little more sleek and dark, like an old French railway car.

Babcock was sitting on a bar stool, twiddling a swizzle stick in one hand. His drink and cell phone rested on the bar in front of him. He looked tall, handsome, and available, and Carmela had the feeling that more than a few predatory single women had already noticed him and scoped him out.

She slipped onto the bar stool next to him. "Hello, handsome," she said. "Buy you a drink?"

He swiveled toward her. "Sorry, ma'am, but I'm with someone." Then he grinned and leaned forward to give her a kiss. "In fact, I'm with you." He kissed her again and they snuggled closer, touching and bumping shoulders. "What would you like to drink?"

"Just a Diet Coke," said Carmela. "I'm rushing off to the Click! Gallery tonight."

"Where they'll undoubtedly be well stocked with cheap white wine," said Babcock. "The art gallery's stock in trade."

"Probably brought in from New Jersey in tanker trucks." She waited as Babcock ordered her Diet Coke and then got another ginger ale for himself. Then she said, "I've got something I want to run by you."

"Shoot," said Babcock.

"It turns out everybody and his brother-in-law knows about those stupid postcards I got," said Carmela. "Including the people at KBEZ-TV."

Babcock frowned. "Who spilled the beans?"

"Ava."

"Ah, she can be quite the motormouth."

"Anyway," said Carmela, "Ed Banister asked if I'd be willing to let them do a story about the postcards. A sort of TV sidebar. You know, something that's peripherally related to the murder?" Even as she spelled it out, it sounded like a terrible idea. "So, what do you think? Good idea? Not so good?"

"It's a terrible idea," Babcock sputtered.

"So what do you *really* think?" Carmela asked.

"I'm radically opposed to the idea," said Babcock, "because there's no earthly reason to believe the postcards are in any way related to Kimber's murder."

Carmela raised an eyebrow. "Oh no? Then why does the sender always ask why I didn't help Kimber? And why are the cards signed with her name?"

"Because some creep thinks it's funny, that's why," said Babcock.

"And you don't think the two are related?"

"There isn't a shred of evidence to suggest they are," said Babcock.

"Okay," said Carmela. "I guess that settles that." She took a sip of Diet Coke and said, "Is Sugar Joe a real suspect?"

"Joe Panola?" said Babcock. "Not really. He doesn't have any priors, nor does it appear he had a motive. Unless, of course, something pops up on our radar screen."

"Good," said Carmela. "Excellent. Then what about Whit Geiger?"

"What about Whit Geiger?"

"Kimber was doing some sort of investigative report on him," said Carmela.

"Let me guess," said Babcock. "So now *you're* investigating him."

"It could lead to something," said Carmela.

"And it could lead to nothing." Babcock leaned forward and rested his elbows on the bar. "I received a rather interesting tape this afternoon. Or, rather, DVD."

"Oh?" Carmela took another quick gulp of Diet Coke.

"From Raleigh, the cameraman." His finger poked out and spun his cell phone around.

"Uh-huh," said Carmela, watching the slice of silver spin like a top. *Lots of information locked up in there,* she thought.

Babcock narrowed his eyes. "You know exactly which DVD I'm referring to, don't you?" He was no fool. He knew she was tight with Raleigh.

"Um . . . maybe."

"A video of the party that was going on in the Bonaparte Suite?"

184

"Anything interesting on it?" asked Carmela.

"Possibly," said Babcock. "Oh crap." He scrunched to one side, then pulled out the beeper that was clipped to his belt. He squinted at it, sighed, and said, "Gotta make a call. Excuse me." Then he was gone. Out the back door and onto the patio where he could do his police work relatively undisturbed. And where she couldn't eavesdrop.

Carmela sat up straighter and gazed out a sliver of window. Yup, he was out there all right, pacing back and forth. She wondered what was going on. A new development in the case?

When Babcock returned she asked him.

"So what's up?"

He made a face. "Just this drug thing I'm working on. There's a whole roster of new street drugs out there — spice, K2, Ivory Wave — you name it. And we can't seem to get a handle on the crew that's behind them."

"Tough," said Carmela. New Orleans, being a port city, meant ships were coming in from everywhere. The Caribbean, South America, Asia.

"Those drugs are bad news," said Babcock. He hesitated for a moment, then said, "Did you know the TV station might try to

185

offer some kind of reward?"

Carmela gazed at him. "For information leading to?"

"Exactly," said Babcock. He eyed her. "I'm guessing they figured you wouldn't consent to an interview, so they cooked up the reward."

"There really is a reward? When did this happen?"

"We got the call a couple of hours ago," said Babcock.

"Maybe offering a reward is a good idea," said Carmela. *Better than me going out on a limb.*

"And maybe we'll get a million calls from everybody who's either dead broke or paranoid," said Babcock. "No, I basically hate the idea of a reward. It ties up critical manpower and the information rarely pans out."

"You've always got me," Carmela joked. "I'll help out."

Babcock held up a hand. "Please. Don't do any more than you already have."

"I'm just saying . . ."

Babcock slid off his bar stool and circled his arms around her. "I just want you to stay safe, okay?"

"Okay," said Carmela. *Okay* to her meant, *Okay I hear you.* Not, *Okay I'll stay in the background.*

"I'll be back in two shakes," Babcock told her. "I have to run out and have a word with Gallant. He should be parked out front by now."

As Babcock dashed off, Carmela's eyes drifted to his cell phone, just sitting there next to his drink.

Do I dare?

She dared.

Quickly, Carmela flipped through the address book. When she came to the name Billy Laforge, she studied the address. Two eighty-one Longfellow Road. Yup, she could remember that.

In fact, she might even take a trip out there and pay Billy a friendly visit.

CHAPTER 13

The Click! Gallery, owned by Clark Berthume, was a long, narrow gallery wedged in between Calliope Antiques and Shooters Oyster Bar. Normally, its shiny white walls were hung with photographs. Black-and-white shots of St. Louis Cemetery No. 2, architectural studies of the French Quarter, moldering old plantations out on River Road. Sometimes the shows were more colorful, offering moody portraits of shrimpers working the Breton Sound, serene ibis and egrets hovering over the Baritaria Bayou, or fantastic shots of torchlight Mardi Gras parades.

Tonight Carmela could see big, color-splotched paintings gracing the walls. And the gallery was already humming with noise and thronged with people.

"Looks like their opening reception is a huge success," said Ava, as they stood in the doorway. Somewhere, beyond the jostle of beautiful people, was a DJ spinning music. Carmela thought it might be a mash-up of Lady Gaga's "Marry the Night" and Katy Perry's "Firework."

"It's a success only if they sell paintings," said Carmela, "not if a bunch of freeloaders show up to guzzle wine and snarf their food."

"Like us?" said Ava, grinning.

"Excellent point," said Carmela. "Except we're *invited* freeloaders."

Ava gazed around. "So, who's the artist?"

"Probably someone who does landscape paintings or sentimental stuff," said Carmela. "That's what they usually . . ." As her eyes searched around, they landed on a large poster balanced against a wooden easel. "Whoa! Was I ever off base! It's Sullivan Finch."

Ava eyed the poster. "You know this artist?"

"Sort of. I happened to see one of his pieces when I stopped by KBEZ-TV yesterday. It was hanging in their lobby."

"So you like this guy's work?" said Ava.

"Eeh." Carmela held up a hand and made a seesawing motion. "Maybe a little too quirky for my taste."

"Really," said Ava, pushing forward. "Now I'm intrigued."

But as Ava disappeared into the crowd, Carmela's way was blocked by Shamus, who seemed to lurch out of nowhere to corner her.

"You came!" Shamus cried. He leaned forward to give her a big sloppy kiss, but Carmela managed to turn her head just in the nick of time. A damp ear was infinitely better than a wet cheek.

"Are you drunk?" Carmela hissed. Shamus had that off-balance stance that only serious drunks and sea captains seemed to share.

"Been drinking a little," Shamus admitted. He held up his drink to show her and in the process sloshed a few drops of amber liquid on the floor. "Oops." He let loose a giggle.

"This is how you act at a charity event?" said Carmela. "Where you probably have to glad-hand clients?"

Shamus peered over the rim of his glass at her. "Huh?"

"Never mind," said Carmela. *I'm not your babysitter anymore.* She glanced past him and saw the broad-shouldered Sugar Joe elbowing his way toward them.

"Carmela!" exclaimed Sugar Joe. He looped an arm around her and gave her a warm squeeze. "You're looking absolutely gorgeous! Did you come here tonight just to break my little old heart?" Sugar Joe might be a terrible flirt, but he was harmless.

"I'm here because Shamus got down on his hands and knees and begged me to come," said Carmela.

Shamus nodded. "I thought she might add a little class to this event." He took a quick sip of his drink. "And you know what else?" He winked at Sugar Joe. "I think I got Carmela to call off the Doberman pinschers!"

Sugar Joe grinned from ear to ear, as if this were the best news he'd ever heard. "You convinced your detective boyfriend that I'm not a suspect?"

Carmela shrugged. "Maybe." She had no intention of talking to Babcock, but what these two didn't know wouldn't hurt them.

"What'd I tell you!" cried Shamus. "Carmela's got clout with the NOPD!" He looked infinitely pleased, as if he'd just soloed Everest or pulled off some equally heroic feat.

"You gave the cops what for," proclaimed Sugar Joe. "Wow. How can I thank you?"

Carmela poked a finger into Shamus's chest. "For starters, make sure this doofus gets home safely. Don't let him drive."

"I won't," Sugar Joe promised.

"You're my goodest, bestest friend," Shamus slurred to Sugar Joe.

And maybe your only friend, thought Carmela. "Listen," she said to Shamus, "did you find out anything more about Whitney Geiger?"

Now Shamus looked indifferent. "Only that his company, Royale Real Estate, is incorporated in Florida."

"I wonder why Florida?" said Carmela.

"Gotta be the favorable tax laws," said Shamus. Carmela knew that Shamus despised paying taxes and tried to claim every possible deduction and write-off he could find. Then again, he'd written off their marriage, hadn't he?

"Tax reasons," said Carmela. "Okay. But can you dig a little deeper?"

Shamus looked pained.

"Do it for Carmela," urged Sugar Joe. "We owe her big-time."

"Okay . . . okay," said Shamus.

"Shamus!" An ungodly, piercing voice suddenly rose above the din of conversation and music.

Carmela took a step back and saw Glory Meechum, Shamus's older sister, elbowing her way through the crowd straight toward their cozy little group. Glory was half a head taller than Shamus, with a helmet of gray hair. She was an indeterminate age, though Carmela figured she was mid-fifties, and had beady, wonky eyes that didn't always work in tandem. Tonight she wore her usual shapeless black dress and sensible squatty heels.

"Shamus!" Glory snapped again, "we're supposed to present the check now. Your presence is required."

"Nice to see you, too, Glory," said Carmela.

Glory turned and gave her the flat-eyed stare of a rattlesnake. "Carmela. What are you doing here?" Glory had always hated Carmela. She hadn't wanted Shamus to marry her, and then she didn't want Shamus to divorce her. Go figure.

"Shamus invited me," said Carmela. She dimpled prettily. "Didn't you, Shamus?"

Shamus nodded. "Yeah, I guess." He edged closer to Sugar Joe, as if for protection.

"Since you're still able to stand," Carmela said to Shamus, "you'd better go play big-time donor and present your check. You certainly don't want to keep the crowd waiting."

Glory held up her almost-empty glass and wiggled it in the air. "Get me a bourbon first, Shamus," she said. "Before you do anything else."

"Sure thing," said Shamus, shuffling away.

Two minutes later, Carmela caught up with Ava. She was chatting with two men who were grinning at Ava as if they'd just hit the hottie patottie jackpot.

"Carmela!" cried Ava. "I want you to meet my two new friends." She pointed at a dark-haired guy. "Arnett." Then indicated a blond guy. "And Earl."

"I'm Arnett," said the blond guy. He indicated his buddy. "That's Earl."

"Whatever," said Ava. "And this is Carmela."

They chatted together for a few moments, then Carmela touched Ava on the arm. "Can I talk to you for a minute?"

"Excuse us," Ava said to the two men. "And if you gentlemen want to fetch us a couple more glasses of champagne, we surely wouldn't mind."

"Maybe we should take off," Carmela said, once they were alone.

"What?" Ava was shocked. "We just got here! Besides, I'm having fun."

"Seriously?" She knew that Arnett and Earl weren't Ava's type at all. They were waaaaay too conservative for Ava's liking.

194

"It's kind of amusing here. And have you even had a chance to peek at the artwork?"

"Not yet," said Carmela. *Maybe not ever.*

"Some of it's really quite stunning," said Ava. "Kind of . . . visceral."

"You think?" said Carmela. Together, they turned and stared at an enormous red-and-orange painting. To Carmela, it looked like a final sunset on a deserted beach after the world had imploded.

"Powerful stuff, huh?" cooed Ava.

"Er . . . I certainly admire the artist's technique," said Carmela. "I'd say he wields a serious palette knife and isn't afraid to slather on multiple layers of paint."

"Thank you," said a male voice behind them.

They both whirled to find a tall, shaggy-looking man giving them a crooked grin.

"Let me guess," said Carmela, "you're the artist?"

"Sullivan Finch at your service," said the man, giving them a wide smile. He had the scruffy look of an artist. Shoulder-length hair, watery blue eyes, drooping mustache, and tweedy but slightly frayed jacket worn casually over blue jeans.

"Nice to meet you," said Ava. She touched a finger to her chest. "Ava." She pointed toward Carmela. "And this is Carmela."

"How absolutely grand," said Finch. He looked like a hippie but affected the bored manner and tone of a smart-ass, erudite Ivy Leaguer. "Now if either of you would care to put a red dot on one of my paintings, I'd be indebted for life."

"A red . . . oh," said Ava. "You mean *buy* one?"

"Only if you can't bear to live without it," said Finch. He made a fluttering gesture with his hands. "I only want my paintings going to loving homes where they'll be appreciated and cherished forever."

"Forever's a long time," said Carmela. This guy was too much.

"Then how about until the paintings take a nice leap in value?" said Finch.

"Now you're talking," said Ava. She wiggled her hips as they moved along to the next painting. "A dog," she said. This painting was a smaller, slightly derivative version of the piece Carmela had seen at KBEZ-TV.

"Fun," said Carmela.

"Fun?" said Finch. He cocked his head like an inquisitive magpie.

Carmela gave him a look dripping with sincerity. "Your work is meant to be interpreted as a dystopian fantasy, right? So it's going to be a little loose and . . . dare I say it? Cheeky?" Was she good or what? All she had to do was spout a snatch of copy from his brochure!

Finch's face lit up like a neon sign. "Thank you, dear girl! So few people actually understand the gestalt of my work! Tell me, are you an artist yourself?"

"Carmela's a designer," said Ava. "Plus she owns a scrapbooking shop."

"Then you have studied art," said Finch.

"Guilty as charged," said Carmela. "Design major."

"I can always tell," said Finch, as they edged their way to the next painting.

Ava suddenly stopped dead in her tracks. "Whoa!" she exclaimed. "What's going on here?"

Carmela gazed at the next painting. It was a portrait of a blond woman with haunted, sunken eyes and a slash of purple down the middle of her chalk-white face. Unsettling to be sure, but there was also something extremely familiar about this woman. Carmela racked her brain, then was startled as comprehension dawned. Oh no, it couldn't be! No, the gallery wouldn't dare put this on display, would they?

"It's one of my death portraits," said Finch, regarding the painting with a somber yet paternal gaze.

"It's Kimber Breeze!" exclaimed Ava.

"Yes, it is," said Carmela. For some reason, the tiny hairs on the back of her neck were standing at full attention.

Finch nodded. "Death portraits are one of my specialties."

But Carmela was still taken aback. "When was this done?" she asked. She couldn't believe what she was seeing. A death portrait of Kimber Breeze? And to put it on display here, tonight, seemed in awfully poor taste!

"I painted this nearly a year ago," said Finch. "Before she . . ." Finch looked suddenly mournful.

"It's like a portent or premonition," Ava whispered. "Of what was to come!"

"Did Kimber know you painted this?" asked Carmela. She needed a little back story here.

"Are you kidding?" said Finch. "Kimber *posed* for it. Like I said, it's my thing. Death portraits of living people. You'd be surprised how many people commission me to do portraits like this."

A hand reached out of the crowd and clamped down tightly on Finch's right shoulder. It was Clark Berthume, the chubby, genial gallery owner. "Are you ladies monopolizing my artist?" he asked.

"Are we ever," said Ava.

"I need to grab him for a few moments," said Berthume. He dropped his voice. "Sully, I think I have a buyer for your *Other World* piece."

Finch nodded, then turned his gaze to Ava. "Can I call you? I'd love to take you to dinner sometime. Or perhaps even have you pose."

"Sure," said Ava, digging eagerly in her clutch purse. "Here, let me give you my card." She handed it to Finch. "Call any time." She grinned. "Day or night."

"I'll do that," said Finch, as he hurried off with Berthume.

"Interesting that he wants to take you out," said Carmela under her breath. She wasn't jealous, she just thought Finch seemed more interested in hustling his paintings than flirting with women.

"He seems awfully nice," said Ava.

"Don't you find it strange that he did a death portrait of Kimber?" asked Carmela.

"He said he did it a year ago," said Ava, "so it's really just a wacky coincidence."

"But Ava, you've always been a *huge* believer in coincidences."

Ava tried to shrug off Carmela's warning tone. "Still," she said, "sometimes things are just . . . happenstance."

"Okay," said Carmela. She'd just spotted

another painting she found singularly strange. One that Ava had her back to. "What about *this* particular painting?"

"Huh?" Ava whirled to check out the painting, then stared in confusion. The subject of the painting was a man in a white tattered costume standing against a red velvet curtain.

"What does that look like to you?" asked Carmela.

Ava clapped a hand to her mouth then released it. "Shoot! It's a clown."

"But look at the costume," said Carmela. Now she was getting a weird vibration in the pit of her stomach.

Reluctantly, Ava said, "It kind of reminds me of the clown we saw on Raleigh's DVD."

"Yes, it's very similar," said Carmela. "Which I find particularly creepy."

"So . . . what?" said Ava.

"Thinking back to the clown on the DVD," said Carmela, "makes me think I should check out the local costume rental shop to see who might have rented that costume."

"You think the costume leads to the killer? You think Sullivan Finch *knew* the killer?"

Or was the killer? Carmela thought to herself. Then she said to Ava, "I don't know,

200

but I think the costume shop might be a good place to start."

CHAPTER 14

Saturday morning dawned cool and overcast. Carmela and Ava rendezvoused at her apartment, then drove over to St. Louis Cemetery No. 1 in Carmela's little two-seater Mercedes, a long-ago gift from Shamus.

"Can we drive right in?" asked Ava. "It looks like it's about to pour buckets any second and I don't want to slop through puddles in these shoes."

"Perhaps five-inch platform sandals dusted with glitter aren't the most practical shoes for a day like this," suggested Carmela, glancing down at Ava's bedazzled feet.

"If they're good enough for Lady Gaga, they're good enough for me."

"Ava Gaga." Carmela chuckled. "It does have a certain ring to it."

"Hah," said Ava. "I was rocking sky-high stilettos and crazy pumps when she was a kid wearing sneakers and jeans."

"You always talk like you're ancient," said Carmela, "and you haven't even hit thirty yet. *I* haven't hit thirty yet."

"Time's a-wastin'," said Ava, sounding a little annoyed with herself. "I thought for sure I'd be married and divorced by now. Enjoying a little alimony and setting a leg trap for husband number two."

"You don't think that's a bummer attitude?"

"That's reality, chickie-poo." Ava pulled a bloodred lipstick from her bag and smeared it across her voluptuous lips. She smacked her lips together, fluffed her mass of curly hair, then turned to Carmela and asked, "How do I look?"

"In those shoes, that lipstick, and your tight leather jeans, you look like you're trolling for a hot date at Dr. Boogie's jazz club." *Not attending a funeral.*

"Exactly the look I was aiming for," said Ava, happily.

Carmela drove through the stone gates of the cemetery, passing under a scroll of antique wrought iron. Then she slowed as a uniformed police officer stepped out and waved her down. She lowered her window and said, "Problem?"

"You here for the funeral?" he asked. Looking bored, sounding bored.

"That's right."

"Which one?"

"Kimber Breeze," said Carmela.

"You and everybody else," wheezed the officer. "Ah . . . we've been asked to keep the looky-loos away."

"I was told to meet up with Detective Babcock here," said Carmela. "He's with the Robbery-Homicide Division. "We're . . . uh . . ."

Ava leaned over. "She's being coy. Carmela and the officer in question are officially an *item*."

"Okay," said the officer. "Whatever." He stepped back and waved them through. "Go ahead."

"That was so helpful," said Carmela, as she tromped on the gas pedal.

"You're welcome," said Ava. "Besides, we don't want to miss the festivities."

"What do you think is going to happen here?" asked Carmela. "A keg party and barbecued ribs?"

"No, but . . ." Ava grinned. "TV cameras?"

"Ah, that's why you're so jazzed," said Carmela, as they crunched their way up a circular drive littered with white gravel. "And all duded up." At the top of the rise, an enormous stone angel watched solemnly over acres of tombs and headstones. Now

Carmela slowed. Which way?

"There!" Ava announced, pointing left. "It's gotta be over there. Oh man, look at all the cars! Look at all the big black shiny limos. It's like . . . I don't know . . . a Hollywood premiere or something."

"Or a funeral," said Carmela. They pulled in behind a gold Lexus and got out, Ava hitching up her tight black skirt while adjusting her low-cut purple sweater even lower.

"Be careful," Carmela said, out of the corner of her mouth. "You don't want to show too much skin."

"This is my *conservative* outfit," said Ava. "You should have seen my first choice . . ."

"Dear Lord," breathed Carmela. At least Ava hadn't worn one of her leather-studded bondage costumes.

"But look," said Ava, pointing, "it kind of *is* like a red carpet. They have velvet ropes set up around the grave site and everything." She stiffened suddenly. "Oh, Lordy Lordy, what if we can't get in? And me all gussied up."

But as they approached the partitioned area, Carmela could see Ed Banister, the station owner, greeting guests and looking somber in a three-piece black suit.

"Carmela," Banister said, stretching out a

hand. "And Ava. Glad you ladies could make it." They mumbled greetings back and strolled in, aware there was a growing contingent of curious onlookers who hadn't been invited into the inner sanctum.

"I was right," said Ava, nudging Carmela. "There is a camera. They're going to tape the whole thing."

Carmela wasn't sure how she felt about taping Kimber's funeral. Maybe that it was a bit too commercial? A little too intrusive? Then again, what wasn't these days?

Carmela glanced over to where a sleek silver coffin rested atop a mound of unnaturally bright green plastic funeral grass. No red carpet for Kimber today, just a tacky green one. Beyond the grave site were three rows of black metal folding chairs, half occupied. Nearby, a cluster of mourners milled around. And, behind all of that, the camera on a tripod.

"Is that Raleigh?" Carmela asked, squinting. "Manning the camera?"

"I don't think so," said Ava.

Carmela surveyed the scene again and spotted Raleigh hanging out with a small group of people, probably KBEZ-TV staffers. He looked drawn and hunched in an ill-fitting dark suit, a radical departure from his usual outfit of chinos, T-shirt, and baseball cap.

"And there's Zoe," said Ava.

Carmela's eyes lasered on Zoe. Unlike Raleigh, Zoe Carmichael looked completely poised and pulled together as she wove her way through the crowd, touching an arm here and there, whispering to coworkers.

"She looks like she's actually enjoying this," observed Carmela. Then decided the girl probably was. Zoe had waited a long time to come into her own, and now Kimber's death had opened the door. The question was, had Zoe helped kick that door open?

As more and more mourners arrived, Carmela and Ava grabbed seats on a fourth line of chairs that had been hastily set up by a nervous, pacing funeral director.

"This has turned into a really big deal," said Ava. She was sitting up straight and craning her neck, the better to be in line with the camera lens.

Carmela looked around for Babcock but didn't see him. She had a feeling, though, that he'd show up. That he'd put in an appearance.

Finally, the last of the mourners filed in and a pink-faced minister wearing a black suit and clutching a Bible walked to the head of the casket. He waited there as Ed

Banister, Zoe, Davis Durrell, and a skinny guy in a shabby black shirt and slacks took their places in the front row.

Carmela studied this peanut gallery of sorts. She understood why Banister and Zoe were there. They were Kimber's coworkers and in charge of filming this spectacle. They were the director and producer, so to speak. As far as Durrell . . . well, he was the mournful boyfriend, so that made sense, too. But who was the other guy? The skinny, scruffy guy?

The answer suddenly hit her.

"That must be Kimber's brother!" Carmela whispered to Ava.

Ava bent sideways to look. "The alligator farm guy?"

"I think so, yeah."

"Judging from how poorly he's dressed," said Ava, "I don't think Kimber exactly shared her success."

But the surprises just kept coming. Now a gospel group in long purple robes filed in. Then the red eye of the camera winked on and the gospel singers sprang into action, beginning with a rousing chorus of "God Walks the Dark Hills."

The singers were really quite good, Carmela decided, their voices joined in a lovely harmony that managed to be both uplifting but mournful, too.

When the song had concluded, the minister stepped closer to the head of the casket, lifted his hands, then spread them apart.

"Dear friends," said the minister, "we are gathered here to bid farewell to a woman who was taken from us in the bloom of her youth . . ."

As the minister continued his soliloquy, Carmela glanced around the audience. She recognized the receptionist from KBEZ-TV, as well as the weatherman and the evening anchorman with his trademark blow-combed hair. They all looked properly sedate, as did most of the other mourners, even the ones who had probably come out of sheer curiosity.

Glancing down the row to her left, Carmela gave a start. There was a face she recognized from last night! She nudged Ava. "Your artist friend is here," she whispered.

Ava hunched forward in her chair. "Finch? Really?"

Carmela nodded. It seemed strange to her that Sullivan Finch had shown up here. On the other hand, he had painted a portrait of Kimber. So there was that connection. Maybe artist and subject had been closer than anyone really knew?

The mousy smile on Ava's face told Carmela that Ava would be hotfooting her way to Sullivan Finch as soon as this service was concluded. Ava was clearly interested, which worried Carmela a little. She let her mind veer off course a bit and hoped that a death portrait wasn't a dire portent of things to come.

No, that wouldn't happen, would it? Couldn't. Not to Ava anyway.

As Carmela ruminated, Ed Banister stood up and gave his heartfelt tribute to Kimber. His voice shook when he talked about her devotion to the station and her superior work ethic.

Really? Carmela thought. She'd never thought of Kimber as a particularly hard-working journalist, had always thought she was in it purely for the glamour and TV face time.

Banister's hands trembled when he concluded his eulogy. Then he reached out and gently touched her coffin with his fingertips, bidding Kimber a tearful farewell.

Just as a thin rain began to filter down, the gospel singers kicked it into high gear again with a rousing rendition of "The Old Country Church." Their voices rose, blended, and harmonized, echoing off nearby tombs, providing a brief moment of joy. But as their final notes hung in the damp air, people stirred, looked around, and stood up. The service was concluded.

"Just think," said Ava, "this was all captured on tape."

"Film at eleven," said Carmela.

Ava lifted her chin, threw back her shoulders, and said, "Excuse me, *cher*, I'm gonna say my how-do's to Sullivan Finch."

"I figured you might," said Carmela.

She watched as Ava nimbly negotiated her way down the row to end up in front of Sullivan Finch. She saw Finch grin and put his arms around Ava. It was a gentle hug, but a hug nonetheless. And it made Carmela nervous.

On her own now, unsure of what to do next, Carmela found herself edging toward Zoe.

When Zoe noticed Carmela, she gave a quick wave and a decorous smile.

"I thought I might see you here," said Zoe. She was wearing a sedate black suit with a plain white blouse.

"And I knew I'd see you here," replied Carmela.

"Such a sad day." Zoe half-managed to arrange her features into a look of sadness.

"So the station filmed the entire service?"

"That's right," said Zoe. "We'll probably

use a few judicious clips on the news tonight."

"And you guys are still working on your
documentary?"

"Oh sure," said Zoe. "In fact, we'll be at it
all weekend, right up until midnight on Fat
Tuesday."

"When the police come out and spray
everyone with fire hoses," said Carmela. It
was New Orleans's friendly way of saying,
*Okay, you've partied your brains out and
we've been more than tolerant, now it's time
to go home.*

"Don't you just love our Mardi Gras
traditions?" said Zoe.

"I've been meaning to ask," said Carmela,
"will you continue to work on the investigative reports that Kimber had started?"

Zoe shifted from one foot to the other.
"Hmm?"

"Remember? You told me Kimber had
launched a couple of investigations?"

"Sure," said Zoe, "but I don't really know
much about them."

But Raleigh does, thought Carmela. *So
why don't you? Or do you know more than
you're letting on?*

"I have to kind of wait until Mr. Banister
gives me some clear direction," said Zoe.
"You know, whether I'll work on fluff pieces,

features, or even hard news."

"What do you want to work on?" asked Carmela.

Zoe considered this for a few moments. "Everything!"

Carmela milled around with the rest of the group for a few more minutes until she connected with Raleigh.

"A sad day," he said, shoulders hunched, a hangdog look on his face.

"Indeed," said Carmela. Then, "I understand you sent the police a DVD of the Bonaparte Suite party."

"That's right," Raleigh said, "one to them, one to you."

Carmela was a little surprised at that. "Nobody else?"

"You're the only guys who want to investigate," said Raleigh. "The only ones who really care."

After giving Raleigh a slightly clumsy good-bye hug, Carmela decided to make a run at the cameraman. He'd finished shooting the funeral footage and was now packing his camera into a foam-lined case and coiling up wires. She also recognized him as the one who'd worked with Zoe the night of Kimber's murder.

"Excuse me," said Carmela, "we met the

other night? At the Hotel Tremain?" They hadn't been formally introduced, but he might remember her.

The cameraman, a skinny guy with curly brown hair, gazed at her for a second, then snapped his fingers. "You were one of the witnesses? You went out on the balcony and . . ."

"That's right," said Carmela. She licked her lips and plunged ahead. "I understand you were working with Zoe that night?"

The cameraman nodded. "Uh-huh, shooting the Loomis parade."

"So you and Zoe were together the entire evening? I mean, up until the time you were called to the Hotel Tremain?"

"Yeah, I guess." Then he shrugged. "Well, not exactly the whole time. Zoe had to do her thing. Go off in the crowd, scout out people to interview. Try to come up with some meaningful story lines."

So Zoe could have slipped away, thought Carmela. *And if she was really quick and really determined, she could have killed Kimber.*

"Will you continue to work with Zoe?" Carmela asked him.

The guy made a face. "Jeez, I hope not." And went back to packing his equipment.

Ava was suddenly plucking at Carmela's

sleeve. "Guess what?" Excitement shone on her face.

"What?" said Carmela.

"I've got a date with Sully."

"Now you're calling him Sully? You do fast work, lady."

"Better believe it," said Ava, giving a wink.

"So you two are going out . . . when?"

"I invited Sully to Baby's party," said Ava. She hesitated. "You don't think she'll mind, do you?"

"Baby loves extra guests." *But I'm not so thrilled.*

Ava peered at Carmela. "You look like you just ate a sour pickle."

"It's that apparent?"

"Yeah," said Ava. "You don't like Sully, do you?"

"I don't know Sully."

"But you've got your pretty pink thong in a twist all because of that clown painting last night. And that death portrait. Those paintings kind of freaked you out."

"Yes, they did. And for your information," said Carmela, glancing around, "I don't wear thongs. Not my style." She'd caught a glimpse of Kimber's brother out of the corner of her eye. Now she was wondering where he'd gone? She wanted to meet him and offer her condolences. And maybe ask a few questions, too. "What happened to Billy Laforge?" Carmela said to Ava.

Ava looked around. "I don't know."

"Doggone, I wanted to talk to him."

"Now who's pushing the envelope?"

Carmela considered this. "Me, I guess." She searched the crowd again, looking for Laforge. What had been a large group had dwindled down to about three dozen people, but Laforge was still nowhere to be seen. Had he dashed off as soon as it was over? Probably. Carmela thought about the address she'd cribbed from Babcock's cell phone. Was it worth going out there? Try to converse with Laforge on his own turf? Well . . . why not? What did she have to lose? After all, this whole case was really quite fascinating.

"Would you be willing to take a ride out to Theriot with me?" Carmela asked.

Ava stared blankly at her. "*Pour quoi?*"

"I was able to, um, obtain Laforge's address from Babcock. And I'd kind of like to corner the guy at home, where he might be more relaxed and amenable to talking to me."

"You think he's going to confess to murdering his sister?" asked Ava.

"No, but we might be able to get some idea as to his state of mind," said Carmela.

"You know, is he sad? Is he angry? Is he indifferent?"

Ava considered this. "So a fishing expedition."

"Well, yes."

"I suppose I could ride along, sure. Miguel's at the store today and so is Talley." She looked suddenly hopeful. "If we're driving out that way, maybe we could stop for lunch at the Blue Tick?" The Blue Tick was one of Ava's favorite roadhouses, a place that served killer andouille sausage with sauce piquant.

"I think lunch could be arranged."

"Excellent," said Ava. "I'm just gonna run over and say bye-bye to Sully, okay?"

"Bye-bye away," said Carmela. Her eyes had landed on Davis Durrell, who was shaking hands with Ed Banister. Then Durrell walked slowly over to Kimber's coffin, placed his hands flat against it, and bowed his head. She wondered whether Durrell was feeling sadness, relief, or guilt. Or all of the above, or none of the above?

Then, like a signal to end his show of grief, Durrell's phone jangled, and he whipped it out of his pocket and hastily held it to his ear.

Carmela could see Durrell's mouth moving but couldn't hear his words. Though she sincerely wanted to.

So . . . did she dare?

She dared.

Edging closer to Durrell, Carmela dodged around Kimber's casket and tiptoed across the hideous funeral grass. Then, using a large white marble sarcophagus for cover, Carmela moved stealthily closer to Durrell. He was speaking loudly now and sounding almost argumentative.

Hassling with a client? Or someone else?

Carmela put her back against a tilting marker, feeling the cool of the marble, and slid around it. Durrell was ten feet away from her now, wandering slowly through a small grotto of head-high aboveground tombs. His black suit was in stark contrast to the whitewashed stone as he railed angrily at his caller.

Carmela cocked her head, trying to concentrate. And listen.

"What? Not until Monday night?" Durrell complained. "I got people *waiting* on me. Seriously heavy-duty people, if you catch my drift."

Carmela strained to hear more. But now Durrell, as if sensing he was making too much noise, as if fearing someone might overhear his conversation, was hunched over and mumbling.

Carmela eased closer.

Durrell raised his voice a final time. "Yeah, yeah, I got it," he snarled. "Eleven. Monday. Just be there!"

Durrell stabbed a finger at his phone, then whirled around. At the same time Carmela jumped behind her tombstone, hopefully out of sight. Her heart thudding with excitement, she wondered exactly what that call had been about. What was Durrell up to? And what, pray tell, was supposed to happen Monday at eleven?

Just as Carmela slid out from her hiding place, Babcock approached her.

"What are you doing over here?" he asked. Suspicion was written all over his face.

"Just looking around," Carmela told him. "I haven't been here for a while. It's . . . interesting."

Babcock grunted.

"I figured you'd show up here eventually." Carmela smiled at him, but he seemed distracted. Maybe even distraught. "What?" she asked.

"Oh, nothing's falling into place," said Babcock. "This whole Kimber Breeze investigation's a mess."

"Sorry to hear that."

"Are you really?" he asked.

"Yes! You know I'm your biggest booster."

"I wish I could believe that," said Babcock. His eyes focused on Durrell, who had rejoined the dwindling crowd of mourners. "Durrell was out last night."

"How do you know that?"

"I have my ways."

"What?" Carmela asked. "You tapped his phone?"

"Nothing that illegal," said Babcock. "We had a squad sitting outside that enormous house of his. Really not that far from your old place."

"Where did Durrell go?" asked Carmela.

"Bar in the CBD," said Babcock. The CBD was the Central Business District, which had become revitalized of late with new condos and clubs. "A place called Augie's."

Carmela knew that Augie's was one of the hot new places. A sleek, contemporary bar where thirty-something ad guys, lawyers, and media people got together to drink, put each other on, and hook up.

"So what happened?" she asked. "Did Durrell pick someone up? A woman?"

"No," said Babcock, "but he met with someone."

"Who? Somebody from his firm? Another money guy?"

Babcock made a face. "That's what we're

trying to figure out."

Carmela thought about the conversation she'd just overheard. Should she tell Babcock about it? Tell him that Durrell was supposed to connect with someone? Or just let it go for now? Something inside her head flashed a yellow warning light that said . . . *just let it go. For now.*

CHAPTER 15

"I've got the burps," said Ava. They were in Carmela's car, speeding south along Highway 315. They'd just passed through Houma and were coming up on Theriot. Just as Ava had hoped, they'd stopped at the Blue Tick, a roadhouse that served gumbo, po'boys, and red beans and rice, and had themselves a proper lunch. Carmela had ordered crawfish cakes topped with spicy aioli. Ava had thrown caution to the wind and ordered andouille sausage smothered in onions, okra, and green peppers, and a bowl of turtle soup for a chaser. Now she was paying the price.

"You gonna be okay?" asked Carmela.

"I think I need an entire jar of Pepcid AC," said Ava. She was holding her stomach and grimacing every couple of seconds. Ava cupped a hand in front of her mouth. "Plus I've got dragon breath from all that spicy food."

"I'm sure the alligators will be highly offended," said Carmela.

"No, they won't," said Ava, "because we're not gonna get that close." She hesitated. "Are we?"

"We just want to talk to Kimber's brother," said Carmela. "Not check out the actual farm."

"What do you suppose they do on an alligator farm?" asked Ava.

"Mmm . . ." Carmela was trying to drive and read the directions on her cell phone, though she'd be the first to admit she wasn't the most skilled multitasker. "I suppose they raise baby alligators into big ones and then sell them."

"For meat?"

"And hides," said Carmela. "Alligator's crazy popular right now. You go into any fancy store and they've got all these cool-looking alligator bags and shoes."

"In great colors," said Ava. "Though I suppose those skins are dyed."

"No," said Carmela, "I think there really are genetically engineered purple and red alligators."

"Purple . . . ?" Ava burped again, then grinned. "Oh *you*!"

"I think if we turn onto Country Road Six,

we'll coast right in," said Carmela. "Or at least come close. In theory."

She hung a left onto a narrow blacktop road that took her through large fields of sugarcane, then dipped and curved its way through stands of pine and oak. After eight miles, she turned onto Longfellow Road, a humpy bumpy dirt road that jangled their fillings as well as their nerves.

"This is awful," Ava complained. "My stomach finally settled down and now it's gettin' all twittery and nervous again."

"Hang tight," said Carmela. They spun around a sharp curve and suddenly a silvered wooden sign peeped out from a copse of ragged bamboo. It read *Laforge Alligator Farm*.

"Dear Lord," said Ava, "this is it? Are we here?"

Carmela took her foot off the gas and let her car coast to a stop. "I think so." Across an acre of green, she could see blue glints of water. Slightly off to their right was a small wooden house built on stilts. Next to that was a tumble-down structure that could be a barn or a garage. Hard to tell from this distance. In front of all that was a maze of dilapidated wooden and wire fencing.

"Now what?" said Ava.

Carmela tilted her head back and

squinted. "I see a pickup truck parked over by the house. So I guess we just head that-away."

"Can we drive over?" asked Ava, still mindful of her shoes.

"Mmm . . ." Carmela pulled forward a couple of feet. "The gate's chained and padlocked, so no. We're gonna have to go in on foot."

"How are we going to slip through the gate?"

"We're not," said Carmela, "we're going to go *over* it." She opened the car door and stepped out. Humidity riding on a cool breeze struck her, lifting the hair gently off her neck. The air felt thick, but refreshing at the same time. And the long vista was peaceful and lovely. A symphony of crickets serenaded them.

But Ava hung back, half in, half out of the car. "You think we'll be okay?"

Carmela was anxious to get going. "Sure, why wouldn't we?"

Ava gingerly extricated herself from the car. "I guess we'll be okay."

"You worry too much," said Carmela.

"And sometimes you don't worry enough," said Ava.

They hoisted themselves over a metal swing gate that hung off a tall wooden pole and started hiking up the curved driveway.

"Kinda muddy here," observed Ava.

"Let's walk on the grass," said Carmela. They stepped out of the muddy track and onto soft, spongy grass. "Better."

"I still don't see any alligators," said Ava.

"And you don't want to," said Carmela. "Besides, they're probably all in pens. Past the house, way down where that bayou comes in. The gators probably like it all damp and swampy."

Yeah, probably," said Ava, picking her way carefully, moving farther off to the right. But after five minutes of twists and turns, they didn't seem to be any closer to the main house.

"This is a pain," complained Ava.

"The shortest distance between two points is a straight line," said Carmela. She raised a hand, held it vertical, and sighted the house up ahead.

"What's that supposed to mean?"

"It means we aim directly for the house, even if it means climbing over a couple of fences. Kind of like . . . orienteering in the woods."

"I was never a Girl Scout," said Ava, "but count me in. This slogging is getting tedious."

"These must be old alligator pens," said

Carmela, after they'd climbed over three separate fences.

"Good thing they're not *ocupado*," said Ava.

"Laforge probably sold off most of his stock for the season," said Carmela.

"You think?" said Ava. "Then how does he get baby alligators?"

"I don't know," said Carmela, "maybe you just need the eggs or something. You keep them warm under special lights and they just hatch by themselves."

"Sounds right," said Ava. "Maybe they even feed them using little baby gator bottles." She paused. "Do gators even drink milk or are they —"

"What?"

"I said do they . . ."

Carmela stopped in her tracks and flapped a hand. "No, I heard something." She listened again. "Do you hear a hissing sound?"

Ava stood stock still and listened. She shook her head, her dark hair swishing about her face. "No."

"Because I thought . . ."

"I hope —"

"Sssh," said Carmela. She touched a finger to her mouth.

Startled, Ava cocked an ear and listened

carefully.

A low hissing sound seemed to emanate from the tall grass off to their left.

"Sounds like a tire losing air," said Ava, taking a step forward. "Nothing to . . ."

Carmela reached out and grabbed Ava's arm, then jerked her backward. "I don't think so. I think it's . . ."

Ava hesitated for all of one second, then screamed, "Alligator!"

They both backpedaled like mad, then spun about and sprinted for the fence they'd just clambered over.

Even with their feet pounding the damp earth, the two women could distinctly hear something following them. A whooshing sound, almost like a reptile effortlessly skimming its belly over wet grass.

"Faster!" screamed Ava. Her longer legs had put her a step ahead of Carmela.

Carmela watched Ava leap up and over the fence. And then, one step from the fence herself, she managed a quick glance over her shoulder and wished she hadn't. A ten-foot-long alligator, its mouth wide open, rows of jagged teeth sparkling, was slithering toward her. Its body made little swish-swish sounds as it moved in a super-quick rocking motion toward her.

"Hurry!" screamed Ava, as Carmela made

a flying leap onto the fence.

Then Carmela was scrambling up the wooden fence, which was reinforced at the bottom with metal screen.

Just as Carmela cleared the top rail, she ventured another look back. There was a rushing sound as the alligator leaped, propelling itself almost four feet into the air, and then there was a tremendously loud snap as his jaws clapped together!

"Holy buckets!" cried Ava. She was standing on the other side of the fence, breathing hard, clutching her side. "That monster almost had us!"

"Almost had us for lunch!" cried Carmela. She stood rigid with fear, still panting from her exertion, while the alligator gazed at them with a placid look, then languidly spun around and slithered off.

"Next time I buy a pair of alligator shoes," said Ava, "I'm gonna hope they were cut from that critter's hide! I want some serious revenge!"

"What are you doing over there!" called an angry voice.

Carmela and Ava looked around and finally spotted a skinny man who was now hustling over toward them. Dressed in olive-drab coveralls and wearing black, knee-high rubber boots, he had dark hair that hung lank about his angry, dark face. This guy was dressed in work clothes, but Carmela was pretty sure it was the same guy who'd attended Kimber's funeral this morning.

"Is that him?" Ava asked in a low voice. "Kimber's brother?"

"I think so," said Carmela. "Looks like the same guy." He had a hound with him, a dog with a brown spotted coat and gray muzzle. *Old dog*, Carmela thought. The dog looked sorrowful, as if it knew this was all a big mistake.

Billy Laforge tromped over to them and glared. "Are you girls crazy?" he screamed at the top of his lungs. "This is private property! Can't you read the signs? This is an *alligator* farm! You don't just stroll through these pens! That's pure crazy!"

"Sorry," said Carmela, feeling thoroughly chastised.

"I've got traps set out here, too!" cried Laforge. "For nutria."

"Really, we meant no harm," said Ava.

"You've no reason to be here!" Laforge shrilled. "Now get out!"

"We knew your sister," said Carmela. She said it in a quiet voice meant to disarm him.

It didn't.

"You're not hearing me!" Laforge screamed. "Get out!"

"We were at the funeral this morning," said Carmela.

"We're sorry for your loss," said Ava.

That seemed to punch the air out of Laforge. He shook his head, as if in disbelief, then placed both hands atop it. "What are you *talking* about?" he asked. But this time some of the venom had gone out of him.

"We know your sister was murdered," said Carmela.

"That's right," chimed in Ava. "We were there. Carmela went out on the balcony and found her."

"What right do you have to come here and say these things?" asked Laforge in a quavering voice.

"None whatsoever," said Carmela. "Except we're looking into things."

"The *police* are looking into things," said Laforge. "You're obviously not the police!" He glowered at them.

"But we're kind of working with them," said Carmela. It was a little white lie, but she had to tell him something.

"Who are you again?" asked Laforge. He pulled a faded blue kerchief from his pocket and swabbed at his face. Now he just seemed exhausted and confused.

Ava pulled her iPhone from her purse,

aimed it, and snapped a picture.

Laforge threw up an arm. "Stop that! Go back to wherever you came from and leave me alone!" With that, Laforge turned and stalked away.

"Nice guy," said Ava.

"You didn't really think he'd welcome us with open arms, did you?" said Carmela.

"I didn't think we'd get chased by an alligator, either!" said Ava. She reached out, touched Carmela's arm. "Come on, let's go home. This trip is a bust."

"At least we learned one thing," said Carmela, as she turned to go.

"What's that?" said Ava.

"Kimber's brother is a lot more than angry, he's also fearful."

"Fearful of what?"

"I don't know," said Carmela. "That maybe he's next?"

"Are you trying to freak me out?" asked Ava, as they walked back down the road.

"Nothing of the sort. I'm trying to figure this out."

"Maybe we should leave that to Babcock and company," said Ava.

"Maybe," said Carmela, though she didn't believe that for one instant.

"This whole alligator episode has given me a splitting headache," said Ava. She put two fingers to her forehead and massaged gently.

"I read about a surefire headache remedy in of those women's magazines you see at the checkout counter," said Carmela.

"Like the *Tattler* or *Shooting Star*? Now Ava was interested. "I love all that celebrity news. I mean, those magazines are *good*."

"What you do," said Carmela, "is cut a lime in half, then rub it against your forehead. The sugar or enzymes or whatever supposedly make the throbbing go away."

"Yeah?" said Ava. "If I had my druthers, I'd rather drop a lime into a nice glass of vodka."

"I hear you," said Carmela.

CHAPTER 16

The interior of Grand Folly Costume Shop glowed like a theater marquee as overhead pinpoint spotlights bounced and reflected off racks of glitzy, glamorous costumes. Sequins, spangles, and gold lamé seemed to be the watchwords here, along with velvet Venetian costumes and shimmering black witches' gowns. On shelves overhead, plastic, faceless heads showcased hats, wigs, sparkly tiaras, and majestic crowns of every style and color. Amid all this faux splendor, the smell of mothballs, cigarettes, and cleaning fluid hung redolent in the air.

A slim young woman with pale skin and maroon-colored hair stood behind the front counter. She held a small sewing tool in one hand and appeared to be ripping the back seam out of a black taffeta vampire costume.

"Excuse me," said Carmela. She'd dropped Ava off at her shop and hustled over here, hoping to find some answers.

The girl looked up and Carmela recognized her. In fact, the girl had worked here for a number of years. "You used to have blue hair, didn't you?" asked Carmela.

The girl smiled faintly. "Not for a couple of years, but yeah. That was me. In my blue period." She chuckled. "Just like Picasso." Then she gave Carmela her full attention. "I'm Beth. What can I do for you?"

"I'm looking for a costume," said Carmela.

"Sure," said Beth. She nodded toward the crowded racks that seemed to extend deep into the shop. "Pick out whatever you want. Or is there something specific you want me to pull?"

"How about a little information?"

"Pardon?" said Beth.

"Here's the thing," said Carmela. "A friend of mine rented a clown costume here recently. And I was wondering if it's been returned yet."

Beth's brows knit together. "You want to rent it?"

"That's right," said Carmela. *And I want to know who rented it.*

"We've got a boatload of clown costumes," said Beth. "Our Bozo and Clarabelle costumes are extremely popular."

"This was a specific clown," said Carmela.

"An opera character by the name of Canio? Do you suppose you could check your records?" When Carmela had been here before, the shop had used a little ledger to check costumes in and out.

"Everything's on computer now," said Beth. "Listed by category."

"Okay, so if you entered clown and last Wednesday's date, the rental information might pop up?"

Beth frowned. "That should work. Theoretically."

"Can you give it a try?"

Beth hit a few keys, waited for a list to come up on the screen, then hit another couple of keys. "Okay, I've got one rental here for a clown costume. Our number one thousand and forty-six." She glanced up. "But it doesn't say what type of clown."

"When was it checked out?" asked Carmela.

"Checked out Wednesday morning and returned the following day."

"Do you know who rented it?"

"Doesn't say," said Beth, "because they paid cash."

"Do most people pay cash? Or do they put it on a credit card?"

Beth shrugged. "Usually a card, because we require a small deposit."

"So that particular costume is back in stock?" asked Carmela. "Number one thousand and forty-six?"

Beth hit another couple of keys. "I don't see that it was . . . yeah, it should be here."

"Can you show me the rack?"

Beth led Carmela past racks of showgirl, cowboy, and vampire costumes. At a pile of fright masks, made even more terrifying by strands of long black and white goat hair, they hooked a left and ducked into a kind of alcove. Leering clown masks and floppy clown gloves hung on the walls. Oversized clown shoes littered the floor. An enormous rolling rack of clown costumes was jammed against the wall.

"The costumes look kind of creepy this way," said Carmela. "Like any minute they might become . . . animated."

"Clowns always scared me as a kid," said Beth, giving a little shudder. "Maybe they still do. Anyway . . ." She backed away. "Just holler if you need help with anything."

"Thanks."

"And if you need any last-minute costumes," said Beth, "we're gonna be open until midnight every night up until Fat Tuesday."

Carmela pawed through the rack for a few minutes until she found the Canio costume.

It hung on its hanger looking limp and inert. Grabbing the hanger, Carmela hooked it onto the rack, then spread out the costume. Was it the same one? It sure looked the same. White with pompoms down the front, gathered at the wrists. And voluminous enough, Carmela thought, to hide any figure, large or small.

So who had worn this costume?

Had it been stashed in Zoe's tote bag? Or had someone shucked into it while hidden in a nearby room or convenient broom closet? Maybe Durrell or Sullivan Finch or even Billy Laforge? And what about Joubert, who gave her the creeps and seemed so interested in all things horrifically odd? Or Whitney Geiger, whom she was still trying to track down? Lots of suspects, not much information.

Carmela reached up and pulled down the mask. Mirthful eyes stared at her along with an upturned mouth. *Who wore you?* she wondered. *Who slipped inside your silky folds and turned you into a capering, creeping being?*

And most important, *Were you there when Kimber Breeze was killed?*

With her questions unanswered and her mind in a whir, Carmela sought out the familiar and the comforting. Her scrapbook shop on Governor Nicholls Street.

"What are you doing here?" asked Gabby, giving a start as Carmela walked through the front door. "I thought you went to Kimber's funeral."

"The operative word being *went*," said Carmela.

"Okay. So how was it?"

"Strange," said Carmela. "The entire KBEZ-TV contingent showed up and captured the entire service on film."

Gabby's face fell. "Are you serious? That's just awful." She shook her head dismissively. "Don't you think the media's gone plum crazy? And not just our local media, but national, too. I can't stand all those talking heads spouting their own political manifestos or fawning over celebrities."

"Take a number and get in line," said Carmela. "You're not the only one who thinks it's nuts, that news isn't really news anymore." She glanced toward the back of the shop, where two women were working away on scrapbook pages. "Have we been busy?"

"Not too much," said Gabby. "A little flurry of customers this morning, but now it feels like everybody's taking a breather and gearing up for tonight. For a big Saturday night."

"I suppose," said Carmela, touching a finger to a packet of charms that included miniature keys and cameos.

"Do you have plans?" asked Gabby. "With Babcock, I would imagine?" She smiled shyly.

"Just coming back here," said Carmela.

There was confusion on Gabby's face, and then she said, "For . . . ? Oh, you mean the open house? At Oddities? You're really *going* to that?"

Carmela nodded. "Ava's all hot and bothered about it, so yeah, I guess I'm going."

"For some reason I wish that shop weren't smack-dab next to ours," said Gabby. "It's just way too creepy for my taste."

"You mean creepy Joubert," said Carmela. "You get a bad feeling from him."

"Yes, I do," said Gabby. "You know me, I'm pretty easy going and amenable. And I don't usually take an instant dislike to someone. But that guy gives me the willies."

"Interesting," said Carmela. Gabby was a fairly decent judge of people. If she'd detected an odd vibration, there just might be something there.

"So please be careful tonight," said Gabby.

"Don't worry," said Carmela. "It's an open house, the joint will probably be mobbed, and we're only staying for a short time."

"Doesn't matter," said Gabby. "Just take care."

"This is like déjà vu all over again," Carmela joked. Just when she thought she'd escaped the weird vibes of the costume shop, Ava had brought over an armload of outfits for them to try on.

"Look at this one, *cher*," said Ava, excited to the point of being practically breathless. "Midnight-blue velvet with a va-va-voom neckline. I think it's the inner *you!*"

"You realize," said Carmela, "this isn't a costume party tonight. It's merely an open house."

"But we're going to Oddities. Which means we really should dress the part."

"Then we should be contemplating dead squirrel hides and finger bone earrings," said Carmela. "Instead of glamour gowns."

"You're no fun," grumped Ava. "You're just not getting *into* this." She dug through her mountain of dresses, pulled out a different one, and held it up for inspection. "Mmm, maybe this yellow taffeta number?"

Carmela gazed at the poufy sleeves, flouncy skirt, and black trim on a yellow bodice. "Maybe a trifle too saloon girl?"

But Ava wasn't about to give up. "Try to pep it up, *cher*. After all, it's Mardi Gras, our most favorite time of year. And we are gonna party! Perhaps if *I* put something on, you might catch a wee bit of spark?"

"Do that," said Carmela, feeling bad that Ava was trying so hard. "And I'll go get us each a glass of wine." Happy to distance herself from the costume caravan for a short while, Carmela went to her kitchen and poured out two glasses of Merlot. While she really had very little interest in attending the Oddities open house, she did have a passing curiosity about Joubert, the owner. For some reason, he'd tweaked her inner early-warning radar. And he'd for sure raised Gabby's hackles.

"Oh, *cher*!" Ava called from the other room. "Come take a look at this."

Carmela padded back into her bedroom, followed by Boo and Poobah. The dogs were regarding this costume activity with great suspicion. Then again, dogs weren't big on dressing up. In fact, whenever Carmela saw dogs sporting little coats and sweaters, they always looked embarrassed. As if they knew, deep down, that the grand creator of canines had never intended for them to wear Gucci or Burberry.

"What do you think?" asked Ava. She

stood before the mirror in a floor-length black crepe dress with a V-cut, ruffled bodice. She'd added a black leather lace-up corset to accentuate her narrow waist and ample derriere.

"You look like you just stepped out of *The Hunchback of Notre Dame*." Carmela chuckled. When Ava frowned, she added, "You know, the character Esmeralda?"

"Think of a better analogy," Ava replied in a slightly frosty tone.

Carmela didn't miss a beat. "You look like Morgana, the gorgeous witch in *Camelot*."

This time Ava smiled broadly. "Much better."

CHAPTER 17

The *Vieux Carré,* or French Quarter, after dark was like stepping into the distant past. Narrow brick buildings stood shoulder to shoulder with their second-story balconies of wrought iron. Old-fashioned streetlamps cast a warm, intoxicating glow. The clip-clop of horses' hooves rang sharply off the cobblestones as liveried carriages rolled by carrying enthralled tourists. And, a few blocks over, on the black ribbon of Mississippi that looped through the city, the mournful toot of a tugboat echoed softly.

Governor Nicholls Street was lit up like a Christmas tree this Saturday evening. Visitors thronged the sidewalk, peering into antique store windows where sterling silver teapots, oil paintings, and fine china enticed under pinpoint spotlights. Tunes cranked loudly from Dr. Boogie's music bar down the street. Waiters from the St. Honoré Chowder Restaurant were standing on the street giving out free samples. And outside Oddities, a good-sized crowd seemed to be lining up.

"Yipes," said Ava, "you think they're only letting in the beautiful people? That it's like Studio 54 or something?" She'd been whipped up ever since they'd parked the car around the corner on North Rampart.

"That's right," said Carmela, "it's probably exactly like a club scene. There's a selection process to admit only the hot, young kids. So maybe we should just turn around and leave while we're ahead."

Ava plucked at her cape. "No way. I've been looking forward to this event for days."

"You've only known about it for days."

"Whatever," said Ava, stepping up her pace.

Carmela adjusted the stand-up collar on her jacket. She'd finally settled for a snugly tailored black patent leather jacket paired with slim black slacks. Ava said it was a contemporary revival of the Yves Saint Laurent smoking jacket look from the seventies; Carmela just thought it looked a little S&M.

As they got closer to Oddities, Carmela realized that the cluster scrum at the front door was centered on Ed Banister and Raleigh from KBEZ-TV. They were there with cameras and a small crew that consisted of a sound guy and a grip.

"Look at this!" Ava exclaimed. "They're setting up to film!"

"Wonderful," Carmela said, in a tone that indicated it really wasn't wonderful at all. She hadn't given Ed Banister a definitive no on the TV interview and was hoping he wouldn't bring it up. Just let the whole thing die a slow death.

But Ava, ever eager to have her mug appear on camera, raced to greet them. "What are you guys doing here?" she asked, dancing around excitedly.

"Filming the open house," said Raleigh.

"Ongoing footage for our documentary," explained Banister.

Carmela came up to join them. "You're still working on that?" she asked.

"Oh, sure," said Banister. "We've maybe got only a third of what we actually need."

"How long is your doc going to be?" asked Carmela.

"Maybe fifty minutes to an hour," said Raleigh.

"An hour at least," said Banister.

"And this is a legitimate documentary you're producing?" asked Carmela. She was still suspicious that her postcards or Kimber's murder might somehow creep in.

"Absolutely aboveboard," said Banister.

Tonight, instead of his business suit and gold Rolex he was wearing khakis, a charcoal sweater, and, this time, a stainless steel Rolex. "This is all about real people in New Orleans who participate in Mardi Gras. We've already filmed a couple of krewes and interviewed some of the float builders."

"And you're not going to include anything about Kimber's murder?" asked Carmela.

"No way," said Banister, shaking his head. "Not in the documentary. In fact, we're hoping to enter it in some regional film festivals, so there's no way we'd include that type of thing." He directed his gaze at Carmela. "You know, since you're so gun-shy about doing a story on the postcards, why don't you at least be interviewed on camera? You'd already consented to an interview last Wednesday night . . ." His voice trailed off, obviously thinking about how Kimber's untimely death had brought that evening to a crashing halt.

"Carmela would love to be in your documentary," said Ava, dimpling prettily.

"Thank you, but I think I'm going to take a pass," said Carmela.

"But if we could do anything to help . . ." Ava offered.

"Maybe you could," said Banister, stepping toward them. "We'd love to get into one of the float dens and maybe even one of the big private parties."

You know," said Carmela, thinking of the Pluvius krewe's party tomorrow night and then Baby's big party on Monday night, "maybe I could put in a word."

"Anything you do would be greatly appreciated," said Banister. "I know you're very well connected . . ."

"She is," gushed Ava.

"Not really connected," Carmela corrected, "but I know a few folks who might be open to your filming."

"Fantastic," said Raleigh. "We definitely need more behind-the-scenes footage."

"Let me make a couple of calls," said Carmela, "and I'll get back to you."

"Appreciate it," said Banister.

"That was very sweet of you," said Ava, as they walked into Oddities.

Not that sweet, thought Carmela. It had suddenly occurred to her that being around the TV people afforded her a direct pipeline to any new information about Kimber. And maybe, just maybe, she could offer some of that information to Babcock.

They were hit with a wall of sound and a crush of people. "Grenade" by Bruno Mars blared out over the sound system. Guests dressed as vampires, fairy princesses, skel-etons, Chinese courtesans, and Venetian lords were crowded elbow to armpit within the narrow brick walls of Oddities. Other guests were glamorously attired in black tie and ball gowns. Carmela figured that most of the guests, especially those costumed and finely garbed, had stopped by on their way to fantastical Mardi Gras balls. Some guests, like her and Ava, had dressed up just be-cause it was Mardi Gras and the New Orleans tradition pretty much dictated you wear a costume.

"This is some place, huh?" said Ava. She gaped at the glass cases filled with strange curiosities. "Look over there, I see some hu-man skulls and an old butterfly collection."

"Did you catch the Egyptian mummy?" asked Carmela. A painted wooden sarcopha-gus leaned against the wall. She wondered if a real, bandaged mummy slumbered inside. And, if they burned tannin leaves at midnight, would the creature suddenly come lurching out? Carmela shook her head to clear it. Strange thoughts had been swirl-ing in her brain for the past couple of days. Too strange, she told herself.

"*Cher*," said Ava, "have a drink." A tall, ethereal-looking waiter in a shiny black tuxedo held out a tray of drinks. Ava had already helped herself to a goblet filled with a lethal-looking red potion. A green gummy worm curled over the side of her glass.

"What are these?" Carmela asked, as she took one.

"Cosmopolitan," said the waiter. He gave a sickly grin and said, "Enjoy."

Carmela took a sip. The drink was strong, slightly sweet, and, when she swallowed, it warmed her gullet thoroughly. "Good," she rasped to Ava.

But Ava was suddenly enchanted by a stuffed monkey. "What is that thing?" she asked.

Carmela gazed at the slightly dusty little creature who was locked forever in a comical pose, wearing a red velvet jacket and cap. "I don't know. Maybe a spider monkey or a capuchin? I'm not all that familiar with monkey varieties."

"It's a rhesus," said Joubert. He seemed to materialize in front of them like a vampire emerging from the fog surrounding Carfax Abbey.

"Mr. Joubert," said Carmela. She knew she'd run into him sooner or later. After all, his shop was barely twelve hundred square feet.

"Oh hey," said Ava, a grin lighting her face. "I've been looking forward to meeting you." She held out her hand. "I'm Ava Gruiex. Proud proprietor of Juju Voodoo."

Instead of shaking Ava's hand, Joubert bent forward and solemnly kissed her knuckles. "Charmed," said Joubert, which prompted a stream of giggles on Ava's part.

"You've got a terrific shop," said Ava. "All these darling collectibles make me want to swoon."

"Really great," said Carmela. She didn't want to appear uninterested in his merchandise, even though she pretty much was. Dead monkeys and dried bones just didn't trip her trigger.

"From a lifetime of collecting," Joubert simpered.

"Did the TV people interview you?" Ava asked. "We ran into them outside."

Joubert gave a quick smile. "They certainly did. I have a nice collection of antique Mardi Gras masks as well as some vintage ball invitations, and they were quite interested in those." He glanced at Carmela. "Ephemera, I believe you'd call it in your line of work. The invitations, I mean."

"Just make sure you keep your vintage invitations stored between sheets of acid-free paper," said Carmela. "Otherwise mold and all sorts of other nasty things have a way of creeping in."

"Thank you for your suggestion," said Joubert. "When things quiet down I may have to slip next door and purchase a few items from you."

"Do that," said Carmela, edging away from him. She was getting the same creepy feeling from him that Gabby had. Carmela wasn't sure what it meant. That she thought Joubert might come on to her, that he possessed some ulterior motive, or that he was just plain creepy? Good question. The fact remained, something was off-kilter.

Twenty minutes later, having toured the shop, chatted with a couple of acquaintances, and made small talk with Devon Dowling, the chubby, affable, ponytailed owner of Dulcimer's Antiques, Carmela was ready to leave.

But leaving wasn't so easy.

For some reason, Carmela found herself in a small alcove, staring at an antique dagger, her exit cut off by a smiling, looming Joubert.

"I see you found your way into my little den of death," said Joubert.

"That sounds fairly ominous," said Carmela. She tried to make a joke of it, but her words felt hollow.

Joubert gave an appropriate smile. "It's supposed to." He picked up a battered, primitive-looking pistol and turned it so the handle pointed to Carmela. "This is one of the guns that wounded Cole Younger, one of the members of the James Gang."

Carmela gingerly accepted the gun. "The James Gang?"

"Jesse and Frank James and Cole Younger and his brothers? The outlaws who terrified the Midwest and robbed that bank up in Northfield, Minnesota?"

"Oh, those guys," said Carmela. "Long time ago. The Wild West."

"That's what makes it so interesting," said Joubert. "As well as highly collectible."

"And pricey, I would imagine."

Joubert gave a knowing smile. "I'm asking four thousand dollars for that particular weapon."

"Good luck to you," said Carmela, finally managing to slip past him.

Skittering around a glass case that held a wrinkled Amazonian mask, Carmela looped an arm through Ava's and gave a tug. "Time to exit stage left."

Disappointment flared on Ava's face. "So soon?"

Not soon enough, Carmela thought to herself. "Just meet me outside, okay?"

The cool air that greeted Carmela was a

welcome relief after the warmth and press of bodies inside. Plus, there'd been some strange aroma in the air. Incense, maybe? Or some type of scented candle? Whatever aroma had wafted through the shop, it had been strong and pungent and almost head-ache inducing.

"Carmela." Ed Banister was suddenly at her elbow.

"Hey," she said.

"I understand you're looking into things." He cleared his throat and dropped his voice. "Concerning, uh, Kimber's murder."

"How do you know that?" she asked. She gazed over at Raleigh, who had his camera pointed at a woman in an expensive-looking red suit. She was extremely animated and talking loudly about the fancy Mardi Gras brunch she was throwing for her friends tomorrow. "Oh, Raleigh told you?"

Banister nodded. "He mentioned it. And I think what you're doing is a good thing, a smart thing. Especially since you have an in with one of the investigators."

"I haven't come up with a single piece of usable information yet," she told him.

He looked thoughtful. "Yes, but maybe you're the one who'll cast a fresh pair of eyes on this tragedy. Maybe, as an outsider without any predilections, you'll spot something the police won't. Or haven't."

"Maybe." But Carmela wasn't all that convinced she would figure things out.

"Anyway," said Banister, as Ava swooped over to join them, "good luck."

"I was having so much fun!" Ava whooped. "And what a place. Did you see that life-sized Day of the Dead skeleton playing a guitar? I'd *kill* to have him serenading in my shop."

"Make Joubert an offer," said Carmela, as she and Ava ambled slowly down the street. "Because I don't think the existing inventory is going to exactly fly off the shelves."

"But it's such neat stuff," said Ava.

"It's . . . unusual," agreed Carmela. "I'll grant you that."

"I got an idea," said Ava. "Let's stop by Mumbo Gumbo. I bet the joint is rocking."

"We're going to be partying our brains out tomorrow night, as well as Monday and Tuesday, so let's not," said Carmela. "Besides, I'm ready to throw in the towel." She glanced around. "Where did we park anyway? I thought we were right in front of Rendezvous Antiques."

"Nope," said Ava, pointing down Rampart. "We're in front of that little souvenir shop."

They strolled along, dodging dozens of

folks who were cruising from bar to bar, carrying plastic *geaux* cups filled with liquid fortitude.

"It's funny," said Carmela, as they wandered past Pansy's Fine Collectibles, then Dugan's Used Books. "My shop is something like a block away, but I hardly ever find time to browse these places."

"That's because you're all business," said Ava. "When you get up in the morning, you click directly into business mode. I do the same thing. It's like having blinders on. I just focus on what's ahead for the day."

"But that's why Juju Voodoo is prospering," said Carmela. Ava had built her business from the ground up. Starting with a small counter in Beckett's Antiques where she sold saint candles and love charms, then moving to her current space as she expanded into wooden skeletons, masks, voodoo dolls, and evil eye jewelry.

"I guess," said Ava. She stopped abruptly and stared into the window of a souvenir shop. "I just wish these other shops didn't try to cut into my business." She pointed to a display of small voodoo dolls sitting in the window. With their blank faces and rudimentary outlines, they looked like white cotton gingerbread cookies. "Look at this. Voodoo dolls from some awful factory city in China. They're pure crap. Don't people realize these are faux dolls, while mine are sanctified at midnight in Bayou Terrebonne by granny witch Cheniere?"

"Are they really?" said Carmela.

"No, but it's a dandy story. Maybe if I . . ." Ava prattled on, but Carmela was standing stock still, her nose pressed against the window.

"Ava! Look at this!"

"Huh? What?"

"Look at the postcards in that little spinner rack."

"They're just tourist things," said Ava. "They're . . ." She peered at them closer. "Holy baloney! They're a lot like those crazy postcards somebody sent to you! The Kimber cards!"

"No," said Carmela, "they're *exactly* like them." She dashed past Ava, eager to push her way into the Dreamland Gift Shop.

But it was closed.

CHAPTER 18

"Oh, shiznit!" said Carmela, anxious to get a closer look at the postcards. "We'll have to come back tomorrow." Ava twirled her cape as they walked to Carmela's car. "Kind of crazy, seeing those postcards, huh?"

"I never thought to look at where they came from," said Carmela. "If they were printed locally or what."

"Maybe only a couple of shops carry them," suggested Ava. She climbed in and pulled her seat belt across. "I've never seen anything like that before. So maybe if you check with the clerks, they might remember who they sold them to."

"It's possible, because the postcards don't seem like they'd be that popular." Carmela turned the key in the ignition, checked the street, and pulled out. "I mean, who would want cemetery postcards?"

"Actually," said Ava, "lots of people probably would. That's why they come to New

Orleans. To drink our booze, eat our fattening food, and get their pants scared off when they wander our cemeteries."

"And they come for the music," added Carmela.

"Absolutely, the music," said Ava. "Zydeco, jazz, blues."

"Plus Caribbean."

"Love it," said Ava. As they zoomed down Burgundy Street, she scrunched down in the seat and let loose a big yawn.

"It's been a crazy week," said Carmela. She cut across a lane of traffic, turned onto Bienville, then bumped down the narrow alley adjacent to her apartment. "With the three biggest days of Mardi Gras still to come . . ."

Ava suddenly sat bolt upright, like an alert prairie dog sniffing the air for danger. "Do you smell something?"

Carmela coasted into her garage and they both scrambled out of the car.

"Fire?" said Carmela. There was a hint of something burning in the air and the atmosphere seemed a little hazy.

Bonfire? Outdoor grill?

But deep inside her chest, Carmela's heart did a slow flipflop.

Fire around here? On our block?

"Criminy!" Ava whooped, as she took off

running. "I hope it's not my freakin' shop!"

Carmela was right behind Ava, running an all-out sprint, trying to keep pace with her friend's longer strides. But when she followed Ava through the porte cochere into their shared courtyard, she was shocked beyond belief to see clouds of gray smoke pouring from *her* apartment!

"Ava!" Carmela's scream was shrill and piercing. "The *dogs* are in there!" She whipped her head back and forth frantically. "Oh, dear Lord, they're trapped! You call 911, I'm going in!"

Ava caught her arm. "You can't go in there! That place is smoking like a chimney! You'll die of smoke inhalation!"

Carmela shook her off roughly. "I have to save them!"

Crashing through the front door, Carmela hesitated for all of two seconds and grabbed a damp towel off her kitchen counter. She pressed it to her mouth, then plunged headlong into the smoke, crying, "Boo! Poobah! Come on kids, Momma's here!"

Poobah came running to her immediately, eyes rolling wildly, looking terrified. "Good boy!" she crooned. Then, grabbing him by the collar, she dragged him to the front door.

"I called 911!" cried Ava, who was pacing

in the courtyard along with three other curious but worried neighbors. "Fire department's on its way!"

Carmela handed Poobah off to Ava. "I'm going back for Boo!" Carmela shrilled.

"You can't!" Ava called back. "Too dangerous!" But Carmela had already disappeared.

This time, the smoke was thicker and more acrid, and Carmela stumbled when she was barely ten feet in.

Where to go? Where would Boo go to seek refuge? Bedroom. She's gotta be in my bedroom.

Carmela crouched low where the smoke wasn't as thick and pushed forward.

Boo was curled up in a tight little ball in the middle of Carmela's bed, panting hard, eyes closed tight, looking severely stressed.

Carmela didn't hesitate for a second. She swooped down and picked up the chunky little dog in her arms. Boo resisted for a moment, then seemed to go limp.

Now to get out of here!

The smoke had gotten much worse and Carmela began to cough. Thankfully, she knew her apartment like the back of her hand. Bending low, cradling Boo, she fought her way to the door. But with her breathing compromised, every step was an exertion.

She could barely see and, weighing in at forty-five pounds, her dog was deadweight.

Stumbling across her living room, Carmela banged her knee on the sharp corner of the coffee table.

At least I know where I am! Just go straight ahead and then I can breathe again. We can both breathe again.

A half-dozen steps from the door, still carrying Boo, Carmela inadvertently drew a deep breath and felt her lungs fill with noxious fumes.

Not now! Not when I'm this close!

Carmela faltered. Her eyes burned, her shoulders ached, and she suddenly felt light-headed and stupid. But as her eyes still searched for what she hoped was the doorway, Carmela dropped to her knees. Panic suddenly filled her brain like a wildfire gone rampant.

Now what? Can I crawl and drag Boo at the same time? Do I save myself and leave her?

Her dog was motionless now. Passed out? Overcome with smoke?

No, I can't leave her behind. That's not an option.

Carmela gritted her teeth and fought hard to pull herself to her feet. Her knees felt like lead; she barely made it. But finally she was up.

Just one step. One step at a time.

Carmela took one faltering step and knew she was a goner. Her head was spinning, she was about to pass out. She let loose a growl of anger and frustration. If she could only see . . .

Suddenly, out of the darkness, a hand appeared. Then a complete arm stretched out to her. She batted at it frantically, not knowing who it was, what it was . . .

Then a dark, shadowy figure wearing an enormous coat and respirator appeared in the swirl of darkness and smoke and wrapped a strong arm around her. Still hanging on to Boo, she was suddenly grabbed, steadied, and yanked outside.

Into blessed, breathable, fresh cool air. Bending over, coughing, fighting to clear her throat, Carmela strained to take some fresh air into her lungs.

"I thought you were dead!" Ava screamed, as she rushed up to her. "I though we'd *lost* you!" She was a crazed Medusa, her hair flying everywhere, her shrill voice piercing the night.

But Carmela, standing up straight again, was focused on only one thing now. Boo's furry, limp body was lying on the brick patio. And it looked to her like her beloved little girl wasn't breathing!

"Help her!" Carmela shrieked, starting to cry, clutching the arm of one of the firemen. "Do something!"

Another firefighter dashed forward with an oxygen tank. He knelt down and held a cone-shaped oxygen mask to Boo's muzzle.

Tears streamed down Carmela's face. "Please, oh, please," she cried. She flung herself down and ruffled the soft fur on Boo's shoulder. "Do you think . . . ?" she asked the fireman. "Do you think?"

"Sometimes, if they've inhaled a great deal of smoke it can take a little while to come around," said the fireman. He had kind eyes and the nametag on his jacket read *Jasper.*

"Please keep trying," Carmela pleaded as Ava stood behind her, kneading her shoulders.

Another firefighter came over to watch. Carmela saw only his boots.

"I don't know . . ." said the owner of the boots.

He's trying to tell me there's no chance, Carmela thought to herself. *That it's hopeless. That she's already . . .*

Boo's eyes suddenly fluttered.

"Hey, now," said the fireman, Jasper, who was holding the oxygen mask to the dog's muzzle.

Suddenly, Boo's eyes flew open and she

264

let loose a long wet snort. Then her chest began to move up and down in a rhythmic manner.

"She's breathing!" Ava cried. "She's okay!"

Wiping the tears from her face, Carmela bowed her head and whispered a prayer of thanks. Then she leaned over and hugged Jasper. Truly, this was a miracle.

Some ten minutes later Babcock showed up. Turns out Ava had called him the minute Carmela had dashed back in to grab Boo.

He was wild-eyed and pacing. Angry at Carmela for being so foolhardy, unnerved that someone had done this to her apartment. Babcock conferred with the firemen, even as he kept a constant eye on Carmela, who was huddled across the courtyard with Ava and the dogs. Finally, hands jammed into the pockets of his leather jacket, trying to manage a casual demeanor but really not pulling it off, he came over to talk to Carmela.

"It wasn't a fire," said Babcock. "It was a smoke bomb."

"What?" Carmela was incredulous.

"Looks like someone pried open the side window and tossed it in," said Babcock.

"Who would do that?" asked Ava, incredulous.

Babcock focused a penetrating stare on Carmela. "I don't know, who do you *think* would do that?"

Carmela just shook her head.

"Maybe a better question," said Babcock, "is *why* would someone do that?"

"I have no idea," said Carmela, although now that the dogs were safe and the situation was under control, she was starting to turn the notion over in her mind. A random act, or was this quite deliberate?

But Babcock wasn't finished. "Perhaps someone who wants to send you a message? Someone who thinks you're involved in something you shouldn't be?" His words were sharp and biting.

"Don't threaten her like that," said Ava, suddenly assuming a defensive posture.

Babcock pulled his hands from his pockets and spread them apart. "Who's threatening?"

"You know exactly what I mean," said Ava. "And if you've got a bone to pick with Carmela, this isn't the time or the place. Look at our girl." Ava reached over and tried to rub a smudge from Carmela's cheek. "She's been through hell, so she doesn't need you harassing and haranguing her."

Babcock's eyes blazed and he looked like he was about to explode. Then he wrestled control of his raw emotions and said, "Fine. We'll talk about this later."

"You got that right," said Ava.

Babcock sighed and said, "She can stay with you for the time being?"

Ava was still bristling. "She's sure not going to stay with *you*."

Carmela held up a hand. "I'm okay," she said to Ava. To Babcock she said, "We will talk about this, but not tonight. Okay?" Her eyes sought out his, then went to Boo.

"Okay," said Babcock. "You ladies need help with anything?"

"Just back off," said Ava, as one of the firemen came over to talk to them.

"If you have to," said the firefighter, giving Carmela an encouraging smile, "you can go inside for a couple of minutes. We've got your place all opened up and a lot of the smoke has pretty much gone. Some of your stuff's still gonna smell smoky, though."

Carmela got to her feet. "I'm going in," she said. "I want to get a few things."

"Just for a couple of minutes," Babcock warned.

Carmela crossed the courtyard and

267

stepped tentatively into her apartment. Just as the fireman had said, a lot of smoke had cleared out. It was bizarre, she thought, that just twenty minutes ago she'd been fighting for her life. And now the danger had passed. Just like that. Strange how things could turn on a dime.

After surveying some of the fire and water damage, Carmela took three minutes to grab some clothes, toiletries, and her laptop computer. As an afterthought, she grabbed the DVD that Raleigh had given her.

You never know.

When she emerged, Babcock was talking to a couple of firemen again. He said, "Earl here says it's not such a big cleanup job after all."

The fireman who'd resuscitated Boo said to her, "My brother-in-law owns a company that specializes in water and smoke damage recovery. If you want, we could probably get him to go in tomorrow."

Ava came up to join the group. "Go for it, *cher.*"

"What would they do?" Carmela asked.

The fireman considered this. "Just suck out whatever smoke was left and set up a bunch of ion machines. Clean the carpets and upholstery if they need it. Your place should be good as new in a couple of days."

"I think . . ." said Carmela, "I think that's a good idea."

"Just leave your house key with Detective Babcock here," said the fireman, "so he can lock up. Then my brother-in-law can pick up the key from him in the morning."

Carmela blushed furiously as she said in a small voice, "He already has one."

CHAPTER 19

A tiny ray of sunlight streamed through a crack in the purple velvet drapes, hitting Carmela directly in the eye. For a moment she wasn't sure where she was. Then the chaos and craziness of last night came rushing back to her and all the pieces fell into place. She was at Ava's place.

She rolled over in bed, aware of sore back muscles, and called, "Boo? Poobah?"

There was a wet snort and then Boo was standing next to the bed, looking alert and almost puppyish, ready to lick her face.

"Sweet girl," said Carmela, reaching out to stroke her soft fur. Touching her dog to reassure herself that Boo was okay.

Another snort came from across the room. "You're awake already?" called Ava.

"Yeah," said Carmela. "Checking on the kids."

"What time is it?" asked a groggy Ava.

Carmela blinked at her watch. "Just seven."

"Agh, the crack of dawn." A long pause. "How are you feeling?"

"Okay." Carmela rolled over, stretched, and gave her answer a second thought. Actually, she wasn't okay. She felt violated, a little scared, and increasingly angry. Some moron, some *idiot*, had dared to invade her precious home. No matter that it was a rented home, it was her safe place. Her little sanctuary from the rest of the world. Anger rolled over her like molten lava.

Somebody's going to pay.

But who? Someone she'd been tentatively investigating? Like Durrell or Laforge? Or someone else? Maybe a wild card like Zoe or Finch or Joubert?

Carmela ground her teeth and vowed to renew her efforts. Because now, she wanted to make whoever had done this to her pay big-time. She was determined to exact slow and deliberate justice.

On the other side of the room, Ava stirred again. "There's dog hair all over my red velvet bedspread. I think one of your little darlings snuggled up next to me during the night."

Carmela gazed at Boo, who was suddenly lying on the floor, busily licking her outstretched paws and feigning innocence. "You're sure it's not cat hair?" said Carmela. She had to make a pro forma attempt at deflecting blame from her little sweetheart.

"Unh-uh," said Ava, "Isis always sleeps in the closet. She's extremely partial to this faux fur coyote jacket I have." She yawned. "Faux-yote."

"It was Boo," said Carmela, fessing up. "Sorry about that. Maybe we could just look at it as a creative use of fiber?" She felt bad, since Ava had been so incredibly accommodating last night. Making up a daybed for Carmela to sack out on, putting down a leopard-print throw for the dogs to bunk on.

"Sounds a little crafty to me," laughed Ava as she swung her legs out of bed. "Ah well, why not let Boo off the hook? After what she went through, she deserves it."

"You're very kind to take us in," said Carmela. "Us neighborhood orphans."

"No problem," said Ava. "You would have done the same for me. But I've got some bad news. You guys are probably expecting a tasty eye-opening breakfast and you're not going to get any."

"That's okay," said Carmela. She was just happy her pups were safe.

"The problem is," continued Ava, "all I

have in my larder are Weight Watchers pizzas and a bottle of Veuve champagne." She sighed. "When I get old it'll probably be Weight Watchers pizza and Metamucil."

"We'll go out," said Carmela. "My treat. It's Sunday, so we can catch a good brunch somewhere. Maybe the Praline Factory or Brennan's."

"Then we better make it snappy," said Ava, stretching. "We've got that photo shoot at eleven."

"Crap," said Carmela, wiping at her eyes and feeling crunchies. "I forgot all about that. Let's just cancel it. I'll call Jekyl and . . ."

"No can do, cookie," said Ava. "You need to get that white elephant of a house on the market."

Carmela considered this. "What if I need it? What if my apartment is more trashed than it looks?" Carmela hated to even consider that possibility. She loved her little place across the courtyard and really didn't want to move back into Shamus's old house, even if she did win it fair and square in her divorce settlement.

"Ya gotta stay positive," said Ava. "Just make like a shark, show your pearly whites, and keep moving forward."

"What am I going to wear?" wondered

273

Carmela. "Most of my clothes are still all smoky and the stuff I grabbed last night is all wrong."

"I've got gobs of clothes," said Ava.

"But they won't fit."

"We'll make them fit," said Ava. "We'll grease you up like a slice of prosciutto, wrap you in fishing line, and slide you into something cute. C'mon, it'll be fun. Like playing Barbie dolls."

By midmorning, the world was looking a whole lot brighter to Carmela. They'd stopped by Brennan's for brunch, downed a glass of champagne, and feasted royally on oysters Benedict and shrimp Sardou.

Now they were rolling down St. Charles Avenue, headed for Carmela's Garden District home.

"Will you drive and stop fidgeting!" scolded Ava.

"Your jeans are so tight on me I keep popping a button."

"And I keep telling you, that's the *look*. Skinny jeans are *it*."

"But skinny jeans call for skinny thighs and hips and mine are not . . . um, as toned as yours."

"Boo-hoo," laughed Ava. "At least you got 'em up over your hips. Hey!" She pointed.

"There's Jekyl. Pull in right behind him."

Carmela cranked her steering wheel hard and rolled in behind Jekyl's old Jaguar.

"Have we got a story for you!" cried Ava, jumping out and running to give Jekyl air kisses followed by an expansive bear hug.

"What?" asked Jekyl, glancing back at Carmela. Rail thin, dressed completely in black, Jekyl Hardy wore his long dark hair pulled back in a severe ponytail, the better to accentuate his pale, oval face. "Pray tell, what's up with you two divas?" Then, when he saw Carmela sporting her supertight jeans, he called out, "Car-*mel*-a! Way to rock those jeans, girl!"

"Oh, please," said Carmela, tugging at the waistband again.

Their words tumbled out as they regaled Jekyl with the events of last night. Telling him about the smoke bomb, Carmela's daring dash into her apartment to rescue Boo and Poobah, and Boo's having to be resuscitated.

"Poor baby," said Jekyl, as they went up the walk.

"Poor baby me or poor baby Boo?" asked Carmela.

"Both of you," said Jekyl, reaching out an arm and pulling Carmela close to him. "Sounds like you've been through the

275

wringer."

"I called 911," said Ava, not to be left out.

"And I'm sure you were wonderfully succinct and to the point," said Jekyl. "I'm sure the emergency dispatcher awarded you top priority."

"I'm positive they did," said Ava, pleased.

"This place amazes me," said Jekyl, as they stood in the living room, taking in the marble fireplace, cove ceilings, and Oriental rugs. "Are you quite positive you want to put it on the market?"

"That was always my intention," said Carmela. "I knew I couldn't pry any real cash money out of Shamus, so this house was the next best thing. I plan to sell it and invest any and all proceeds." She reached out and rapped her knuckles on a small wooden side table. "That is, if the stock market cooperates."

"Smart girl," said Jekyl, as he picked up a small bronze statue of a water nymph and glanced at the bottom, studying the maker's mark. "Hmm." His brows pinched together in thought. "Would you take five hundred for this Louchet?"

"Take it," said Carmela. "For gratis."

Jekyl looked deliriously happy. "I couldn't." He glanced at Ava. "Could I?"

"Never look a gift horse in the mouth," said Ava. "Whatever that means."

"Consider the nymph partial payment for setting up this photo shoot today," said Carmela. "And helping art-direct it."

Jekyl grinned and rubbed the bronze against his jacket as if to polish it. "In that case . . ."

They got busy then, dusting tables, mantels, and lamps, turning on all the lights until the place fairly glowed. Jekyl moved chairs, pushed a floor lamp closer to a library table, and created a still life of candlesticks and leather-bound books on the mantel.

By the time the photographer and his assistant arrived, the place had been transformed from stuffy to stylish.

"We're going to need three photos," said Jekyl, spreading Carmela's layout out on a green felt gaming table for the photographer to study. "Two interior and an exterior."

"Where's your ad running?" asked the photographer. He was a fellow by the name of Martin Dunn, a tall, gangly man with a tightly trimmed salt-and-pepper beard. His specialty was home interiors. Upscale home interiors.

"*New Orleans Home*," said Carmela. "And

it's scheduled for the upcoming issue, so ad materials are due to the printer next week."

"Shouldn't be a problem," said Dunn. He glanced around, then said, "We'll shoot in here first. Get a few shots of the fireplace with the wing chairs tucked in close. That should look all cozy and heartwarming. Then maybe we'll shoot that built-in cabinet with the china. Kind of cheat the brocade love seat into the shot, too."

"Good, good," purred Jekyl. "Buyers adore built-ins."

"What else?" asked Dunn, glancing around with a critical eye.

"Maybe the dining room?" said Carmela. "Just because the crystal chandelier gives it a rather grand air and the room can accommodate a table set for sixteen."

"Excellent," said Dunn.

"And then we need a killer exterior shot," said Carmela. "Try to make this white elephant look like a highly desirable mansion."

"No problem," said Dunn, as his assistant set up lights and tested strobes. "We'll futz around in here and shoot a variety of interiors. By the time we're finished, the sun will have risen higher and we should have nice warm light bathing the exterior."

"Love it," said Ava, who'd been making

278

eyes at the assistant.

Dunn and his assistant got busy, doing a little more furniture arranging, taking test shots. Because they were shooting digital, Carmela was able to view every shot on Dunn's laptop.

"These are perfect," she told him.

"If you want," Dunn said, "we can ghost the edges a little. That way you could actually fit three shots across the bottom of your layout. Either way, I'll give you lots of options."

As Dunn worked, Jekyl pulled Carmela into the library for a quick chat. "Are you okay?" he asked her. "I mean really okay?"

Carmela nodded. "I think so. I mean, last night I felt like I was going to fall to pieces, and now I've morphed into being just plain mad. I want to track down whoever dropped that smoke bomb in my place and hold their head underwater or something."

"Waterboard them with chloroform," growled Jekyl. "So, do you have anyone in mind?"

Carmela brought him up to speed on her suspect list.

"Mmm," said Jekyl, "be careful of Davis Durrell. With his money he's going to have friends in high places."

"How much do you know about him?"

Carmela asked.

Jekyl did his trademark eye roll. "Please, sweetheart, Durrell is one of my clients. I sold him the most fabulous seventeenth-century Flemish painting."

"I guess he does have money."

"And rather good taste," said Jekyl. He glanced sideways at her. "You realize, Carmela dear, that Durrell is practically your next-door neighbor."

Carmela frowned. "What are you talking about?"

"Don't you know?" said Jekyl. "He bought the old Hollister mansion, just two blocks from here."

"I didn't know that," said Carmela. Although she kind of did. Babcock had mentioned something about Durrell living near her old place, but she hadn't thought much of it at the time. She'd been focused on other things.

"How *would* you know?" Jekyl chuckled. "For the past couple of years you've been little Miss Bohemian Chic. Turning your back on the swanky Garden District to live in the uber cool French Quarter."

"Is that what I did?" asked Carmela. "I thought I just moved out and got a divorce."

Jekyl snorted. "Well, you did. But it sounds better the way I tell it. Everything needs a titch of embellishment."

But Carmela's curiosity was suddenly amped. "What else do you know about Durrell?" Jekyl could be an untapped resource of information.

"Besides the fact that he has discriminating taste and oodles of money?" asked Jekyl. He tapped an index finger against his slightly pointed chin. "Well, I know he sits on the City Opera's board of directors."

"Excuse me?" said Carmela. "Durrell's an opera fan?" The image of the opera clown suddenly capered through her memory.

"We have to *assume* he's a fan," said Jekyl. "Perhaps you should quiz your good friend Baby about him. She's served on every board in town at one time or another."

"Maybe so," said Carmela.

"Oh, chickens!" Ava was suddenly in their face and clapping her hands like a strict schoolmarm. "We're ready to shoot outside!"

"Just as I'd hoped," said Dunn. "Plenty of sunshine. And with most of the leaves off the trees we get a sort of pure, unfiltered light."

Dunn and his assistant worked away, taking lots of shots, moving out into the street to capture the home in its entirety. At one point Carmela and Jekyl even blocked traffic at either end of the block, so that Dunn could shoot uninterrupted.

"Be sure to get the corner turret in the shot," Carmela called, as she stepped back onto the lawn.

"Got it," said Dunn, who suddenly looked around. "Is that my phone or yours?"

"Mine," said Carmela, pulling her ringing phone from her suede bucket bag. "Hello?"

"Sweetheart," said Babcock in her ear. "You okay?"

"Pretty good," said Carmela. "We're just finishing the final shot on the Garden District house."

"I meant you. After last night."

"I don't feel scared anymore," Carmela told Babcock. "Just angry."

"Don't let your emotions lead you into a bad situation," Babcock warned.

"By *bad situation* you mean *don't investigate*," said Carmela.

"Very good. That's exactly what I mean."

"So are you?" asked Carmela. "Investigating, I mean."

"Sometimes it feels like that's all I do," said Babcock. "It never stops. Murder, robberies, arson, and dope dealing."

"How about smoke bombs?" asked Carmela. "Anything on that?"

There was a long pause, then Babcock said, "A window was pried open, the thing was tossed in. That's not a whole lot to go on."

"Which means nothing's going to happen," said Carmela, suddenly feeling a little bereft. And Boo had practically died last night!

"I'll try," said Babcock, "but . . ."

"I get it," said Carmela, sounding a little snappy. "I get it. Hey, gotta go. Talk to you later, okay?" She pushed the Off button, not waiting for his answer.

"That's it," said Jekyl, as Dunn held his hand over the viewfinder and clicked through the shots for them to see. "He's got it."

"Fabulous," said Carmela. She touched Dunn's arm. "Thank you so much."

"Too bad you have to sell this old place," said Dunn, a little wistfully. "It really is gorgeous."

Carmela gazed at the home she'd moved into when she was first married. She'd had such high hopes and grandiose plans. Then she shook her head. "Can't keep it," she murmured. "Just too many bad memories."

"Are we done here?" asked Ava. She'd been

283

sitting on a low brick wall that belonged to one of the neighbors, catching a few rays. Jekyl had just roared away in a cloud of exhaust fumes and burning oil, and Dunn and his assistant were almost packed.

"Yes," said Carmela, "but I want to drive by Durrell's house before we take off for good."

"Sure," said Ava. They climbed into Carmela's car and crept down the block, Carmela keeping a watchful eye out. She *thought* she remembered which home it was.

They turned a corner and Carmela said, "I think that's it."

"The Greek revival with the octagonal turret?" said Ava. "And the peaked roof?"

Carmela nodded. "I guess so."

"It kinds of looks like a cross between the *Addams Family* and the *Real Housewives of Beverly Hills*. In other words, spooky and big," said Ava.

"Spooky, big, and expensive," said Carmela.

"Durrell must be rich, huh?"

"Jekyl says he is. And he's right around the corner from Baby's place," Carmela observed.

"Who knows?" said Ava. "Maybe she'll invite him to her party. You know, as the new guy on the block. The new *single* guy."

"Isn't Durrell supposed to be in mourning?" asked Carmela. "Shouldn't he be swaddled in black and beating his chest?"

"That's only old women who do that," said Ava. "Women who live in tiny villages in Greece or Sicily. Here, in New Orleans, when a man loses his wife or girlfriend, he's out partying in the French Quarter the very next night. And the awful thing is, he's considered a good catch just because he proved he was able to commit!"

"Maybe even commit a crime," Carmela murmured, as she pulled away slowly.

CHAPTER 20

Carmela had to detour a few blocks to dodge minor Mardi Gras parades that were snaking their way throughout the city. But she finally made it back to the Dreamland Gift Shop in the French Quarter. And on this fine afternoon, with the sun shining down and revelers crowding the streets, the place was definitely open for business.

"Typical T-shirt shop," Ava snorted as they cruised in. "Too *many* darned T-shirt shops in the French Quarter, if you ask me. Popping up like noxious mushrooms."

The shop was a mash-up of T-shirts, Mardi Gras beads, colorful masks adorned with feathers, and boxes of pralines, as well as posters, pennants, foil balloons, and ashtrays. All emblazoned with Mardi Gras images or some sort of New Orleans logo.

Carmela grabbed the three cemetery postcards that were left in the spinner rack and carried them to the counter. She waited while the clerk rang up two young men who were buying multiple strands of oversized purple and gold beads. When the clerk had given the men their change, Carmela laid the postcards out flat on the counter and said, "Do you sell many of these?"

The clerk, a young woman with spiky black hair, eyes rimmed in kohl, and a pierced nose and eyebrow, nodded and said, "Oh yeah. Quite a few. Tourists seem to get a kick out of them."

"These seem to be the last of the cemetery cards. Do you know, are they printed or distributed by a local company?"

"Jeez," said the clerk, wrinkling her nose, "I don't know. I just work here part-time."

"Okay," said Carmela, as another customer came up behind her. "I'm going to take these."

"Three for two dollars," said the clerk. She popped the cards into a brown paper bag and handed them to Carmela.

"What'd you find out?" asked Ava. She was prowling the shop, still grousing over the imported voodoo dolls.

"Zip," said Carmela. "But maybe we can track down the printer or something. Maybe the postcards are done locally. Maybe there'll be some clue."

"Do you think I could send this company

a cease-and-desist?" asked Ava. She tapped a finger against the voodoo doll kit she'd been in such a snit over last night. Still was.

"What do you mean?" said Carmela. "File suit against the Chinese manufacturer?"

Ava nodded.

"On what grounds?"

"Unfair business practices?" said Ava.

"Nice try, counselor," said Carmela. "Except I think you might need a couple more episodes of *Judge Judy* under your belt before you venture into the realm of international law."

"Whatever," grumped Ava.

But as they were leaving, the clerk caught Carmela's eye and called out to her. "You know," said the girl, "if you want more of those postcards, you can buy them at our other shop."

Carmela stopped in her tracks. "You have another shop?"

"Where's that?" asked Ava

"Just a few blocks over," said the clerk. "In the Faubourg Marigny."

"Interesting," said Carmela, as they left the shop.

"What's up?" asked Ava.

"Maybe . . . let's just go check out that other shop."

They hopped in the car, and had to make

yet another detour because of a marching band and a pod of food trucks selling everything from po'boys to fried alligator. But ten minutes later, they pulled up in front of Dreamland Two.

"So they have another shop," said Ava. "So what?"

Carmela studied the street. "This shop's in the same block as Davis Durrell's office."

"Yeah?" Ava was curious now.

"Yup. His office is three doors down from here, in the Gallier Building."

"Which means Durrell could have ankled down here and bought himself a stack of those postcards," said Ava.

"And then hand-delivered them to me," said Carmela.

"But why would he do that?" asked Ava.

"I don't know," said Carmela. "To warn me off the investigation? To show how clever he is? Because he's diabolical? Take your pick."

"Is he?" asked Ava. "Diabolical, I mean?"

"I don't know," said Carmela. "But I'd sure like to find out."

Carmela had just paid for her purchase, six more cemetery postcards, two of which were different from the ones she already had, when her cell phone blipped. She looked at the Caller ID and pursed her lips. Shamus.

"What?" she said to him.

"Holy horse pucky!" Shamus exclaimed. "I just heard about the fire at your place! Are you okay?"

"I'm fine," said Carmela. "And it was a smoke bomb, not actual fire and flames."

"What about the dogs?" asked Shamus. "How are my precious little babies?"

"They were a little shaken up," Carmela admitted. She didn't want to tell Shamus how bad the smoke had really been, or that Boo had passed out and needed to be revived. It would freak Shamus out too much. He'd probably get a court order that accused her of being an unfit pet mother.

"I gotta tell you," said Shamus, "I went totally bonkers when I heard about the fire."

Carmela didn't say anything. Shamus went totally bonkers if they served him Johnnie Walker Red instead of Bush-mills.

"Where are my little darlings now?" he asked.

"They're with me. Staying at Ava's."

"Doesn't she have a *cat?*" Shamus spit out the word like he was referring to a venomous reptile.

"Yes, she does, you know that. And Boo and Poobah get along famously with Isis. They all play together and love each other."

"I'm not buying it," said Shamus. "Boo is extremely sensitive to cat dander. If her allergies kick in, I'll never forgive myself."

"She's fine," said Carmela. "No sneezing or anything."

"No," said Shamus, "I think it would be better if I came over and got them. Yeah, that's it. I want the dogs to stay with me. They need to be with their daddy after experiencing such a terrible trauma."

"No way," said Carmela. "You're going to be partying your brains out over the next couple of days and won't even be home." She knew how crazy Shamus got during Mardi Gras. Drinking, carousing, doing whatever he did with women. "You'll be at the Bacchus Parade tonight and then hanging out at your float den party until all hours."

"So what," said Shamus, sounding grumpy. "You're running around trying to solve a murder."

Touché, thought Carmela. "Shamus, the dogs will be just fine at Ava's. But once Mardi Gras is over, once Fat Tuesday has come and gone, then you can have them for a couple of days, okay? You do have . . . um . . . parental visitation rights."

There was a slight hesitation and then Shamus said, "Okay. I guess." More hesitation. "So you're gonna be there later tonight? At the Pluvius den?"

"I've been invited, yes."

"I suspected as much. So maybe I'll see you there."

"Maybe."

"What was that all about?" asked Ava, as Carmela dumped her phone into her purse.

"Shamus is all wound up about the dogs," said Carmela. "He wanted to come over and get them."

"I hope you told him no way."

"I did."

"Good. Because we got some stuff to figure out," said Ava. "Important stuff."

"Like what?"

"What fabulous thing are you gonna cook for dinner tonight? And what are we gonna wear to the Pluvius den party to make everybody's eyeballs fall out of their heads?"

"These are the things that matter," said Carmela.

"Dang straight," said Ava.

They jumped back into Carmela's car and zipped up to Riley's Market. It was a neighborhood fixture that carried a general array of groceries as well as luxe staples such as artisan cheese, Beluga caviar, and truffle oil. The front part was an open-air fruit market displaying mounds of oranges, apples, lemons, and limes, and, as Carmela grabbed a shopping cart, she also picked out a nice bunch of grapes.

Pushing the cart inside, being trailed by Ava, who looked slightly bewildered by all the groceries, she grabbed a package of chicken breasts, a carton of eggs, a box of crackers, and a jar of honey. She figured she could manage her honey crunch chicken tonight without too much effort in Ava's bare-bones kitchenette. Halfway through their foray, Ava abandoned the shopping expedition and wandered down the candy aisle, where she picked up some GooGoo Clusters, a couple of pralines, and a package of marshmallow top hats.

When they returned to Ava's apartment, Carmela was happy to see the fire and smoke restoration team across the way, working on her apartment. She dumped the grocery bags on the counter and ran downstairs to check how the cleanup was going.

"Hey," she said, to a man in gray overalls who was holding a clipboard and scratching notes. "How's it going? Any problems?"

The man turned his head and peered at her from beneath beetled brows. "You the homeowner?"

"Renter, yeah."

"Piece of cake," said the guy. He stuck

out his hand. "Ralph. Ralph Bagley, proprietor of Bagley's Restoration Services. Nice to make your acquaintance. Considering the circumstances, that is."

"Carmela," she said.

"Those smoke bombs are a heck of a thing," said Bagley. "They look like Armageddon if you're stuck in the middle of one, but they clear out pretty quick."

Carmela pointed toward her apartment. "Does it still stink to high heaven in there?"

"Some," said Ralph, "but we set up four ion machines, so any residual odor should dissipate in a couple of days. Then your place will be good as new."

"Excellent," said Carmela.

"The landlord came by before," said Ralph. "I think he's nervous you're gonna sue or something."

"Good," said Carmela. "Thank you."

Ava ghosted through the kitchen for the third time in twenty minutes. "Mmm," she said, "that chicken smells dang good."

"It's just something I throw together," said Carmela. "Very quick and easy to prep, seeing as how we're going out again tonight." They were planning to hit the Bacchus Parade and then mosey on over to the party at the Pluvius den.

But Ava was overjoyed at the prospect of chowing down on Carmela's chicken. "Thanks so much for cooking a real dinner," she chortled. "It's like having Wolfgang Puck drop in for a visit."

"I'm not sure Wolfgang would deign to bake his chicken in a crumpled pie tin," said Carmela, "but it's what you had and I'm happy to accept the compliment."

Ava dipped a finger in the honey jar for a taste. "So good. I can hardly wait."

She really didn't have to wait. Just twenty minutes later, the oven timer dinged and the honey crunch chicken was done. Carmela plated the golden-brown chicken atop two small green salads, Ava popped the cork on her champagne, and they sat down at Ava's rickety table to eat. Two dogs and a cat lined up to carefully observe.

"So, did you take another look at those postcards?" Ava asked between bites.

Carmela nodded. "They were printed by a company called Devoux Printing."

"Local?"

"That's what I'm guessing," said Carmela.

"What are you hoping to find out if you do locate this printer?"

Carmela shrugged. "Not sure. Maybe distribution or quantities, that type of thing. Or did they do a print run for a specific group or organization? Maybe even a church?"

"That's smart," said Ava, pointing a fork at her. "You're good at figuring this stuff out."

"I wish," said Carmela, as her cell phone tinkled from the counter. She got up, slid her chair back, and grabbed the phone. "Yeah?" She expected the caller to be Babcock or Shamus.

"Your apartment caught fire?" came Gabby's agonized wail. "Are you okay?"

"I'm fine," said Carmela, "but how did you know?" Out of the side of her mouth she said, "Gabby" to Ava.

"It was on the news," said Gabby.

"Let me guess," said Carmela. "KBEZ-TV."

"That's right," said Gabby. There was a pause. "Carmela, where are you now?"

"Eating chicken at Ava's," said Carmela. "Then we're going to the Bacchus Parade and will probably hit the Pluvius float den."

"You don't sound very worried," said Gabby, who did.

"You should have seen me last night," said Carmela. "I was a basket case. But the cleanup guys were just here and it all seems to be shaking out okay."

"Wow," said Gabby. "You're really fine?

The dogs are okay?"

"Hanging in there," said Carmela. "So for gosh sakes, stop worrying about us, okay?"

"I'll try," said Gabby, "but it's difficult, after all the weird things that have happened."

"Force yourself," said Carmela. "And we'll maybe even see you tonight."

The Bacchus Parade was often singled out as the rowdiest of all the big Mardi Gras parades. Here was the thinking: Revelers had all day Sunday with not much to do but drink. Then the Bacchus Parade, appropriately named for the god of wine, rolled out Sunday evening and people suddenly went bonkers.

By the time Carmela and Ava took up a spot on the corner of Napoleon Avenue and St. Charles Street, it wasn't completely crazy yet, but a current of electricity rippled through the air. Packed shoulder to shoulder, eager to catch a first glimpse of what was always a spectacular parade, the parade-goers looked like happy refugees from Party City. They sported gold Mardi Gras crowns, king cake earrings and pendants, glitter top hats, and crazy masks. Some even wore costumes. Many regulars who knew the drill had constructed elaborate viewing stands, stepladders with platforms that held two and even three people.

Carmela felt the first vibrations of a bass drum down in the pit of her stomach. Everyone around her quickly picked up on it. Cries of "They're coming!" split the air, and the level of anticipation ratcheted even higher.

"I can hear the band!" exclaimed Ava.

Then, as if a light switch had suddenly been thrown, the first float, the Officer's Float, glided out of the darkness. An enormous grinning Bacchus face, ringed with bright lights, suddenly appeared and the crowd cheered wildly. Then, all hell seemed to break loose. Marching bands streamed by along with traditional flambeaus, dancing and twirling their fire-lit torches. Men in gilded masks astride prancing horses clopped alongside enormous floats that sparkled and glowed like Christmas ornaments.

"Don't you love it?" asked Ava, sagging against Carmela. "Isn't it spectacular?"

Carmela nodded even as a wide grin split her face. This was the absolute best. This enormous parade that completely jangled your nerves and sensibilities with strobing lights, brilliant colors, bulbous heads, and blaring music.

And the throws, the marvelous throws! Crews of fifty and sixty costumed men rode atop each float, tossing out beads, medallion necklaces, plastic cups, and even Moon-Pies. There were frenzied grabs, midair snatches, and heartfelt pleas of "Throw me somethin', mister!"

The Bacchus Parade, like all the major Mardi Gras parades, was a collective crowd experience. Everyone was delighted and dazzled and never disappointed.

"Here comes the Bacchawhoppa!" screamed Ava. "I love this crazy thing!" The Bacchawhoppa float was an eighty-five-foot giant humpback whale that held sixty-eight krewe members. Its rounded blue whale head seemed to poke up into the stratosphere and its enormous body held a seething mass of krewe members, all garbed in white and tossing strands of green and purple beads.

A dozen more floats and another fifteen marching bands streamed by, each more dazzling and dizzying than the next. Until, finally, the last float, the last horseman, clattered past and the aura that was part spectacle, part Venetian *carnivale* faded back to reality.

Ava held a hand to her heart. "Whew."

"Amazing," said Carmela. She felt like she

wanted to go home and curl up in a cozy armchair and replay every single visual image that had been seared into her brain.

The crowd around them was still jubilant, but a little subdued now. Fantasy time was over; reality was beginning to set in. Time to walk back home or try to find their car, wherever it might be parked. Or towed to.

Carmela and Ava sauntered down the sidewalk, content to be carried along with the crowd. Until Carmela suddenly spotted a familiar face. Zoe Carmichael from KBEZ-TV!

"Hey!" Carmela cried, as they approached Zoe and a cameraman. Zoe was dressed in a sophisticated red suit with a slim, short pencil skirt. She was busily coiling a cord around a small handheld microphone, while her cameraman was still up on a stepladder, getting crowd shots.

"Carmela," said Zoe, smiling. "And . . ." She searched for Ava's name.

"Ava," said Ava.

"Great parade, huh?" said Zoe.

"Fantastic," gushed Ava. "One of the best I've ever seen."

"Did you guys shoot the whole parade?" asked Carmela.

"Pretty much," said Zoe. "Plus some interviews and crowd reactions."

"Is this more footage for the documentary?" asked Carmela.

Zoe shrugged. "Some of our stuff might make it into the doc, sure. More likely it'll run on our ten o'clock news tonight or the morning news tomorrow. But mostly they'll just use snippets, kind of like video postcards."

"Postcards," said Carmela. "Interesting choice of words."

CHAPTER 21

The band that rocked the Pluvius krewe's float den this Sunday night called themselves the Blond Zombies, but they weren't blond and they didn't appear to be stumbling zombies. Rather, they were eager young rockers who wailed away with macho enthusiasm, playing a medley of Springsteen, Black Eyed Peas, and Lady Gaga.

"Finally," said Ava, as they pushed their way into the enormous float den, "a real party."

Located in the CBD, the Pluvius den was a cavernous, barnlike building. Enormous, colorful floats ringed the outer walls, while in the center, the party swirled madly around the band and a three-sided bar that had been installed temporarily. Krewe members and their guests stood four deep at the bar, clinking glasses, laughing, and boasting to each other. A few dancers were jigging to the music.

Jekyl came rushing up to greet them immediately. "The floats aren't done yet, but all my volunteers are two sheets to the wind!" he cried. He wore a red sequined jacket, matching red slacks, two tiny devil horns glued to each side of his forehead, and a look of utter panic.

"You've got time," said Carmela. "You've got another forty-eight hours before these floats have to roll."

"You think?" asked Jekyl. He looked as if he wanted to climb onto the bandstand, grab the microphone, and threaten everyone with a hot glue gun. Then, of course, he'd conscript them all into gluing glitter and tacking crepe paper streamers onto his floats.

"This happens every year," said Carmela, trying to impart some degree of calm. "You think the floats won't get done, but they always do."

"Last year my Cassiopeia float rolled without all her stars in place," muttered Jekyl.

"And nobody noticed," said Ava. "Because everything else about it was perfect. Your overall *design* was perfect."

"You think?" Jekyl was one of those artistes who was never convinced his work was good enough.

Carmela grabbed Jekyl's arm and pulled him close. "What's your theme this year?"

"Oh," said Jekyl, brightening suddenly, distracted by her question, "it's Myth and Man. But we're specifically featuring mythical animals. Unicorns, centaurs, fauns, and satyrs, that sort of thing."

"I'd love it if you showed us," said Carmela.

"Let's see the unicorn," said Ava.

They walked into a quieter part of the den where an enormous float depicted a sprightly woodland scene complete with moss-encrusted trees and a leaf-covered forest floor. Smack-dab in the middle, rearing up on its hind legs, was an enormous white horse with a silver horn sprouting from its forehead.

"Fantastic!" said Carmela. "You sculpted this?"

Jekyl nodded, pleased. "I started with a chicken wire frame and just kept building with papier-mâché. Once the basic horse outline was pretty much established, I used wood putty to refine it."

"It doesn't look like putty," said Ava, peering at the enormous unicorn, which looked ready to leap off the float. "In fact, he looks all fuzzy. Kind of like a teddy bear."

"That's because once I finished sculpting

him, we glued on white feathers," said Jekyl.

"Feathers?" said Carmela. She studied the horse's pelt more closely.

"Buckets full of feathers," said Jekyl. "It looked like a pillow factory had exploded in here. But we overlapped each feather just so, to achieve real depth and dimension. You oughta see the unicorn when the blue and green spotlights are turned on. Spectacular! Ethereal, really."

"It looks great now," said Carmela.

They strolled back to where the party was happening. The Blond Zombies launched into a rockin' rendition of Springsteen's "Born to Run" and Ava, who was practically tapping her toes, said, "I'm gonna find myself a handsome dance partner."

"Go for it," said Carmela.

Then Jekyl said, "Let's ankle up to the bar and get a drink, shall we?"

They pushed their way through the crowd and up to the bar, where three bartenders were working frantically. When one finally glanced up, Carmela said, "Could we get two glasses of red wine, please?"

The bartender shook his head. "No wine. Just Abita Blue, Wild Turkey, Jack Daniel's, and some really rotgut whiskey."

"Two Jack and Coke then," said Carmela, glancing at Jekyl, who nodded. As the bartender hurriedly fixed their drinks, Carmela said, "Shamus must be in charge of the bar this year. Those are all his faves."

At which point a familiar baritone voice broke in with, "Did I just hear my name taken in vain?"

Carmela spun around. "Shamus!"

Shamus Allan Meechum beamed down at her. "Hey, babe," he said. "Long time no see." Dressed in black slacks and a tailored black button-down shirt, he had an impossibly young woman in a gold sequined dress hanging on one arm.

Carmela grabbed her drink, took a fortifying sip, and said, "Did you forget? We just saw each other two nights ago."

Shamus rocked back on his heels and looked surprised. "We did?"

Carmela cast a glance at his young date in her sparkly dress and six-inch platforms and said, "Sure, at the Click! Gallery. Remember?"

Shamus let loose an annoying chuckle. "Heh, heh, I guess you're right, babe. It just *seems* like a long time."

"And your frantic call yesterday," Carmela reminded him.

Shamus frowned through his alcohol haze. It was all coming back to him now. "Oh yeah, about the —"

"I'm Jekyl Hardy," said Jekyl, sticking his hand out to greet Shamus's date. "And this is Carmela Bertrand."

Carmela pounced on Jekyl's deft change of subject. She leaned toward the girl and said, "And you are . . . ?"

"Tinsley Wyatt," said the girl, in a high squeaky voice. She peered at Carmela, wrinkled her perfectly unlined brow, and said, "Wait a minute . . . you're Carmela? That means you're . . ."

"The ex–Mrs. Meechum," Carmela filled in. "Yup, that's me. Nice to meet you, Tinsley. Having a good time?" Carmela's grin was wide and cheesy. Inside she felt the tiniest little pang. Shamus was dating a girl who was barely in her twenties, barely . . . legal.

But Tinsley seemed utterly thrilled to be here. "This is fantastic!" she cooed. "I've never ever been to a float den before. I feel like such an . . . an insider!"

"That fluttery feeling should last for about two more minutes," Jekyl said in a caustic tone. "Until reality sets in."

"Be nice," Carmela warned, under her breath.

"As nice as you are," Jekyl whispered back.

"Shamus," said Carmela, "you still owe me some information."

Shamus glanced around, obviously looking for a getaway. When he didn't find one, he tried to focus on Carmela. "Huh?"

"About Whit Geiger?" said Carmela, snapping her fingers under his nose. "Remember?"

"Uh, he's here tonight," said Shamus. "You should talk to him yourself."

"Really," said Carmela. This was opportune news. She quickly slid in between Shamus and Tinsley and grabbed Shamus's arm. "Be a gentleman and introduce me, will you?"

Jekyl, who always had Carmela's back, smiled at Tinsley and said, "How would you like to see a unicorn float close up?"

"Would I ever!" whooped Tinsley, who suddenly skittered over and attached herself to Jekyl.

"You're an evil witch," said Shamus, as he and Carmela strolled through the crowd.

"That's why you married me," Carmela said, in an airy tone. "You always did enjoy a challenge."

"Still do," said Shamus, suddenly gazing at her with brown puppydog eyes.

Carmela shook a finger at him. "Unh-uh, I know what you're thinking and you can *forget* it. We're divorced. Remember?"

"How can I forget?" Shamus grumped. "You took my house and everything!"

"Glory's house," corrected Carmela. "The house you were always complaining about. The garage wasn't big enough, the yard was too big, the wiring was kaput . . ."

"But now I'm left with nothing," complained Shamus.

"Cheer up," said Carmela. "When Glory kicks the bucket you'll probably inherit the whole chain of Crescent City Banks."

"That's a terrible thing to say," said Shamus. "About Glory, I mean." But he said it with a big smile.

They paused at the corner of the bandstand.

"Over there," said Shamus, inclining his head. "That's Whitney Geiger."

Carmela gazed at a tall, silver-haired man who was holding court with a group of six people. Geiger had the air of an imperious CEO who was used to serious eye contact and deferential treatment. "He likes to talk," she said. "He enjoys being the center of attention."

"And how," said Shamus. "Geiger is fairly new to the Pluvius krewe, but he's always yapping about some dang thing. Why don't we increase membership? How can we start our parade planning earlier? I don't know why he doesn't just shut his trap and have fun like the rest of us."

"Maybe," said Carmela, "because he's a real businessman?"

"A cutthroat businessman, from what I hear," said Shamus.

"I thought you didn't know anything about him," said Carmela. "Just that he owns Royale Real Estate and his company's incorporated in Florida."

"I don't know much," said Shamus. "But I was talking to Dickie Winthrop earlier tonight . . . you remember Dickie Winthrop?"

"The dopey-looking guy who fell off the sea serpent float last year and broke his collarbone?" said Carmela.

"That's our Dickie," said Shamus. "Anyway, Dickie was telling me that some TV station was gonna do a story about Geiger."

Carmela did a slow reptilian blink. "What?" she said.

"Yeah," said Shamus. He paused. "Something wrong with that?"

Carmela clutched his arm. "Never mind, let's just go find Dickie. Is he here?" She gave Shamus a sharp yank to show she was serious. "I want to talk to him."

"Yeah, he's here. Whoa, babe, you're spilling my drink!"

They found Dickie Winthrop on the dance floor, looking like he was in the final throes of an epileptic seizure.

Shamus tapped Dickie on the shoulder of his white *Saturday Night Fever* three-piece suit. "Dickie, Dickie, I gotta talk to you!"

Dickie's dance partner, grateful for the interruption, spun away with a look of sheer relief on her face.

Dickie was six feet tall and weighed maybe one hundred and fifty pounds sopping wet. He grabbed Shamus by the lapels. "Did ya see us?" he wailed, his face shiny with perspiration. "We were doing the hustle. Remember the hustle? The L.A. hustle, the Latin hustle, just like Travolta used to do? I'm good, man. I've still got it." Dickie had to be midfifties, so he probably had grooved to the Bee Gees and *Saturday Night Fever.*

"Dickie," said Shamus, "you remember Carmela, don't you?"

Dickie, who'd clearly hit his limit on drinks, blinked and said, "Carmela. Whoa, aren't you a cutie!" And to Shamus, "This chick's your date?"

"I'm his ex," said Carmela, an edge to her voice. "Don't you remember, Dickie, you were at our wedding?" *In fact, you spazzed out at our wedding and pretty much cleared the dance floor.*

Dickie pulled out a hanky and made a big show of mopping his face. "Oh yeah," he muttered. "Sorry things didn't work out for y'all."

"Don't be sorry," said Carmela. "Just try to be lucid for one minute."

"Carmela wants to ask you about Whit Geiger," put in Shamus. "Remember, you were saying something about him earlier?"

Dickie nodded. "Yeah?"

"You mentioned to Shamus that Whit Geiger might be interviewed for TV?" Carmela prompted.

Dickie furrowed his brow as if deep in thought, then said, "Not exactly interviewed. What Geiger told me is that some TV station wanted to do a story about him."

"About his real estate dealings?" said Carmela.

"That's right," said Dickie. He nodded to himself as if recalling the conversation, then poked an index finger at her and chuckled. "And Geiger told me he dodged the bullet."

"Really," said Carmela. "What do you think he meant by that?" She tried to line up her thoughts. "What exactly did Geiger tell you?"

Dickie fixed her with a soggy smile. "Remember that crazy broad who got killed a few days ago? The one who got hung during the parade?"

312

"Kimber Breeze," said Carmela, trying to quell the flutter that had started up in the pit of her stomach.

"That's the one," said Dickie.

"What about her?" asked Carmela. Pulling information out of Dickie was like pulling taffy. Sticky and lugubrious. Plus he kept drifting off course.

Dickie glanced over his shoulder, as if the CIA might be monitoring his every word. "Geiger told me she was planning to do an exposé on him," he said in a scratchy whisper.

"An exposé about what?" asked Carmela, determined to get an answer.

Dickie shrugged. "I dunno exactly. But I got the feeling it was something to do with real estate. Maybe . . . eminent domain housing that he bought for a song from the city?" Dickie winked. "Lot of that going on."

Carmela found Ava lounging at the bar, sipping a drink.

"What's that?" asked Carmela, pointing to her glass.

"Red Rooster," said Ava. "Vodka, orange juice, and cranberry juice. Really quite delicious."

"How come I could only get a crappy Jack

Daniel's when you scored a tasty mixed drink?"

"You have to flirt with the bartenders," said Ava. She twirled a finger in the air, then pointed at a dark-haired, mustachioed bartender, who smiled engagingly and gave her a slow wink.

"I gotta talk to you about something," said Carmela.

"Shoot," said Ava.

"You remember Dickie Winthrop?" asked Carmela.

Ava thought for a minute. "The dumb-ass who broke his arm when he fell off a float?"

"Collarbone," said Carmela. "But, yes, that's the Dickie we all know and love. Anyway, I was asking him about Whit Geiger, that real estate guy I told you about, and Dickie said Kimber was trying to do an exposé on Geiger."

"Do tell," said Ava. She took another sip of her drink. "So that means what exactly?"

Carmela lowered her voice. "I think it means that Geiger should be on my suspect list."

Ava grimaced. "Because Geiger had an ax to grind with Kimber?"

"He might have wanted her out of the way."

"Jeez," said Ava. "I'd say that's . . . significant."

"I think so, too," said Carmela.

"The thing is," said Ava, "are you going to tell Babcock about this latest wrinkle?"

Her question gave Carmela pause. "I'm not sure."

"Well you better decide fast," said Ava, "before somebody else gets whacked!"

CHAPTER 22

Carmela walked with her shoulders hunched and her head thrust forward, headed for Memory Mine and the start of what would probably be a very busy day. But scrapbook albums, rubber stamps, and cute embellishments were the last thing on her mind right now. She was thinking about Whitney Geiger, the prominent real estate developer who'd been hailed as a business leader by the chamber of commerce, and quietly pointed out to her as a man who was known to dabble in shady deals. And, after getting an earful from Dickie last night, Carmela was still pondering whether Whitney Geiger might be a legitimate suspect in Kimber's murder.

Could Geiger have been worried sick that Kimber was planning to do an exposé of his real estate schemes? It was possible, she decided. So the next question was, could Geiger have donned a costume and slipped into the Bonaparte Suite? Yes, that was possible, too. But now came the biggie. Could Geiger have sneaked out on the balcony and strangled Kimber?

That was where it all got elusive and fuzzy for Carmela. She could imagine any number of people doing exactly that. But who was numero uno? Who was the killer? That, unfortunately, was still up in the air. Which meant the killer was still free as a bird.

Shivering against a cool breeze, Carmela spun around a corner and turned onto Governor Nicholls Street. She sailed past Oddities, thinking briefly of the strange Mr. Joubert, then smiled at her own display of party invitations and cigar box purses in her front window.

Just as she punched her key in the lock, Carmela noticed a piece of paper stuck in the door.

Oh no. Not another . . .

Oh yes, it was. Another postcard.

Snatching the postcard from where it had been stuck, she pushed her way into her shop. Feeling nervous, like someone might be spying on her and relishing her nervousness, she flipped on the lights. Their reassuring glow and the warmth of her shop helped calm her.

Carmela shrugged out of her corduroy

jacket and set the postcard on the counter.

Okay, let's take a look.

It was the same type of postcard that she'd purchased yesterday at the Dreamland Gift Shop. And this one had writing on it, just like the previous two postcards she'd received. This message read *I'm still waiting.* And it was signed *Kimber.*

Isn't this just ducky.

A rattle of the brass doorknob sent Carmela's heart lurching and a shot of adrenaline speedballing through her veins.

"Carmela?" called a voice. Then Gabby's smiling face appeared.

Carmela stood rooted to the spot, unable to answer, looking more than a little stunned.

"Sorry we didn't make it last night," said Gabby. "Stuart had to —" She suddenly noticed the look of fear on Carmela's face and put two and two together. "Oh, don't tell me. Another one turned up?"

Carmela nodded wordlessly.

Gabby hastily latched the door behind her. "Please don't tell me somebody broke in here again."

"No," said Carmela, "it was stuck in the door."

Gabby grimaced. "Let me see."

Carmela handed her the postcard.

"Same kind," said Gabby. For some reason, she was a lot more composed. Maybe she was getting used to these crazy postcards. "Who the heck is doing this?" She gazed at Carmela. "Do you have any idea at all? Does Babcock?"

"Not really," said Carmela, "though the suspect list does seem to be growing."

Gabby waggled her fingers. "Who else? Tell me."

So Carmela told her about the information she'd gleaned about Whit Geiger and how Kimber had been planning an exposé on mortgage fraud and now she obviously wasn't.

"Whit Geiger," murmured Gabby. "I know that guy. I mean, I've *met* him. He's on the board of the Riverview Pediatric Hospital. We even attended their charity gala."

"That's nice," said Carmela. "And I found out from Jekyl that Davis Durrell is on the board of the City Opera."

"So what are you saying?" asked Gabby.

Carmela shrugged. "Rich people behaving badly?"

"I'd say it's more than just behaving badly. And it's not all rich people, just . . . one."

"That's all it takes," said Carmela. "But, the rotten thing is, I seem to have hit an impasse. In other words, I've narrowed it down to a handful of suspects, but have no real proof on anyone."

"What does Babcock think?" asked Gabby. "He's the pro, he should have figured something out."

"Ah . . . he's not exactly a happy camper right now. After the smoke bomb Saturday night, he's pretty sure somebody is trying to tell me to back off. So we're not on the best of terms."

"He's right about sending a warning," said Gabby. "And they didn't just *try* to, they did send it!"

"Point taken," said Carmela, giving a half-smile.

"Speaking of the smoke bomb," said Gabby, "how is your place?"

"Coming along," said Carmela. "The cleanup crew left a bunch of fans and ion machines cranking away and they seem to be doing the trick. I checked this morning before I came in."

"When can you get back into your own apartment?"

"I don't know," said Carmela, "maybe a couple of days?"

Gabby took off her coat, then said, "This situation is getting serious. You must be on to something."

"Maybe," said Carmela, "but for the life of me, I don't know what it is."

By nine o'clock, Carmela had Tate Mackie on the line. The owner of Byte Head Computers, Mackie was a jack-of-all-trades. He fixed computers, set up computers, and did a booming business in computer security and computer special effects.

"Do you know anything about setting up a teeny, tiny little camera?" Carmela asked Mackie.

"For your store?" Mackie asked her.

"That's right. I want a camera to cover the front door. And I guess there should be another one at the back door, too."

"I take it you're worried about Mardi Gras hoodlums breaking and entering?"

"Something like that," said Carmela. "The important thing is, can you do the installation?"

"Of course I can," said Mackie. "Piece of cake, really. If you want, I can even link the camera feed to your computer or smartphone."

"Are you serious?" said Carmela. "If you can make that happen, it'd be phenomenal."

"Technology," said Mackie, "you gotta love it."

■ ■ ■ ■

"I'm having cameras installed," Carmela told Gabby. "The guy from Byte Head is coming over in a few minutes."

Gabby put a hand to her chest and patted it gently as she breathed a sigh of relief. "Excellent. Maybe we'll even catch the perpetrator in the act."

"If some idiot delivers more postcards, we might," said Carmela. She picked up a package of gold brads and worried it with her fingers. "This is getting stranger and stranger."

"I know you've got an entire roster of suspects, but tell me, who's your front-runner?"

"For Kimber's murder or the wacky post-cards?"

"Mmm," said Gabby, considering her words. "I've been assuming it's one and the same."

"Maybe it is. Probably it is. That scenario feels right anyway." Carmela thought for a few seconds. "If I had to venture a guess at this point, I'd say Davis Durrell."

"The boyfriend," said Gabby, pouncing on her words. "I knew it! It's always the boyfriend. Haven't you noticed that whenever some poor girl falls down a flight of stairs or takes a swan dive off a cruise ship, it always comes back to the boyfriend!"

"Not always," said Carmela, as the phone on the counter started to ring. "Sometimes it's the husband."

"Oh, you!" said Gabby as Carmela reached for the phone.

"Memory Mine," said Carmela.

"Carmela?" came a girl's voice. "This is Beth at Grand Folly Costume. I don't know if you're still interested, but we rented that costume again. The clown costume."

"Oh! Do you know who rented it?" *Could it have been Sullivan Finch? The man who painted the clown portrait as well as Kimber's?*

"Sorry, I don't," said Beth. "I wasn't here and whoever came in paid cash again."

Carmela thought for a moment. "You said *again.* That implies it was the same person."

"Oh," said Beth. There was a moment of silence, then she said, "Now why would I say that? Why *did* I say that?"

"Think hard," said Carmela. Was there a reason? There had to be a reason.

"Maybe because the whole outfit was rented," said Beth. "The silk clown costume, the mask, and the shoes. Even the white silk gloves."

"The whole shebang," said Carmela,

fervently hoping that Canio's smiling, leering face wasn't about to turn up at her shop. "Thanks, Beth, I appreciate your call."

Carmela was busy pulling sheets of yellow and gold banana leaf paper for a customer when Tate Mackie showed up. "Excuse me," she said to her customer, then quickly slipped away to greet Mackie. "Hey," she said, "thanks for coming over right away."

"No problem," said Mackie. With his close-shorn head, green army jacket, blue jeans, and pierced eyebrow, Tate Mackie looked like a slacker. But he owned his own shop, moonlighted in movie graphics, and had built quite a reputation for himself in the French Quarter.

"Got any film gigs going?" asked Carmela.

Mackie gave her a wide grin. "Oh yeah. Since I got myself listed on the New Orleans Film Commission's Web site under production services, I've worked on a couple of features. A movie called *My Spy* and another one as yet untitled."

"That's fantastic. You've gone Hollywood."

"Don't I wish," said Mackie. He opened a battered leather messenger bag and showed her two small cameras.

"Amazing," said Carmela. "They don't

even look like cameras. More like cigarette lighters or something."

Mackie winked. "That's the whole idea. Like a nanny cam. Heck, these days you can get smoke detectors, thermostats, wall clocks, and silk flower arrangements that masquerade as cameras."

"I'll remember that next time somebody sends me flowers," said Carmela.

Mackie glanced around the store and pointed. "How about I tuck a camera right up in that front corner? That way we'll have a good shot of the cash register, the door, and most of the store."

"What I really need," said Carmela, "is tight surveillance on the front and back doors."

Mackie's brows shot up. "You've had problems with break-ins?"

"You could say that."

"Tough," said Mackie. He scratched his nose and wandered over to the front door. "Inside or out?" he asked.

"Outside would be better," said Carmela. "Can you do that?"

Mackie thought about it. "I can run a wire through . . ." The rest of his words were lost in a ruminating mumble. Then he turned and said, "Yeah, I can do that."

■ ■ ■ ■

While Tate Mackie was working on the camera installations, Carmela pulled Gabby aside.

"I don't want to freak you out or anything," said Carmela, "but I wanted you to see these." She pulled the cemetery postcards out of their flat brown bag.

Gabby *was* freaked. "Don't tell me you've been holding out on me!" she squealed, her eyes suddenly the size of saucers. "Don't tell me you received a whole raft of these cards!"

"No, no," said Carmela, quickly trying to put Gabby at ease. "I bought these. Three from Dreamland Gifts down the street. Six more from their other shop over in the Faubourg Marigny."

"Really?" said Gabby. She peered at the cards, as if they possessed magical properties. Black magic. "You think that's where your mysterious pen pal purchased his cards?"

"I don't know, but I think so. That's what I'm trying to figure out."

Gabby frowned. "How are you going to do that?"

"I'm going to start with the printer and

hope I get lucky."

But when Carmela finally got hold of Devoux Printing, they weren't much help.

"We're not doing that line any more," said the woman who answered the phone.

"Because it wasn't selling or . . . ?"

The woman cut her off. "Because we just change designs every couple of years. We have tons of images archived already, stuff that's in the public domain. Plus photographers are always trying to peddle new stuff to us."

"I see," said Carmela. "So . . . do you think you'll be doing more cemetery images?"

"I don't see why not," said the woman. "They've always been perennial best sellers."

"Just not that same line and not for a while," said Carmela.

"That's right," said the woman. "We've still got a couple cartons of our current antique cemetery cards in the warehouse."

"Do you know . . . have you had any large orders for those particular cards?"

"Not that I know of," said the woman. "And I'd be the one the order would come through." She paused. "I don't know what you're looking for, but I'm sorry I couldn't be of more help."

Carmela hung up her phone and thought for a moment, as images of the gritty black-and-white postcards flitted through her brain. If someone had been sending her a not-so-subtle message, had it been Whitney Geiger?

Flipping open her phone directory, Carmela dialed KBEZ-TV and got Ed Banister, the station manager, on the line.

"Carmela!" he said, greeting her with great enthusiasm. "I talked to your friend Baby Fontaine and she's agreed to let us film at her party tonight!"

"That's terrific," said Carmela.

"It's fantastic!" Banister raved, "and I owe it all to your good connections. It isn't often we get to film in the Garden District's inner sanctum."

"You won't be disappointed," Carmela promised. "Baby puts on a terrific masked ball and the food is to die for." She paused, then said, "I have a question for you that may or may not be related to Kimber's murder."

"Okay," said Banister.

"I was wondering," said Carmela, "if you guys are still doing that investigative report on Whit Geiger?"

There was silence for a moment, then

Banister said, "On who?"

"Whitney Geiger," said Carmela. "The Royale Real Estate guy who built a slug of mega mansions over in Lake Vista." When there was more silence, Carmela added, "Apparently, Kimber was working on some kind of exposé?"

"I'm pretty sure his company's been a sometime advertiser," said Banister. "But I don't know anything about an exposé."

"You didn't hear about it or see a proposal?" said Carmela. "From Kimber?"

"I'm afraid not," said Banister. "If this was a project Kimber was spearheading . . ." Banister coughed loudly, then cleared his throat. Kimber's death was obviously still very painful for him. Then he said in a slightly choked voice, "I hate to phrase it like this, but I'm guessing any project she was working on died with her."

"He didn't know about it," Carmela said out loud in her office after she'd thanked Banister and hung up the phone. "Hmm."

She wasn't sure what that meant exactly. That Kimber had been doing this exposé on the down low? That Kimber didn't run every project past her boss? Or that Kimber hadn't even gotten a toehold on the project yet?

Carmela figured there might be one way

to find out.

"Raleigh," she said, "can you hear me?" She'd called Raleigh on his cell phone and gotten him immediately, though the connection felt tenuous.

"Who's this?" he asked. His voice crackled out from a din of background noise and musical notes.

"It's Carmela," she said.

"Oh, hey. What's up?"

"Where are you?" she asked.

"Over in Gretna. The Somerset marching band is just setting up. They're gonna march across the bridge, do a concert in Woldenberg Park, and wind up as part of tonight's Proteus parade. Lucky me, I get to document the whole thing."

"Listen," said Carmela, "I was wondering . . . is there any way I could get a look at the footage you shot on Whit Geiger?"

"There isn't any footage," said Raleigh. "The story never got that far. It was all research on Kimber's part."

"Research," said Carmela. She was disappointed there wasn't anything tangible. Footage that might have shown a twitchy Whit Geiger, a man who had a possible motive to put a decisive end to Kimber's story. And to the indomitable Kimber. "So what happened to the research? To Kimber's notes and things?"

"I don't know," said Raleigh. "It's probably all still in her office. Zoe's office now."

"Is Zoe with you today?"

"Of course she's with me. You don't think they're giving her the plum assignments yet, do you?"

"Can you put Zoe on the line?" said Carmela.

"No can do," said Raleigh, "I don't even know where she is right now. Maybe . . . hiding behind a bass drum?"

CHAPTER 23

"Carmela." Tate Mackie hovered in her office doorway. "You're all set. I've got the cameras tucked away where nobody can see them."

She straightened in her chair. "Unless somebody's looking for them."

"Then you're dealing with a different kind of thief," said Mackie. "Someone who possesses a high degree of sophistication when it comes to breaking and entering, not just some goofball off the street."

They went to inspect the cameras, and then Mackie spent another five minutes showing Carmela how to pull up the images on her smartphone.

"This is very cool," said Carmela.

"Hey," said Mackie, "it's what I got."

Carmela, wondering if her little video leg trap would catch the postcard perpetrator, wandered back into her shop. And realized that Memory Mine was suddenly busy. Two women were looking at leather-bound albums, another customer was selecting rolls of colorful ribbon, and — wait a minute, was that Tandy standing at the counter? Sure it was.

"I can't believe you came in today," said Carmela, hustling up to greet her friend.

"Hey you!" said Tandy, whirling about and quickly administering a series of elaborate air kisses. Wearing a red sweater that matched her curly red hair, she looked skinny as ever. "I was just telling Gabby that I can't believe you guys are *open* today."

"Strange as it sounds," said Carmela, "the day before Fat Tuesday often turns out to be one of our biggest days."

"It sure does," agreed Gabby. "Everybody seems to be in a blind panic over having enough paper and cards and ribbon."

"There you go," said Tandy. "I guess that explains why I'm here, too." She lowered her voice and aimed a concerned look at Carmela: "Gabby tells me your apartment got smoke-bombed." She rolled her eyes. "Must have been awful!"

"There were a few panic-filled moments, yes," said Carmela. *Were there ever!*

Tandy frowned. "Who would do such a horrible thing? And, more importantly, why?"

"Babcock thinks it might be the same person who killed Kimber Breeze," said Carmela. "He thinks the killer was sending me a warning."

"Scary," said Tandy. "What do you think?"

"Not sure," said Carmela.

"Yes, you are," said Tandy. "I bet you know *exactly* why you were targeted."

Carmela shrugged. "I guess so. I mean, I suppose Babcock might be right."

"Which tells me you're trying to solve this Kimber Breeze murder," said Tandy. She looked both skeptical and curious. "I know you and Ava were *there*, but . . ."

"I'm just kind of muddling things around," said Carmela. *At least that's what it's been so far.*

"You know what?" said Tandy, waving a birdlike hand. "I'll bet you *do* come up with something. You've got a heckuva knack for this kind of stuff. Remember poor Byrle? In St. Tristan's Church? You were the one who figured it all out."

"I got lucky on that one, but this Kimber Breeze case is totally different," Carmela explained, as she followed Tandy back to the craft table.

Tandy dropped her plaid tote bag onto the floor. "I bet you figured out some suspects, huh?"

"A few," Carmela admitted.

"And you're gonna be careful, right?" said Tandy, peering at her through red-rimmed half-glasses. "Not take any silly chances?"

"I'll try not to," said Carmela.

"Good girl," said Tandy. She dug into her tote bag and pulled out scissors, paper, rubber stamps, and, finally, a plastic container. "I brought you some homemade biscuits to help you keep up your strength." She popped off the top. "Sweet potato biscuits."

"Thanks," said Carmela, selecting a golden-brown biscuit and taking a bite. "Mmm, delicious."

"Thought you might like 'em," said Tandy. "Now I've got a crazy question for you." She put her hands on her skinny hips. "Have you ever done a dog scrapbook?"

"Not a crazy question at all," said Carmela, as she popped the remaining bit of sweet biscuit in her mouth. "Because the answer is yes."

Tandy nodded. "I thought you might have." She pulled out a packet of photos. "Here's the thing. We've got tons of photos of Buster and I've never so much as scrapped a single page on the little guy."

"And you're feeling guilty?" said Carmela, shuffling through the photos of Buster, an adorable black-and-white Boston bulldog.

"As only a pet momma can," said Tandy with a laugh.

"Then let's play around a little," suggested Carmela. "Shop the store and see what might work for you." She led Tandy over to her floor-to-ceiling racks of paper. "We've got tons of dog motif paper here," she said, grabbing a few sheets. "And we've got breed stickers, dog bone stickers, tennis ball stickers, and dimensional ID tags."

"Excellent," said Tandy.

"And," said Carmela, "I just happen to have these neat leather albums with a photo window on the front cover."

"Just stick Buster's photo in there," said Tandy, smiling. "Easy peasy."

"Right," said Carmela. "Now, these albums are small, just six by nine inches, but if you use eight-and-a-half-by-eleven-inch paper and cut the sheets in half, it works like a charm. Plus the album ends up being cute and manageable."

"Just like Buster," said Tandy, "so I'm gonna do exactly that." She was grabbing paper and stickers by the handful. "Hoo-ee! This is gonna be great!"

Because Gabby seemed to be handling the onslaught of customers just fine, Carmela sat down with Tandy and decided to do a scrapbook page herself. She hand-lettered the words *Lucky Dog* at the top of a page with pawprint borders, deciding the words would serve as a sort of talisman for Boo and Poobah's safety. She added a photo of Boo and Poobah cuddled on their beds, then punched it up with some glitter bone buttons and two metal ID tags.

Tandy, meanwhile, had stenciled the words *Bad to the Bone* at the top of her page and was busily trimming and fitting photos.

Perfect, Carmela decided. She was doing a great job.

"Whatcha wearing to Baby's party tonight?" asked Tandy. Her curls bobbed as she labored over her page.

"Ava and I are going to pick something from that Voodoo Couture line she's supposed to be acting as muse for," said Carmela.

Tandy lifted her head. "That's funny. Ava as muse. So what kind of clothing will it be?"

"Probably lots of black lace and satin," said Carmela.

"Ooh, sexy stuff."

"Hopefully not over-the-top sexy," said Carmela. "Maybe a little more Goth."

"Please," said Tandy, snickering, "if the company chose Ava as their spokesperson or muse or hot mama or whatever she's supposed to be, then the clothes are gonna be *beaucoup* sexy."

"Carmela," Gabby called from the front counter. She waggled the phone, indicating she had a call.

Carmela dashed into her office. "Carmela here."

"Meet me at the Café du Monde in ten minutes, okay?" It was Babcock, sounding harried.

"You okay?" asked Carmela. She hated to see him frantic and chasing his tail, like he had been for the past week.

"Hanging in there," he said. "I just need a serious infusion of caffeine. And I'd like to see you. Talk to you."

"Okay then," said Carmela, "I'll be there."

The Café du Monde was a french quarter fixture, an open-air café with green-and-white striped awnings. But the real selling point, besides the great French Quarter views and serenading street musicians, was the rich chicory coffee and sweet beignets. Ah, those beignets! Three to an order, nestled in a tidy little cardboard container, there wasn't a tastier, sweeter, more lethal doughnut to be found. Beignets were, literally, delectable little gut bombs drenched in powdered sugar. To eat one was to love one, and to love one was to be hooked.

Carmela was the first to arrive, so she hastened to the counter and grabbed two cups of coffee and an order of beignets. By the time she threaded her way to an empty table, she could see Babcock approaching. Dressed in an Etro sport coat and James Perse slacks, he looked debonair, au courant, and all those other good things. Except for the slight bulge under his left arm, where his service revolver was holstered in a custom leather harness, he could have been a male model taking a break from a magazine shoot.

"You look good," Carmela told him, when he got to her table. She'd noticed two blond women at a nearby table noticing him, too. *Mine*, she wanted to tell them. *Hands off*.

"So do you," he said. Settling into a chair, he leaned over and gave her a quick kiss.

"Too quick," she said. "Again."

"Gladly."

This time his kiss was a little more lingering and Carmela noticed that the two blondes had suddenly lost interest. Good. "What's up?" she asked him.

He pointed toward the steaming coffees. "Is one of those for me?"

"Your jolt of caffeine," she said, then

indicated the beignets. "And a sugar hit, too."

"There's a problem," said Babcock.

"Concerning?"

"The party tonight."

"Don't tell me you can't come."

"I can't come," said Babcock.

"Oh rats." Carmela grabbed one of the beignets and took a bite, cognizant she'd just given herself a powdered sugar mustache. She wiggled her nose, trying to wipe it away surreptitiously.

"Correction," said Babcock. "I can attend Baby's party for a short while, and then my presence is required elsewhere."

"Care to share what that 'elsewhere' is?" asked Carmela. She shoved the remaining beignets toward Babcock. There was no reason she should pack on the pudge and Babcock should remain trim.

"Not really," said Babcock.

"Does this have anything to do with Kimber's murder?"

"Nope." Babcock grabbed one of the proffered beignets and took a bite. "Good," he said. With his mouth full it sounded like "Guuuh."

"Does it have to do with the smoke bomb at my place?" Carmela asked.

Babcock eyed her with amusement. "What

is this, twenty questions?" He finished chewing then said, "Okay, this is strictly confidential."

"Of course."

"Remember that drug thing I told you about? The cartel?"

"Sure." Carmela had a vague memory of him mentioning something about illegal drugs coming in from South America.

"That's what I'm working on."

"Isn't that more DEA territory?"

"Not when it's in my territory," said Babcock.

"So, a stakeout? A drug bust?"

"Nothing that exciting or dangerous, I'm afraid. It's more like checking out supposedly suspicious activity."

"Okay. So . . . I'll meet you at the party," said Carmela. "That's no problem. Just be sure to wear a costume."

"I'll be the one dressed as a homicide detective. You know, thick-soled Church's shoes, holstered gun, khaki slacks, suspicious air about him."

"I'd say it's going to be practically impossible to pick you out from all the witches and warlocks," Carmela quipped, "but I'll try my best."

Babcock eyed her. "Have you been staying out of trouble?"

His question caught her off guard. "Um . . ."

"What?" Babcock's mood shifted in an instant and he pounced like a hungry alley cat.

Since they were sitting in fairly neutral territory, Carmela decided she could probably tell Babcock about the third postcard that had arrived this morning. Better here than at her office, where he might hunker down and stay forever. Or *his* office, where he could browbeat her to pieces and bring in police reinforcements.

"Another postcard came this morning," Carmela said.

Babcock didn't look happy. "Your place? Or at Ava's?"

"At Memory Mine. It was stuck in the door."

"Ah, man," said Babcock, rubbing his chin. "I hate this weird shit."

"Believe me, so do I," said Carmela.

"Either you have a very strange admirer or you ticked off somebody but good."

"Really," said Carmela, "I didn't mean to."

Babcock leaned back in his chair and gazed at her intently. "Carmela, I think you did."

CHAPTER 24

Tandy was gone by the time Carmela made it back to her shop. But two more scrappers were seated at the back table.

"Do they know we're closing at three o'clock today?" Carmela asked Gabby.

Gabby nodded. "I told them. They're cool." She smiled. "Everything okay with Babcock? He's still coming to the party tonight?"

"He's coming," said Carmela, "just not with me."

"You two having problems?"

"Nothing we haven't faced before," said Carmela quickly. "He's just hard at work on all sorts of things."

"I imagine he is," said Gabby.

Carmela wandered back to where Susan, one of her regulars, was scanning a rack full of rubber stamps. "Help you with anything?" she asked.

"Anything new come in?" asked Susan,

squinting at the floral image she'd just stamped. "You know what a stampaholic I am."

"Let me see," said Carmela, perusing her inventory. "Oh, I bet you haven't seen these Renaissance stamps yet with images taken from Italian paintings."

"I have not seen them," said Susan, "and I can tell you right now, I want them."

"Well . . . good," said Carmela. If only every sale were that easy!

"Oh hey," called Gabby, "the chicken wire guys are here."

"Thank goodness," said Carmela, scooting up to the front of the store. Every year, right before Fat Tuesday, the really big blowout day, she had a couple of guys show up and stretch chicken wire across her front window. It was a smart precaution, since every year, drinks, debris, and even people were tossed through plate-glass storefront windows throughout the French Quarter. Again, just another one of the heartwarming traditions of Mardi Gras.

"Between the chicken wire and the cameras we should be covered," said Gabby. "Ain't nobody gonna get in here!"

"Not unless they're invited," agreed Carmela. Then her eyes widened as the front door opened and Marcus Joubert stepped in.

"Greetings," said Joubert. He gave Carmela a friendly smile and aimed an offhand wave at Gabby.

"Well, hello," said Carmela, as Gabby gave a terse nod and suddenly got busy sorting packets of silver and turquoise beads.

"I just wanted to pop in and thank you for coming to my open house," said Joubert. "And for bringing your lovely friend, Ava."

"She had a blast," said Carmela.

Joubert's eyes darted around the shop. "Are you going to be open tomorrow?"

"Nope," said Carmela. "Tomorrow we're closed. It'll be way too crazy in the French Quarter." She paused. "Why? You're going to be open?"

"Probably for a few hours," said Joubert. "Test the water, so to speak."

"I hope you're planning to get the chicken wire treatment."

Joubert shifted nervously. "Do you think I should?"

"Absolutely," said Carmela. "Unless you want a couple of drunks waking up in your sarcophagus. Just go outside and talk to the two guys who are working on my window. They'll take care of you."

"Thank you," said Joubert.

345

"You're welcome," said Carmela, as the door whooshed closed behind him.

"Welcome?" Gabby muttered. "Not in here. In fact, that guy's about as welcome as a nest of fire ants."

By three o'clock, Memory Mine had emptied out and Carmela and Gabby were ready to lock up.

"Security cameras turned on?" asked Gabby, as she gathered up her coat and purse.

"Oh yeah," said Carmela. "They'll be running 24/7. Tate Mackie even set it up so I can monitor them from my smartphone. I'm all teched out."

"Which probably beats an armed guard and a moat full of alligators," said Gabby. She paused. "Well, I guess I'll see you tonight."

"Baby's big bash," said Carmela. "Oh, did I tell you KBEZ was going to be there?"

"Baby really agreed to that?"

"Guess so. Anyway, they're going to shoot some footage for their documentary, so be sure to wear a costume that's over the top!"

"I'm coming as Annie Oakley, so I'll leave the craziness to you."

"Good thing I'm off to shop the Voodoo Couture line with Ava," laughed Carmela.

"Get ready for your close-up!" said Gabby, chuckling.

Carmela dashed the few blocks to Juju Voodoo and found the place swarming with tourists. "You about ready?" she asked Ava, even though Ava was mobbed.

Ava threw her hands in the air. "Not hardly, *cher*. Look at this place, I'm up to my eyeballs in customers!"

Carmela grinned. "Cool your jets, sweetie, we've got time." She wondered why shopkeepers and restaurateurs always got upset when they were busy. Busy was good. Busy meant you were making money. Busy meant you could pay the rent this month and then some.

Wandering to the back of Ava's shop, where the atmosphere was a little quieter, Carmela stopped to test a bottle of Voodoo Amour perfume. Mmm, a nice tropical scent, maybe a hint of vanilla and frangipani? But would it attract love? Or help intensify desire? That was the million-dollar question.

And what about Ava's saint candles? If you lit a St. Paul candle, it was supposed to protect you from snakes. Good for cruising the bayous, she supposed. St. Thomas Aquinas was the patron saint of scholars.

And here was one she should probably pick up for Babcock. St. Michael, patron saint of police officers. Perhaps lighting this candle would magically assist him in solving Kimber's murder.

Ava was suddenly by her side. "Take that one if you want. It's been sitting on the shelf just gathering dust."

"What if it's lost its juju?" asked Carmela. "Its magic?"

"That candle is one hundred percent guaranteed to work," Ava promised. "And here, take this one, too." She thrust a second candle into Carmela's hands. "St. Andrew, patron saint of spinsters. Lot of good *he's* done me!" She adjusted her tight V-neck sweater, the better to show off her tight décolletage, then said, "Let's hit the trail, cupcake. I can't wait to slither my bodacious bod into one of those dresses for tonight's party."

"I gotta show you something first," said Carmela. She pulled out her phone, jumped on the Internet, and pulled up the Web site Tate Mackie had shown her. Entered her password and . . . bingo!

"Whoa!" said Ava. "That's the front door of your shop. How very cool."

"Gonna catch that postcard jerk," said Carmela.

"Just think," said Ava, "with technology like that, you can solve a crime and still party your head off at Mardi Gras!"

Magazine street was one of the cool streets in New Orleans — a colorful, cosmopolitan stretch where boutiques, trendy restaurants, jazz clubs, avant-garde shops, and art galleries had clustered and thrived. The Latest Wrinkle, Carmela's favorite resale shop, was here. So was Lacy Lady, the upscale retail shop that carried the Voodoo Couture line.

"There it is!" Ava squealed. "Lacy Lady! I can feel a pulsing vibe already!"

"I think that's my transmission," said Carmela, as she nosed her aging sports car into an empty parking spot on the street.

"I just wanna look like a million bucks tonight," Ava sang out as she jumped from the car and sprinted for the door.

"And I just want to keep a low profile," sighed Carmela.

"Then you *didn't* come to the right place," called Ava.

Lacy Lady was a sparkling little jewel box of a shop. There were stacks of J Brand and True Religion jeans, racks of Cosabella lingerie, hand-painted silk scarves, trays of enormous statement rings by Yves Saint

Laurent, bangles by Stella McCartney, skinny T-shirts, racks of elegant evening gowns, a display of neon-colored faux furs, and an old-fashioned dressing table that held long leather gloves, strands of opera pearls, and enormous vintage brooches.

"Tasty, tasty," murmured Ava. A slinky black peignoir paired with black velvet cage boots had caught her eye. "Ooh, and there's Sally. Hey, girl, how you doin'?"

"Ava," said Sally Barnes, exchanging air kisses. "And Carmela. Welcome." Sally was the boutique's manager, a skinny blonde who always wore impossibly skinny jeans, sky-high Manolos, and what Carmela had come to think of as slightly skanky tops.

"I hope you've got some good stuff for us," gushed Ava.

"Not to worry," said Sally. "I've already gone through the new Voodoo Couture line and pulled a few pieces."

"An edit," said Carmela, thankful that someone else, someone with more fashion savvy than she, was making decisions.

But Ava, being Ava, just laughed and said, "I only want to try on the super-sexy stuff. The va-va-voom pieces."

"We like to think all our clothes are inherently sexy," said Sally, tactfully. "It's how a woman carries them off, how she lets her inner self shine through, that's the true test."

"Well put," said Carmela.

"However," said Sally, "I do have one piece in particular that's rather special."

"Let's have a look," said Ava.

Sally ran practiced fingers through a metal rack jammed full of clothes. "This dress," she said, pulling out a full-length strapless gown. "It's called Gothique Lady. You see? A lovely green velvet bodice laced with silver studs, then an enormously full ball skirt of black silk."

"That's it!" declared Ava. "That's my dress!"

"You want to try it on?" asked Sally, delighted by Ava's enthusiasm.

"Absolutely," said Ava. In one fluid motion, she grabbed the dress and zipped into a dressing room.

Sally, still amused, gazed at Carmela. "Now you."

"Gulp," said Carmela.

"Don't want to be such a spectacle?" asked Sally.

"If we can tone it down a little, that'd be good," agreed Carmela.

Sally went back to her rack. "Maybe . . . no. Too revealing." She continued her search. "But how about this?" She pulled out a long black velvet dress with a sweetheart neckline and long sleeves edged with ruffles of black lace.

"I'll give it a try," said Carmela.

But when Carmela and Ava both came out of their dressing rooms, Ava started laughing hysterically.

"You look like a Goth version of Betsy Ross!" howled Ava. "The long sleeves, the ruffles!"

"She looks great," said Sally, through clenched lips.

Carmela put her hands on her hips and gazed in the mirror. She did look like somebody who'd stepped out of the Revolutionary War era. Or someone of that ilk who was in mourning. But, hey, the dress covered what it was supposed to cover and, wonder of wonders, made her waist look teeny-tiny. Which was always a good thing.

"I like it," said Carmela. After all, she was wearing it for one night only. And she'd be attending a masked ball where everyone would be dressed a little goofy.

"Maybe . . . she needs a headpiece?" suggested Ava.

Sally swept in and pinned a swoop of black feather atop Carmela's head.

"You think?" said Carmela.

"Oh, much better," said Ava.

Carmela couldn't tell if Ava was serious

or putting her on. "You guys don't think the feather's too Big Bird?"

"It's great," said Sally. "Really."

"Hmm," said Ava, not to be left out. "Maybe I need a headpiece?"

Sally, ever resourceful, pinned a short black veil on Ava.

"Oh my gosh!" said Ava. "Now I look like the Corpse Bride!"

"That's a good thing?" asked Carmela.

"From the Tim Burton film," gushed Ava. "One of my all-time faves."

"Guess I missed that one," murmured Carmela.

"All we need to do is add a few pieces of jewelry," said Sally, "and I'd say you ladies are good to go."

"Are we ever," said Ava.

"What are we supposed to be again?" asked Carmela. "What kind of costumes are we wearing?"

"Dunno," said Ava. "Gothic rich bitch? Eurotrash witch? Wacky fashionista? Take your pick."

"Ah," said Carmela. "Now I get it."

Ava flounced her way over to the three-way mirror again and smiled at her thrice-reflected image. "You think I need jewelry?"

"Why stop now?" said Carmela.

"Maybe a necklace of jet-black beads and

a huge statement ring?"

"Sure," said Carmela. "Maybe even a tiara and a scepter. Who knows, you could end up knighting someone."

"I love that!" said Ava.

While Sally was up front selecting jewelry, Carmela said to Ava, "The costume shop called earlier today. That Canio clown costume's been rented again."

Ava's finely plucked brows rose in twin arcs. "Do they know who rented it?"

"Unfortunately, no," said Carmela. She hesitated, then said, "But I sure hope . . . no, I shouldn't say that."

"What?" said Ava.

"I hope your friend Sullivan Finch doesn't turn up wearing it."

Ava looked suddenly unhappy. "Ah jeez, why would you say that?"

"You know . . . his painting the other night?"

"You have a very dark and suspicious mind," said Ava.

"I can have, yes. And right now I'm trying to be extra cautious."

"Mark my words," said Ava, "when Sully shows up tonight he'll be looking fine!" She held up an index finger. "But I do share your concern, especially after seeing that sneaky little clown on video. So we better keep an eye out for that costume."

"With something like eight hundred thousand visitors plus the entire population of New Orleans celebrating Mardi Gras," said Carmela, "it's going to be like searching for a needle in a haystack."

"Still," said Ava, "you never can tell."

CHAPTER 25

If the French Quarter was the crown jewel of New Orleans, then the Garden District was its lush sister. Elegant, old world, and opulent, but decaying just enough so that it possessed a mysterious Miss Havisham quality. Here, authors such as Truman Capote and Anne Rice had fallen under its spell, inhaled its rarefied air, and penned their magic. Here, block after block of elegant mansions were tucked amid whispers of foliage and private gardens, all of which harked back to an earlier, more graceful era when carriages, mint juleps on silver trays, and liveried help reigned supreme.

Tonight, however, most Garden District homes glistened like fancy baubles. Lights, action, party! The night air sizzled with electricity, and Baby Fontaine's palatial home seemed to be at the nexus of it all. Lights blazed in every one of the tall, elegant windows, music floated up into the blue-black sky, and a steady stream of eager guests poured up the front walk, eager to dance, carouse, and tip back drinks.

"How do I look?" asked Ava. She was poised on the curb, adjusting her bodice and fluffing her hair. Basically preening.

"You're a knockout," said Carmela. "How about me?" She plucked at a ruffled sleeve.

"Like you should be sewing stars on a flag," said Ava.

"That bad?"

"Not bad, *cher*, just different. If you want to make Shamus jealous, it's totally the wrong outfit."

"Who said anything about making Shamus jealous?" squawked Carmela. Then she did a double take. "Wait a minute, who says Shamus is even going to *be* there tonight?"

Ava looked suddenly nervous, like she'd let the proverbial cat out of the bag. "Well, he is. He and that wacked-out sister of his. Baby told me so herself."

Carmela wasn't thrilled. "That's all I need. Shamus and Babcock in the same room."

Ava clutched her hands together and struck a dramatic pose. "I think it could pan out to be a very romantic, old-fashioned moment. They could fight a duel over you!"

Carmela snorted. "They'll probably just ignore me."

"Never happen," said Ava. " 'Cause even with that dress, you still look dang cute."

"Oh . . . put on your mask," said Carmela. She'd cut eyeholes into thin strips of fine black lace, so all they had to do was tie them on. Instant mask.

"I hate to cover my face," said Ava, "since I'm wearing purple eye glitter and went to the trouble of gluing on two sets of false eyelashes."

"Here," said Carmela. "Take my mask, it's got bigger eyeholes."

"Well, I declare," said Del Fontaine, Baby's handsome husband, as he greeted them at the front door. "It's Madame Goth and . . . er . . ." He peered at Carmela, trying to figure out her costume. "A lovely character straight out of *Barry Lyndon*."

"Works for me," said Carmela.

"Delighted you could make it," said Del, taking her hand. A prominent attorney, he was dressed as a Chinese emperor, complete with long brocade robe. "Oh sweetheart," he drawled to Baby. "Do come and greet our lovely guests."

Baby, dressed in a diaphanous white toga with quivering gold fairy wings on her back, flew across the palatial marble-floored entry to greet them. She embraced them with hugs and cooed greetings, even as she admired their costumes. "Ava!" she cried, "you look so netherworld. And Carmela, you're a . . ." She cocked her head. "A lovely black moth!"

"That's me," said Carmela. "Mothra. Just winged in from Japan." She glanced around, noticed things looked different, and exclaimed, "Oh my gosh, Baby, don't tell me you redecorated again?"

Baby gave a hopeful but slightly guilty smile. "The pink silk just wasn't working. Complementary to the complexion, of course, but Del felt it was a trifle girly."

"So you went with imported toile and raw silk?" said Carmela. A blue-and-white pattern covered one wall, while another was padded in cream-colored tufted raw silk. It was glamorous Park Avenue and Old World New Orleans, all at the same time.

"Well, yes, I did make a few changes," said Baby. "Do you like it?"

"It's fantastic!" said Carmela. "Like slumming at Versailles."

"And it does match my Louis the Sixteenth chairs," drawled Baby.

"Are the TV people here yet?" asked Ava.

She craned her neck, trying to peer over the crowd.

"They're here," said Baby, "and they're out back conducting their interviews." She smiled at Carmela. "It was kind of you to recommend me."

"Au contraire," said Carmela, "it was kind of you to invite them. Most people wouldn't want a TV crew tromping through their home."

"It's just three more people," said Baby, "and what's three more guests when the list already tops three hundred? But here I am, jabbering away when you should be enjoying the party. Go on in and mingle, enjoy the buffet! Tip a glass of champagne!"

"Exactly what I was thinking," said Ava, grabbing Carmela's hand and tugging her into the fray of guests.

"Do you know where you're going?" Carmela asked, as they pushed their way through a crowded parlor into a packed living room. Ethereal strands of purple and green fluttered from the chandelier; a hundred gold candles flickered on the mantel above the fireplace. A man in a Charlie Chaplin costume tipped his hat at them; a werewolf snarled.

"Bar," said Ava. "Gotta be here around here someplace." She paused. "Ooh, a waiter bearing champagne on a silver tray! Even better."

They rocked to a stop in front of a white-coated waiter wearing a Blue Man mask and grabbed their drinks. Then they raised fluted glasses of champagne in a toast to each other.

"Here's to my date," said Ava, "if he manages to find his way here."

"Ditto that," said Carmela, wondering if Babcock would find time to put in an appearance.

"Why is it," asked Ava, "that two hot, highly desirable chicks have to make a grand entrance all by our lonesome?"

"Because the guys we're dating are workaholics?" said Carmela.

"Can an artist be a workaholic?" asked Ava. "I thought they just laid around all day in a dusty garret, smoking stinky French cigarettes and drinking cheap Chianti, dabbling paint when the mood struck."

"I think artists are a lot more into marketing these days," said Carmela. Truth be told, she wasn't all that keen on Sullivan Finch showing up here at all. In fact, if Finch decided to bail on Ava, it would be totally fine with her.

"Woo-ee!" yelped Tandy, as she galloped up to join them with Gabby in tow. Tandy was dressed as Harry Potter, while Gabby was in her Annie Oakley costume, complete with lariat.

"Can you rope a dogie with that lariat?" asked Ava.

"Only if it's six inches in front of me," laughed Gabby.

Carmela and Ava found Ed Banister, Raleigh and Zoe out in Baby's gazebo, a tall glass and wrought-iron structure that always reminded Carmela of a human terrarium. Two brilliant floodlights blazed as Raleigh manned the video camera. Zoe, who was dressed as a witch, appeared to be interviewing the Phantom of the Opera. Ed Banister, dressed as Thomas Jefferson, looked on with smiling approval. Raleigh wore his usual costume of polo shirt and khakis.

Ava nudged Carmela. "Think I could get on camera again?"

"I don't see why not," said Carmela.

Ava gave a quick hip twitch. "Maybe you could put in a good word for me with Banister?"

"I could probably do that." Carmela sidled up to Banister and said, "How's it going?"

"Just wonderful," said Banister. He grabbed Carmela's hand and pumped it vigorously. "Again, I can't thank you enough for putting in a good word for us. This party puts the maraschino cherry on the whipped cream for our documentary. The pièce de résistance."

"I take it you already got some good interviews," said Carmela.

"Did we ever," said Banister. "Some really nice sound bites from a lot of Garden District people." He said it in hushed tones, obviously impressed by the caliber of people here tonight.

"Do you think Zoe would be interested in interviewing my friend Ava again?"

"Voodoo shop Ava," said Banister, remembering. "Sure, no problem."

•

While Ava was being interviewed, Carmela slipped back in to join the party. Big mistake. Because the minute she set a dainty little bootie inside the living room, Glory Meechum cornered her. Dressed in her usual shapeless black dress, clutching a tumbler of amber liquid, Glory looked wonky, angry, and already pickled.

"Nice costume, Glory," said Carmela. "And I love your mask." Glory wasn't wearing a mask.

Glory's mouth puckered into an unhappy O and she snarled, "I still can't believe you're going to sell Shamus's house."

Carmela noted that there was no preamble, no *Hi, how are you*. And definitely no *Gee, it's grand to see my ex-sister-in-law*.

"We've been over this before," said Carmela. "Endlessly, in fact. It's now *my* house. Therefore, in the eyes of the law, and with the blessing of choirs of angels above, it's mine to sell. Lock, stock, and barrel."

"A travesty," spat Glory. She swished her drink around in her glass, then took a big slug.

Carmela glanced about the crowded room. If Glory was here, could Shamus be far behind? She hoped not. She was a damsel in distress who needed serious rescuing. There was a group of vampires swirling nearby, some Venetian lords and ladies, two Scarlett O'Haras circling each other warily, as if getting ready for a catfight, and . . . Ah, there he was, scrunched in the corner, probably droning on about hunting, fishing, or gun dogs, with a gaggle of men equally indolent-looking as he was.

Carmela waved a hand. "Shamus!" He was dressed as a riverboat gambler, complete with cutaway jacket, panama hat, and string tie.

Shamus's eyes flicked her way, then back, as he pretended not to notice.

"Maybe Cousin Emil could *rent* the place," mumbled Glory. One eye stared directly at Carmela, the other twitched left.

Carmela could barely recall Glory's cousin Emil, but knew he was in his eighties and spent pretty much all of his time in a wheelchair. Thus, Cousin Emil probably wasn't a great candidate to be lord and master of an enormous three-story manse that required maximum upkeep just to prevent the siding and roof beams from decomposing in the Louisiana heat and humidity. To say nothing of termites and other critters that threatened to take up residency.

"Shamus!" Carmela called again. When he continued to ignore her, Carmela edged toward him as Glory trailed along, still ranting her discontent.

Finally, Shamus pulled himself away from his group and came over to join them. "What?" he asked bluntly.

"Glory needs a refresher on her drink," said Carmela.

"I can get it myself!" Glory snorted, as she teetered away.

Shamus stared grudgingly at Carmela. "You needed me for *that?*"

"I needed you to break up our little party of two and get her off my back."

"Glory *can* be persistent," smiled Shamus.

"She's tenacious as a pit bull," said Carmela. "And twice as mean."

"Hey," said Shamus. He pulled a fat Cuban cigar from his jacket pocket and twiddled it between his fingers. "I got a major bone to pick with you."

Carmela patted at her hair, which seemed to be going bouffant on her, rising like a pan of Jiffy Pop from the warmth of all the close-packed bodies. "Now what?"

"You promised to call off your enforcer friends."

"Really, Shamus," said Carmela, "what are you talking about?"

"Your cop buddies. They were pestering Sugar Joe again this morning!"

This was news to Carmela. "Who was?" she asked. She was pretty sure Sugar Joe was off the hook.

"Your boyfriend's chief henchman," said Shamus.

"You mean Bobby Gallant?"

"That's the guy." More rapid twiddling of his cigar.

"I imagine they're just looking at all the angles," said Carmela. "I can't help that."

"Sure, you can," said Shamus. "Just make a deal with your boyfriend." Shamus leered at her. "Tell him you'll give him a little somethin' somethin' for backing off."

Carmela stared at Shamus. "You want me to bribe an officer of the law with sexual favors?"

"Well . . . yeah."

"Get lost," said Carmela.

Ava grabbed Carmela from behind. "I did it!" she squealed. "I got interviewed again! And you know what? The documentary KBEZ is doing might even appear on TV! I mean, like, *network* TV. TruTV or the Travel Channel!"

"Big-time," said Carmela. "You'll have Hollywood agents knocking at your door. You'll be right up there with the Kardashians."

"You think?"

"One can only hope," said Carmela, as they surveyed the party guests.

"Mmm," said Ava, "who's the silver fox over there?" Ava sometimes had a thing for older men.

Carmela glanced around and saw Whit Geiger, dressed in a bishop's robe and holding a gold scepter, conversing with a group of guests. *Holy purgatory, Whit Geiger!* "You mean the bishop over there?"

Ava dimpled prettily. "He's got that fat cat look I kind of go for."

"No," said Carmela, "I don't think you'd like that one. I don't think you'd like him at all."

They strolled into the dining room, where the twenty-foot-long buffet table beckoned enticingly.

Baby's dinner buffets were legendary, and this one was no exception. Enormous sterling silver serving trays and chafing dishes were piled high with shrimp stuffed with crabmeat, fried oysters, pan-seared salmon drenched with citrus beurre blanc, veal chops stuffed with bacon and fontina cheese, plump duck sausages, fried plantains, and spicy red beans and rice. Caterers in white jackets seemed to hover like moths, ready to replenish at a moment's notice.

"Some nice light treats," observed Ava. "Ought to tide us over for a while."

"Take a look at the desserts." Carmela giggled. She had a passion for sweets and was known to indulge.

There was crème brûlée, praline cheesecake, banana nut bread pudding with whiskey sauce, chocolate mousse, and an enormous king cake.

"I don't know where to start first," said Ava.

"I'm going to hit the fried oysters hard,"

said Carmela, "and do a little grazing on all the rest."

"Excellent strategy," said Ava.

They filled their plates, then wandered into one of the smaller parlors, hoping to find a place to sit down. What they found was Madame Blavatsky dealing out her tarot cards to a fairly interested audience. They plunked themselves down on a blue velvet love seat and watched with interest as Margo Leland, a Garden District doyenne, got a reading.

"Choose three cards," instructed Madame Blavatsky. "One for past, present, and future."

"A speed read," murmured Ava.

Margo, swaddled in sparkles and fur, made a big show of choosing her cards. Then she laid them on the table facedown. "Now what?" She looked up expectantly, blue eyes shining, masses of blond curls bobbing. Carmela had never seen Margo with so much hair. She must have pinned on at least three Hair U Wears.

"Now we peer into the infinite," said Madame Blavatsky.

"She's good, isn't she?" Ava whispered to Carmela. But Carmela was watching closely.

Madame Blavatsky's nimble hands turned

over the first card. "This represents your past."

"What do you see?" asked Margo.

"The Four of Wands," said Madame Blavatsky. "Prosperity."

"She's right!" shrilled Margo. "My ex-husband Jerry Earl was a whiz at making money!"

"Too bad he's doing two to four at Dixon Correctional for cooking the books," whispered Ava.

"For your present situation," said Madame Blavatsky, turning over the middle card. "The Magician. An indication of creativity and skill."

"That's me," said Margo.

Madame Blavatsky's finger touched the final card and lingered for a moment.

Margo drew an excited breath. "And my future?"

Madame Blavatsky flipped over the Lovers card and smiled. "It would appear love is in your future."

Margo sprang up from her chair, delighted. "Did y'all hear that? I'm gonna find husband number four!"

"Maybe he's here tonight," remarked Carmela, still working away on her plateful of goodies.

"Say," said Ava to Madame Blavatsky,

"can you do a kind of blanket reading? Can you scope out the general tone of this party?"

"I can try," said Madame Blavatsky.

Ava moved over to the chair Margo had just vacated while Carmela looked over her shoulder.

"Same kind of spread?" asked Ava.

"Better that you shuffle the entire deck and draw just one single card," Madame Blavatsky instructed.

"Ooh, I like that," said Ava, as she grabbed the deck and shuffled, fingers working nimbly like a practiced blackjack dealer. "Okay, one card."

"One card," echoed Carmela.

Ava pulled out a single card, then flipped it over.

It was the Seven of Swords.

A look of concern flickered on Madame Blavatsky's face.

"What's it mean?" asked Carmela, curious.

"Deceit," said Madame Blavatsky. "Someone here is planning a huge deception."

"You mean in this room?" Carmela asked. She glanced hastily around. "At this party?"

"Well, that's a buzzkill," said Ava.

But Madame Blavatsky was taking it all quite seriously. "Be careful," she cautioned.

"Someone very close to you is not what they appear to be!"

And who might that be? Carmela wondered. Shamus? No, he was totally transparent. So who else here tonight had deception or treachery on their mind and in their heart? Was it Whit Geiger? Or Zoe? Or the soon-to-arrive Sullivan Finch? Who exactly should she be watching out for?

It would seem there was a veritable roster of folks. And it included Davis Durrell.

CHAPTER 26

"Carmela," called Baby. She came swanning across the dance floor, one hand clutching Durrell's upper arm. "Have you had the pleasure of meeting my new neighbor?"

"Actually, I have," said Carmela, gazing at Durrell. *Or was it my displeasure? Then again, maybe I should be happy he's not wearing a clown costume.* Durrell, tricked out as a cowboy, wore jeans, cowboy boots with genuine spurs, a checkered Western shirt and leather vest, and a ten-gallon hat. A leather holster was slung around his waist and held what looked like a genuine pearl-handled pistol.

"Is that a real gun?" Carmela asked him, as Baby flitted off.

"Of course it is," said Durrell. "This is a Colt .45."

"Loaded?"

Durrell's eyebrows inched up a notch.

"What do you think?"

"Dangerous," said Carmela.

"Only in the wrong hands," said Durrell.

"So," said Carmela, "how are you managing?" She figured she had to somehow reference Kimber's death. Even though everyone here was drinking and dancing and having a grand old time. Probably Durrell included.

"Hanging in there," said Durrell, in a noncommittal tone. "Still hoping the police come up with some answers."

"Me, too," said Carmela.

"Yes," said Durrell, giving a nasty smirk, "your husband told me you're quite the amateur investigator."

"Excuse me?" said Carmela.

"Correction," said Durrell, "your *ex-*husband."

"Tell me again," said Carmela, "how is it you know Shamus?" It worried her that Shamus might have made some offhand remark to Durrell. Shamus could be awfully trusting. And the more he drank, the more he blabbed.

"We're in the Pluvius krewe together," said Durrell. "But I think you knew that."

"Were you at the party last night?" asked Carmela. She hadn't seen him there, but that didn't mean anything.

"No," said Durrell, "I'm afraid I had business."

"Must be those pesky overnight markets," said Carmela.

Durrell's mouth twitched. "How would you know about that?"

His jibe grated Carmela. "Why do you persist in thinking I'm completely unenlightened when it comes to investing?" she asked. "Really, your attitude is quite tedious."

Durrell eyed her with caution. "Apologies, then."

"I understand," said Carmela, deciding to give her investigative skills a workout, "that you've recently joined the City Opera's board of directors."

"That's right," said Durrell. "I was just appointed."

"You're an opera buff?"

Durrell gave an offhand shrug. "As much as anyone."

Should I? Carmela wondered. Then plunged ahead. "What's your favorite opera?"

Durrell regarded her with a steady gaze. "Really, I enjoy them all."

"How about *Pagliacci?*"

"Wonderful," said Durrell, without much enthusiasm.

"Tell me," said Carmela, watching Durrell's face carefully, "what do you know about Canio?"

"We've not met," said Durrell, fixing his gaze somewhere above her left shoulder.

"You're sure about that?" asked Carmela.

"Perhaps when I have a chance to get better acquainted with all the members," muttered Durrell. He looked both embarrassed and confused. "Excuse me," he said, edging away. "There's a . . ." And he was gone.

Carmela felt a thrill of triumph. *He doesn't know. Durrell had absolutely no clue what I was talking about. He's no opera buff. If he's really, truly sitting on the board, and I'm pretty sure he is, then all he is is a big fat poser.*

Carmela couldn't wait to tell Ava. She eased through a crowd of hooded monks, dance hall girls, and World War II–era soldiers, and found Ava sitting on a chair, talking to a Vulcan, complete with *Star Trek* tunic and pointed ears. When she pulled Ava aside, she said, "I just had a conversation with Durrell."

"Okay," said Ava.

"About Canio."

"The clown," said Ava. Then the implication hit her. "Oh!" Her eyes widened. "The clown costume. Did your mention of the clown shake him up?"

"Not in the least," said Carmela. "In fact, Durrell had absolutely no clue what I was talking about."

Ava was surprised. "Seriously?"

"I think Durrell shoehorned himself onto the opera board for the sole purpose of rubbing shoulders with heavy hitters, people with money."

"What a scumbag," said Ava, curling her lip.

"But maybe not a killer," said Carmela. "I'm guessing it wasn't him in the clown suit."

"Maybe not," agreed Ava.

Carmela decided she had to rethink her list of suspects. She wandered past the buffet table, stepped out the French doors onto a brick patio, and wandered toward the far corner of the yard and a lovely vine-covered arbor. She needed a little quiet time, away from the shrieks of the crowd, the guffaws of the heavy drinkers, and the loud, pulsing music from the DJ's turntable.

But when she sat down on a narrow bench woven from tree willows, the bushes next to her shook slightly. And not from the wind.

What? Was someone there?

"Psst!"

There *was* somebody hiding in the bushes!

The leaves shook and jiggled again, this time more vigorously, and a dark face peeped out. Carmela let loose a startled little, "Oh!" in recognition. Because this was the last person in the world she expected to see here!

Then an entire head and shoulders materialized and Billy Laforge said, "Miz Meechum, I gotta talk to you!"

Kimber's kid brother! Here? Why?

Carmela glanced around hastily. There wasn't another soul in sight. Was she safe or should she scream bloody blue murder for help? But when she gazed at Billy's face, there was something there, a funny look, that made her hesitate.

"What are you doing here?" Carmela managed to choke out.

Billy's voice was low and urgent. "Ma'am, I'm sorry for how I treated you the other day. I was upset and I thought you were with the TV or newspaper or something. I thought you were sneaking around trying to take pictures or pressure me for an interview."

"Okay," said Carmela, swallowing hard. "No harm done."

"But I can see you're a nice lady," said Billy. "A kind lady."

"Thank you," said Carmela. His words were so unexpected and strange, considering the circumstances, that she was completely taken aback. Was this the same guy who'd screamed at her just two days ago? The guy who'd basically threatened her life and kicked her off his property?

"That's why I came to ask for your help," said Billy.

"What?" Now Carmela was utterly perplexed. "Excuse me, what exactly are you talking about?"

"About my farm," said Laforge.

Carmela shook her head. This did not compute. "What about your farm?"

Now there was a grudging undertone to Billy's voice. "I need your help, ma'am, because you're one of them. One of the bank people. A . . . a Meechum." He spat out the word *Meechum* as if he were referring to pond scum.

"No, I'm really not," said Carmela. "You're thinking of my ex-husband, Shamus. But we're divorced, have been for a couple of years."

Billy was unrelenting. "But you could ask him to help me. With my farm. He's a big shot at the bank."

"Your farm?" The point of Billy's coming to see her was slowly dawning on Carmela.

Aw crap, it's all because Shamus's bank is foreclosing on Billy's farm. And then a thin, cold wave of fear washed over her. "Wait a minute. Did you follow me here tonight?"

Billy hesitated, then answered, "Yes."

Carmela's heart was suddenly beating out of her chest. "Did you follow me last night?"

Billy blinked, clearly befuddled by her question. "No."

But Carmela wasn't sure if she could believe him. Was Billy lying? Was he trying to scare her? Or coerce her? Her instincts told her to drill him with one very important question.

"Billy, did you send me some postcards?"

Now Billy Laforge seemed totally bewildered. "Postcards? You mean from a trip? I can't take a trip, not with the bank people after me. They already stole my dog and threatened to take my gun."

Carmela stared at him. She was hearing his words just fine, but they didn't make any sense to her. They sounded like gibberish. "Billy, get real. Banks don't do that sort of thing."

Billy's face pulled into an insistent glare. "Yes, they did. A man called me on the phone and warned me they were going to do exactly that. And then yesterday, when I got home, my dog Saber was gone."

"That's crazy," said Carmela. "That's not how banks operate."

"It is, and it's why I need your help!" said Billy. His face darkened and his eyes blazed.

"I can't help you," said Carmela. "Really."

"You have to!"

Carmela felt a sudden uptick in what she gauged as a threat level. *Get out of here!* her inner instincts screamed at her. *Get away from this crazy guy!* And just as she tensed her entire body, just as she was about to bolt, footsteps sounded on the nearby patio. A voice called to her.

"Carmela?" Ed Banister was standing some ten feet away, peering at her through the darkness. "I heard voices. Are you okay?"

Her rescuer!

"Ed!" she cried.

Banister took a step forward, suddenly unsure. "You out here all alone?"

Carmela drew breath, about to say something, then changed her mind. Banister was standing right there. She was safe. Nothing could happen to her now.

"I'm . . . fine," said Carmela. The leaves next to her rustled ever so slightly as Billy Laforge retreated deep into the magnolias and ivy. "What's up?"

"Oh," said Banister, "we're going to shoot a sort of dance scene, where, at the end, everyone rips off their masks for a big reveal. And we wanted you to join us." He cocked his head, as if worried he wasn't getting through to her. "You sure you're okay?"

Carmela heard the faintest of rustling and, seconds later, Billy was gone for good. Poof.

"Really," said Carmela, "I'm peachy."

"Whatcha doing out here all by yourself?" Banister asked.

"Nothing," said Carmela. "Just getting some air."

As Carmela stepped into the house, Ava rushed to greet her. "You gotta hurry!" She pulled her along as Carmela managed to grab a flute of champagne from a passing waiter. "We gotta get in the shot!"

"Wait a minute, wait a minute," said Carmela. "Where's Sullivan Finch?"

Ava waved a hand. "Already here and gone. He had time for one little glug of champagne, then he had to rush back to the Click! Gallery. Some big-shot collector saw his work and wants to buy three or four pieces."

"And you believed him? You trust Finch?"

Ava stopped in her tracks. "Why shouldn't I?"

Madame Blavatsky's warning ran through Carmela's head like chase lights on a theater marquee. "Maybe because your tarot-reading friend said there was deception afoot?"

"I didn't think she meant *him*," said Ava.

"Then who?"

Ava shrugged. "Dunno. But I figured the warning was aimed more at you."

"Ladies." Ed Banister was at their elbow. "The unmasking shot?"

"Let's do it!" said Ava.

Carmela set her glass of champagne down on a circular glass end table and elbowed her way into the crowd. Unlike Ava, she felt no compunction to be front and center. Better just to be part of the swirling crowd. Probably more fun that way, too.

Lights blazed as Raleigh framed his shot. He peered through his lens, made a minor adjustment, then called to the DJ, "Cue the music." Usher's "Without You" blared as Raleigh waved a hand and yelled, "Action!"

Then Carmela was dancing, swept up in the whirling crowd. She danced with a green elf, then suddenly found herself boogying with a Japanese samurai.

"Everybody crowd together!" called Raleigh.

Like a school of sardines, everyone tightened into a jostling swirl. Shoulders touched and elbows jabbed as the music built to a crescendo and the mayhem increased. Carmela wondered briefly if Billy Laforge might be dancing with them. Had Billy donned a mask and costume, the better to stroll among them, just as Plague had in Edgar Allan Poe's "The Masque of the Red Death"? Was Billy watching her right now, planning to prowl after her again? And the real question, the raise-your-hackles question, was: Had Billy killed his sister and smoke-bombed Carmela's apartment? Had his sweetie-pie act in the garden been purely for show? Was he really evil incarnate? Or just kind of sad and crazy?

"As you continue dancing," called Raleigh, his voice rising above the din, "I want you to rip off your masks!"

Carmela tore off her mask, in sync with forty other revelers. Hats, rubber faces, pussycat glasses, giant ears, black veils, and plastic masks all flew into the air, like a bizarre version of graduation day at the U.S. Naval Academy. Tandy's Harry Potter hat went sailing; Gabby tossed her bandana as the dancers continued to swirl in a heated frenzy, laughing, giggling, delighted to be immortalized on film.

"And . . . perfect!" shouted Raleigh.

"Whew!" said Ava, discreetly wiping a sleeve

against her brow. "That was some fun!"

Carmela, slightly breathless from the exertion, glanced around for her champagne. It wasn't there. A small wet ring marked its place.

"What's wrong?" asked Ava.

Carmela frowned. "Somebody made off with my champagne."

"I'm not surprised," said Ava, "considering this crazy, thirsty crowd. But no harm done, we'll just grab a fresh glass from one of the adorable young waiters."

"That's okay," said Carmela. She really didn't want another drink. "I guess what I really need to do is have a word with Shamus."

Ava made a dismissive gesture. "You want to talk to him again? Why do you want to do *that?*"

"Because I'm a masochist?" said Carmela.

"No, you're divorced," said Ava. "And, please, never forget it."

Carmela didn't forget it. Never again would she be beholden to Shamus. Never again would she tolerate a cheating, lying skunk of a husband. Or boyfriend, for that matter.

But, at this exact moment, she needed to ask her cheating, lying skunk of an ex-husband a couple of critical questions.

She found him at the buffet table, loading up on steamed shrimp. "Shamus." She tapped him on the shoulder.

Shamus glanced at her and pursed his lips. "Now what?"

"We need to talk."

"I need to eat."

"Don't be a dolt," said Carmela. "You can eat and talk. Besides, I need to ask you about something."

Now Shamus looked apprehensive. "What?" He scooped a big dollop of rémoulade sauce onto his plate.

"It's about a mortgage customer."

"Jeez, Carmela, how many times do I gotta tell you I don't do mortgages." He put his free hand to his chest, let loose a burp, and gave a sheepish grin.

Carmela took a step backward. "Just hear me out."

"Mortgages are *tough*," he said. "You gotta figure out all that principal and interest stuff. And payment schedules."

"Give me a break," said Carmela, "that stuff's all calculated with garden-variety plug-and-play computer programs."

"That so?" said Shamus.

"C'mere." Carmela grabbed his sleeve and pulled him out into the hallway, where it was quieter. "Do you know who Billy

386

Laforge is?"

Shamus let loose another little Jack Daniel's–fueled burp. He frowned, trying to look serious, then said, "No, should I?"

"Billy is Kimber Breeze's brother," said Carmela.

"So what?" He nibbled on a shrimp.

"Billy Laforge is also a customer at your bank. A mortgage customer who's being foreclosed on."

"I told you . . ." Shamus was starting his broken-record act again.

"I just spoke to Laforge," said Carmela. "And he told me that somebody at Crescent City Bank threatened to steal his gun . . . and made off with his dog."

Shamus looked suddenly pained. "What? You think we can't collect somebody's mortgage, so we go harass them?"

"And steal his dog," said Carmela.

"What kind of dog?" asked Shamus.

"Shamus, it doesn't matter what kind of dog!" said Carmela. "The point is, something weird is going on!"

"The problem," said Shamus, poking a shrimp in her face, "is that you're too involved in this murder investigation!"

"No," said Carmela, "the problem is, there are more darned suspects than dead bodies in a Quentin Tarantino movie!"

"Hah," said Shamus. "Funny."

But it wasn't. Not to Carmela. "And you were supposed to get me some more information on Whitney Geiger and Royale Real Estate."

"Give me a break," said Shamus.

Carmela was about to flip Shamus's plate of shrimp in his face when an ungodly scream rose from the front parlor. A hideous, banshee-like scream that spiraled upward in a shrill crescendo.

"Holy Christmas!" said Shamus. "That sounds like Glory!"

The two of them sprinted toward the front of Baby's house, only to find Glory standing in the middle of the party, screaming her head off. Her face was beet red, her hands were clenched tightly at her sides, and long, undulating screams bellowed from her.

"Shamus," said Carmela, as everyone in the room gaped, "*do* something!"

Shamus gave a reluctant sigh as he set down his plate. "Looks like the party's over."

"Was that the DJ playing crappy sound effects or someone really screaming?" asked Ava. They were in the front parlor now, moments after Shamus had quickly spirited Glory away.

"Take a wild guess," said Carmela.

"Glory? Having one of her usual freak-outs?"

"It would appear so," said Carmela.

"Somebody oughta put a muzzle on that lady," said Ava. "Or shoot her. Put her out of her misery."

"I think that's what her meds are supposed to do." Glory had a few psychoses that even the doctors didn't seem to understand.

Ava shook her head. "They ain't working. She needs stronger stuff. Horse pills, maybe." She glanced around, gave a start, and nudged Carmela with her shoulder. "Hey, looks like your buddy-boy is stepping out early."

Carmela swiveled her head, just in time to see Davis Durrell slip out the front door.

"And the night is still young," said Ava.

Something pinged deep in Carmela's brain. "He's . . . I think he's got some kind of meeting." She paused to gather her thoughts. "Remember, I told you I overheard a phone call he took at the funeral?"

"Yeah. So?" Ava was still mellow from drinking champagne.

"I think it was supposed to be tonight." Carmela let this information cycle through her brain. "Where do you suppose he's off to?" she wondered. *Could it be a meeting with Kimber's killer? Could he be paying off a hired killer? Was that why he had acted so hinky and weird?*

Ava yawned as she struck a pose, the better to show off her curvaceous hips. "I don't know." She snapped her mouth shut. "Oh crap. You want to follow Durrell, don't you? Dang, I *knew* it."

But Carmela had already pulled her car keys from her clutch. "Hurry up," she urged. "We don't want to lose him."

CHAPTER 27

The night was cold and moonless, but up and down Prytania the elegant homes glowed from within.

"Careful," murmured Ava, "don't get too close." They'd hopped into Carmela's car, then prowled slowly down the block without benefit of headlights. And, two blocks later, they were rewarded when Davis Durrell backed his Jaguar down his driveway and took off with a throaty roar. Hanging back as far as she dared, Carmela flipped on her lights and slid into traffic, tailing him for about six blocks until he cut over to Coliseum Street.

"Where's he going?" Carmela wondered out loud.

"Maybe he's got a hot date," said Ava.

"So soon after Kimber's death? Do you think he ever cared for her at all? Do you think he's just a serial Romeo?"

"I don't know," said Ava. "That's what

makes his encounter tonight a potentially hot date."

But Durrell wasn't headed for the jazz clubs of the CBD or even the frivolity of the French Quarter. Instead, he skimmed past Coliseum Square and hooked a right onto BR 90. Still hot on his tail, Carmela whisked across the bridge that spanned the turgid Mississippi. Below, tugboats prodded barges while a paddle wheeler, sparkling like a bedazzled Christmas ornament, churned madly as it carried tourists on a late-night cruise.

Carmela followed Durrell's car into a spiral turn and soon found herself navigating the mash-up of warehouses and industrial complexes in neighboring Algiers.

"Dang," said Ava, as they cruised down a dark street lined with hulking buildings. "This area makes me nervous. Too many big old warehouses and spooky buildings. If something happens, nobody can hear us scream."

"It's Mardi Gras," said Carmela. "People are screaming their heads off all over town and nobody cares."

"That's a great comfort."

Carmela eased her foot off the accelerator. "Durrell's turning."

"Just coast on past," Ava advised.

So, of course, Carmela flipped off her lights and followed him.

"No!" Ava hissed, "what if he spots us! You're gonna get us in deep doo-doo."

"We're like a ghost car," said Carmela. "Gliding through the dark, ethereal and silent. He's not going to see us."

"What if he's got ESP and can spot our ectoplasm?"

"Stop it," said Carmela. "We'll be fine."

Ava leaned forward until her nose practically touched the windshield. "Wait a minute, where'd he go?"

"Huh?" said Carmela. In the inky darkness, she'd lost sight of him, too.

"Where is he? Where is he?" gibbered Ava.

Red brake lights flared some fifty yards ahead of them.

"There!" said Carmela. She eased off the gas again and coasted along.

"He's turning again," said Ava. "Back toward the river."

"Then so are we." Slowly, very carefully, Carmela angled her car into the driveway Durrell had taken. And found herself crunching across a parking lot that was part dirt, part hunks of broken concrete. The lot sloped down toward a long, low wooden building that hunkered directly ahead of her, but there was no sign of Durrell. He'd obviously skirted the building and was parked somewhere on the other side.

"What is this place?" asked Ava.

Carmela cut the ignition and rolled down her window. The place smelled like damp earth, diesel fuel, and something else. *Fish?* "I think this might be some kind of fish-processing plant," she said to Ava.

"So what's Durrell doing here?" asked Ava.

"Darned if I know. But I'm guessing whoever owns it isn't benefiting from his financial advice."

"You don't know that," said Ava. "There could be big money in fish."

"Something tells me," said Carmela, climbing out of her car, "that Durrell's up to no good."

Ava opened her door. "Don't leave me here," she whispered.

"Then come on," Carmela whispered back.

Together they tiptoed across damp earth.

"We look like idiots in these dresses," said Ava, trying to gather up her long skirt.

Carmela had crept to the corner of the building and was peering around it.

Ava touched a hand to Carmela's back. "What do you see?"

Carmela made a little come-hither gesture

and Ava flattened herself against the wooden building and peered around the corner with her.

Durrell was there, all right. He was standing next to his car, gazing out across the Mississippi. Lights from the city gleamed on the surface of the undulating river, sparkling and shimmering. Around the edges of the small clearing, where Durrell had parked, were junked cars, towering piles of scrap metal, and dozens of enormous wooden cargo containers that lay tumbled like wooden blocks.

"Think he's just enjoying the view?" whispered Ava.

Carmela shook her head. "I'd say he's waiting for something."

"But what?"

Carmela held up a hand. A soft putt-putting sound echoed from out in the middle of the river. It mingled with the engine noise and churn from other boats going by, and the rumble of traffic from the bridge downstream. Then slowly, cautiously, a small boat throttled back its engines and pointed its bow toward shore. *And Durrell.*

"That's what he's waiting for," said Carmela. "C'mon, we gotta get closer."

Together, Carmela and Ava dashed forward and took refuge behind a huge wooden crate. Crouching, they spent a few moments trying to catch their breath, then peered over the top of the crate, just the tops of their heads and eyes showing, like a couple of cartoon characters.

"That boat's coming in for sure," whispered Carmela.

"There's a dock?"

"No, but I see pilings where they can pull up and moor."

"Strange time to take a boat trip," murmured Ava.

"I don't think he's going, I think he's expecting something," said Carmela.

"Or someone," said Ava. "What do you think we should do?"

"Just stay low and quiet," said Carmela. "See what he's up to."

Ava's nose twitched. "This crate smells like rotten cabbage. Maybe we should . . ."

Carmela, nervous and on edge, glanced right, then left. And suddenly did a double take. "Oh, no." Her heart sank.

"What?" hissed Ava.

"We're smack-dab in the middle of something," said Carmela, as the boat cruised closer and a spotlight suddenly flicked on.

"Well, I know that."

"No, look over to your left," prompted Carmela. "Tell me what you see."

"Dark stuff. Piles of junk."

"Look harder."

"Um . . . oh!"

"See that brown car?" said Carmela, as the spotlight from the boat began to probe the shoreline. "Tucked close to that enormous scrap heap?"

"Uh-huh," said Ava. "Kind of like the car Babcock drives."

"It *is* the car Babcock drives!"

"Oh, man!" said Ava. "Did we stumble upon some kind of sting operation? Like in the movies?"

"That'd be my guess."

"Now what?" asked Ava.

"Now we exit stage left," said Carmela, her heart beating a timpani solo inside her chest. "As fast as possible. And we don't let Babcock *or* Durrell see us! We don't dare get caught in their little nighttime soap opera, whatever it is!"

"Just tiptoe back the way we came," said Ava, ducking down.

"And do it verrrrry carefully."

"Okay," said Ava, "on the count of three we make a dash for it. One, two . . . three."

They scooted out from behind the crate, heading for the wooden building. Halfway there, Ava stumbled and let out an audible "*Whoof!*" as her heel caught in the hem of her dress. As her arms flailed wildly and Carmela paused to grab her, the boat's searchlight flicked over and caught both women, silhouetting them like dancing images in an old black-and-white movie. Then the light winked out and every thing was plunged into darkness.

Carmela sat on the bed, facing Ava. Wearing a pink velour top and slacks, she looked anything but cozy and ready to tuck into bed.

"Maybe he didn't see us," said Ava. She handed Carmela a mug of cocoa with a raft of tiny white marshmallows bobbing on top. Her concession to cooking.

"Babcock saw us all right," said Carmela.

"Maybe he won't *say* anything."

"He'll have plenty to say," said Carmela, managing a sip.

"You want something stronger in that?" asked Ava. "Brandy or schnapps? Tincture of poison?"

Carmela's phone shrilled. She clenched her jaw and gazed at the small green screen in front of her. Babcock.

"It's him?" Ava asked.

Carmela nodded.

"So don't answer it."

"I have to." Carmela flicked the On button. "Hello?"

There was a burst of static, and then Babcock shouted, "Are you certifiably *insane*? What were you *doing* there? You blew our cover!"

"Sorry," said Carmela.

"Sorry?" he sputtered. "Sorry doesn't cut it with me, Carmela. I'm furious! No, I'm beyond furious!"

"I can hear that," said Carmela.

"If it's not too much trouble, I'd like a reasonable explanation! Like how exactly did you know to turn up there?"

"I . . . er . . . overheard Durrell's phone conversation the other day at the cemetery. And then he left Baby's party early tonight . . ."

"Which you blew off," Ava called from across the room. "Some boyfriend you are."

"Was that Ava?" asked Babcock.

Carmela nodded, then said, "Yes."

"Tell her to shut up!"

"He says to shut up," said Carmela.

"Tell him to taking a flying . . ."

"Anyway," Carmela continued, trying to sound contrite, "I kind of put two and two together . . .

"And I ended up with a big fat zero!" Babcock shouted. "Damn Durrell jumped on the boat and that was that!"

"Really," said Carmela, "this isn't long distance. You don't have to shout, I can hear you just fine."

"You blew it, Carmela." Babcock's voice was cold as ice now. "You blew our drug arrest."

Carmela was contrite. "I had no idea!"

"That's not good enough," said Babcock. "That's not . . . aw, forget it." There was a loud click.

Carmela stared at her phone. "He hung up on me."

"That's rude," said Ava.

"No," said Carmela, "I probably deserved it. "I blew his drug bust."

"Drug bust?" Ava just about choked on her cocoa. "What the heck are you talking about?"

"Babcock was working on this drug deal," said Carmela, "but he never clued me in as to who he was staking out. I didn't know it was Durrell!"

Ava shook her head and pushed a mass of curly dark hair off her face. "Come again? Durrell was involved in drugs?"

"Apparently."

"Jeez," said Ava. "If he's dealing drugs and stuff, maybe Durrell really did kill Kimber!"

"I don't know," said Carmela, offering a glum face.

Ava grabbed a bottle of schnapps, unscrewed the top, and poured a shot into her cocoa. Carmela held out her mug and Ava gave her a shot, too. "Let's think about this," said Ava. "About how Durrell might be a real psycho."

"I've been wondering the same thing," said Carmela.

"So . . . what now?" asked Ava. "You're the one who always seems to fit the pieces together."

"You mean like . . . oh wow!" Carmela looked suddenly stunned. "It just occurred to me . . ."

"What?" said Ava.

"What if Kimber had gotten wind of Durrell's drug involvement?"

"She might have known," said Ava. "She was dating him, after all."

Pieces were rapidly clicking into place for Carmela. "But think about it! Maybe that's *why* Kimber was dating him!"

"Whaddya mean? You're saying she was a cokehead?"

"No," said Carmela. "Maybe Kimber was trying to get a line on this whole drug operation."

"You mean she was *using* Durrell?" said Ava.

"Maybe," Carmela reasoned. "Maybe

Kimber planned to blow the lid off his drug deals and make Durrell the subject of a big investigative report!"

"And Durrell figured it out," finished Ava. "He's smart, so he saw what her motive really was." She puckered her brows. "And so he killed her?"

"Could have happened," said Carmela. There were a few holes in her theory, but she figured she was close. "And then we came stumbling along, into the middle of the NOPD's drug bust, and blew it."

"Which means . . ."

"I don't know what it means! Maybe it means we blew the whole case!" said Carmela, looking miserable. "Oh man, no wonder Babcock never wants to see me again!" She reached down, scratched Boo's ear. "Oh, crap."

CHAPTER 28

Jekyl Hardy lived in Napoleon Gardens, one of the premier residences in the French Quarter. Built of red brick and originally designed as a warehouse, the building dated back to the mid-1800s. Now it had been divided into gorgeous apartments that featured mahogany floors, fourteen-foot-high ceilings, and small wrought-iron balconies.

"I hear there's a five-year waiting list to get into this building," said Ava, as they crept up the stairs. It was eleven in the morning of Fat Tuesday, the big day, and already the French Quarter was cranked and rocking. Jekyl's party had kicked off at nine a.m. sharp, and Ava was terrified they'd missed the best part.

"Take it easy," said Carmela, as she lagged behind. "We've got the whole day ahead of us."

"I don't want to miss a single moment!"

said Ava. She gave a little shudder. "Ooh, I feel so alive!"

"And I feel like leftover pizza," said Carmela. "Cold, flat, tasteless."

"But you look great," said Ava. She'd coaxed Carmela into wearing a pair of black leather leggings with an oversized black pullover sweater. Carmela, sick over Babcock's anger and not really caring what she put on, had complied.

"But this is so not my style," said Carmela.

"It *is* your style," insisted Ava. "Inside that conservative Republican veneer is a boundary-pushing slightly punky fashionista just itching to break out."

Carmela wasn't having it. "The only good thing about this outfit is it matches my mood. And the gloomy weather."

"Come on, *cher*, don't be bummed. This is the most exciting day of the year — better than Christmas!"

But Carmela was clearly miserable. "After last night's fiasco, Babcock's never going to speak to me again."

"Ah, it's not the speakin' part that worrisome, it's the hugging and kissing part."

"That, too," said Carmela. "Besides, Ava, I don't feel like partying. It's just too early!"

"Oh, put a cork in it," said Ava, as she rapped sharply on the door of Jekyl's apart-

404

ment. "And remember, Babcock ain't the only starfish in the sea. There are lots of other . . ." She waited a millisecond, then pushed the door open.

"Oh man," moaned Carmela.

Forty people were crowded into Jekyl's apartment, drinking, toasting, nibbling his trademark vampire wings, which were really chicken wings laced with Tabasco sauce, and Mardi Gras meatballs. Purple and green streamers hung from crystal chandeliers, while enormous purple and green feathers were stuck in large brass vases that flanked his pitted marble fireplace. Dark-blue shellacked walls looked both elegant and ominous, and the room boasted high-backed leather couches as well as overstuffed chairs covered in rich brocades.

Jekyl, dressed in a black sequined tuxedo, greeted them at the door.

"You're late," he told them, administering quick pecks to their cheeks as he managed to balance an enormous martini glass by its thin stem.

"Our Carmela's a little under the weather," said Ava.

"Romance problems?" asked Jekyl, lifting his brows.

"You could say that," said Carmela.

"The only cure for the blues is to help

yourself to a drink," said Jekyl. "We've got Bloody Marys and dirty martinis. We've also imposed a six-drink minimum, and I can pretty much guarantee that by the second drink you won't be feeling a lick of pain."

"Sounds good to me," said Ava.

"In fact, you won't feel anything at all," giggled Jekyl. "And by the by," he added, cocking his head in a magpie gaze, "I do like that sweater-and-legging combo that Carmela is sporting."

"Doesn't she look adorable?" said Ava. "I'm seriously thinking I should launch a second career as a stylist."

"I do believe you could," said Jekyl.

Carmela, in no mood to engage in bright banter, pushed through the crowd and headed for the kitchen. Normally, she adored attending a party at Jekyl's apartment. His décor, the antique smoked mirrors in gilded frames, the fringed lamps, the oil paintings and large brass sculptures of horses, dogs, and Roman statues, were all intriguing and welcoming. But after her conversation with Babcock last night . . .

Carmela just felt dejected.

And rejected.

What if he never wants to see me again? Then what? Then what do I do?

She was too tired, too bummed to contemplate her fate.

In Jekyl's postage stamp–sized kitchen, Carmela grabbed an enormous pitcher of Bloody Marys and poured herself a drink. *Why not start drinking?* she asked herself. *Why not get a little bit tipsy?*

She took a sip. Tasty. Peppery, too.

She took another sip even as she pulled out her phone. Maybe Babcock had called? Or maybe the cameras at Memory Mine had captured some rogue images of strange postcard deliveries?

But when she checked, there wasn't a thing.

Carmela's shoulders slumped and she was about to tuck her phone back in her pocket when her ringtone sounded. She picked up without looking.

Huh? Babcock?

And answered with a tentative, "Hello?"

"Carmela! You're never going to believe what happened," Shamus cried in a breathless rush.

Dang, it's only Shamus.

"When it comes to your self-centered take on life, nothing surprises me anymore," said Carmela. She leaned against an antique Japanese kitchen cabinet, suddenly happy she could vent her anger on Shamus.

But Carmela's words inflicted barely a

sting. "This will blow your mind!" Shamus continued. "I had to rush Glory to the emergency room last night!"

Carmela *was* surprised. "Are you serious? What was wrong with her besides, um, the screaming?" She figured Shamus had just driven Glory home last night so his crazy sister could unwind on her own.

"It was horrible!" said Shamus, now that he had Carmela's undivided attention. "The ER doc thought Glory was experiencing some kind of drug overdose."

Carmela relaxed. "That's generally what happens when you mix pills and alcohol." Glory had a nasty habit of enjoying a few drinks, then popping an Ambien or Xanax. In fact, she popped Xanax like they were M&Ms.

"But she didn't do that," said Shamus. Then he rethought his words and backpedaled slightly. "I mean, she does *some*times, but she didn't *this* time. If that makes any sense."

"Of course, it doesn't, Shamus."

"If you'd stop jumping down my throat," said Shamus, sounding pouty, "I'll explain the whole thing."

"Please do."

"The doc thinks somebody slipped Glory a roofie."

"What's a roofie?" asked Carmela. "Is that like Ecstasy or Zombie or whatever the au courant party drug is?"

"It's the date-rape drug," snarled Shamus.

Carmela stared at him. "Excuse me?"

"You heard me," Shamus said in a sour tone.

"Somebody wanted to, um, rape Glory?" said Carmela. She didn't think anybody in their right mind would try something with Glory, the great stone-faced matriarch of the underworld. People were *afraid* of Glory. Glory made grown men tremble in their Thom McAns.

"Don't be stupid, Carmela," said Shamus. "I'm talking about somebody dropping a drug into her champagne glass."

Carmela froze. "Um . . . they *what?* Wait a minute, what exactly happened? What did Glory *think* happened?"

"Just that she picked up a glass of champagne from that little glass table and drank it. But now we're pretty sure some asshole went and slipped a drug into it!"

That was my champagne, Carmela almost blurted out. But she didn't. She didn't want to tell Shamus that Glory had picked up her glass by mistake. That news would surely send him careering off the deep end.

"Is Glory okay now?" asked Carmela.

"Seems to be."

"Good." She paused. "Listen, Shamus, did you find out anything more about Whitney Geiger and Royale Real Estate?"

"Not really." Now Shamus just sounded bored.

"We had a deal, Shamus."

"Babe, today's the big day! I'm having lunch with Sugar Joe and some of my other buds at Galatoire's, and then there's Zulu, Rex, and our Pluvius parade. Plus I'm supposed to hit six separate parties tonight!"

"So make a couple of calls, then go party your fool head off."

"Are you serious?"

"Yes, I'm serious. Shamus, this is important!"

"I'll make the calls," Shamus grumped, "but I'm not happy about it."

"Look, I just need a little more information, okay?"

"I feel like a Judas," Shamus muttered, "spying on Geiger. Like I'm selling out one of my krewe members."

"Try to think of it as helping solve a murder, okay?" Carmela felt that Shamus was still hesitant, so she tossed out the final clincher. "And a way to get Sugar Joe off the hook."

Shamus relented like she knew he would.

"When you put it that way . . ."

"Shamus," said Carmela, "just get the doggone information."

Carmela hung up and stood there, feeling a little wooden, a lot scared. Who in the world had tried to drug her? Had it been Whit Geiger? Or Davis Durrell? Maybe the culprit was Sullivan Finch, who'd come and gone in a whirlwind. Maybe that was why he'd ducked out so fast.

Or could Billy Laforge have done it? Or Zoe the reporter?

Or is there someone who's flying completely under my radar?

The thought chilled Carmela. So much so that she quickly checked her security cameras again, half-suspecting she might catch someone sneaking toward her shop.

But there was nothing going on. And no spooky postcard stuck to her door.

At two o'clock, Carmela, Ava, Jekyl, and about twenty of the revelers trooped over to Mumbo Gumbo. Quigg Brevard met them with great gusto and Carmela could almost see dollar signs light up in his eyes. Three large tables were hastily pushed together to accommodate their group, which gave the whole event the feel of a Rotary Club dinner.

"We have a slightly limited menu today," said Quigg, hastily passing out printed sheets, "but our tasty gumbos are still headlining."

"And wine," declared Jekyl, "we need wine."

Quigg stood behind Carmela's chair, one hand draped possessively on her shoulder. "I'm sending over a few complimentary bottles of my Bayou Sparkler champagne," he announced to the group. His generosity elicited a spate of applause.

"You're too kind," gushed Ava.

"Think nothing of it," said Quigg, as he squeezed Carmela's shoulder. Then he bent down and whispered in her ear. "What's wrong, darlin'? You look kind of down."

"I'm fine," said Carmela.

"Is that boyfriend of yours not treating you right?" Quigg asked.

"I'll say," put in Ava. "In fact he —"

"He's great," said Carmela. "Things couldn't be better."

"If you say so," said Quigg, but his hand lingered on Carmela's shoulder for a few more seconds.

Jekyl was up, then down, bouncing from table to table, greeting friends in the bar and at various booths. When he came back to their table he announced, somewhat breathlessly, "The Zulu parade is running way late, which means Rex will be backed up, too."

"It happens every year," said Ava.

Then Quigg was back with bottles of his new champagne, popping corks and pouring out the bubbling liquid with a masterful flourish.

"I've got some TV people coming in a little while," Quigg whispered to Carmela, "but I'd love it if you stuck around, so we could enjoy a quiet drink in my private office."

"Excuse me," said Carmela. She slipped out of her chair and made a beeline for the ladies' room.

Luckily, the anteroom to the ladies' room had two pink velvet club chairs facing a large mirror. Carmela eased herself into a chair, grateful for the peace and quiet.

Her gut was still in turmoil over Babcock. She was seriously in like with the man, probably in love. But if she lost him for good, then what?

She stared in the mirror. *Then nothing. Then it would be over. Fini. Kaput.*

No do-over?

Probably not.

Carmela pulled out a tube of Dior Rouge Blossom and applied it to her lips, noting the dark circles that seemed to have settled under her eyes.

I look like a raccoon.

Although Ava had told her that smoky eyes, what Carmela always thought of as ashtray eyes, were still very much in vogue, she wasn't a fan.

Just not for me.

After she'd done her lips and cheeks, Carmela nervously checked her cell phone to see if Babcock had called. Nada.

Then, on a whim, knowing she probably wouldn't see a darned thing, she checked her security cameras.

Nothing. But wait. There was a way to check back through the archived videotape. Tate Mackie had shown her how. She pushed a few buttons, then scrolled through the tape from the past hour. Because it was speeded up, it had the herky-jerky motion of an old-fashioned silent film. People walked by her front door, but nobody stopped. Then, just as Carmela was about to click off, something black loomed in the frame.

What?

Suddenly, bizarrely, there was a grainy image of Joubert, her neighbor from Oddities, skulking toward her front door. She slowed the motion down, just as Mackie had taught her. And watched as Joubert hesitated for a few seconds, then glanced surreptitiously around. When he seemed to be satisfied that nobody was watching, he pulled something out from beneath his cape and hastily stuck it on her front door!

Carmela shut her phone off and hurried to her table. Without any explanation, she quickly told Ava she had to leave and would call later. A few minutes later, Carmela stormed down Governor Nicholls Street with all the bluster of the second coming of Hurricane Katrina. Stopping outside Memory Mine, she paused long enough to grab the newly delivered postcard. Then she was flying though the front door of Oddities.

Joubert was busy with a customer but she didn't much care.

"You!" Carmela called out in a thunderous voice.

Joubert glanced up. He'd been pointing out the fine points of a scarab ring to his customer. But when he saw the postcard clutched in Carmela's hot little hand, his face went slack and assumed a sickly expression.

"You did this!" she cried again.

"Excuse me," Joubert said to his customer. He met Carmela halfway, ducked his head, and said, "You have some nerve!"

"*You* sent the postcards!" she shrilled.

Joubert pulled himself up to his full height and peered down his nose. "I did no such thing."

Carmela thrust her cell phone under his nose. "Exhibit A. Your mug caught on camera! Gotcha!" She showed him the video, at which point Joubert's customer beat a hasty retreat.

Now that Joubert realized he'd been caught red-handed, his reserve crumbled. "All right, yes. I did it and for that I apologize. But, please believe me, I meant no harm."

"No harm?" Carmela screamed. "You were trying to scare the crap out of me! What would you *do* that?"

Joubert looked suddenly miserable. "I . . . I thought the postcards might eventually be collectible. Attached, such as they are, to a local murder."

"Have you lost your mind!" Carmela cried. "Why would you *think* that?" She jammed the postcard up under his nose. "I want an explanation!"

Joubert gave a helpless shrug. "Business is terrible. The economy sucks."

"You cooked up this postcard fiasco to spike *business*?" Carmela sputtered. She'd never heard of anything so preposterous. Or so ridiculous.

"I'm sorry, I'm truly, truly sorry!" cried Joubert. Now he looked ashamed, and ready to burst into tears.

But Carmela wasn't finished. She got in his face again and screeched, "Did you smoke-bomb my apartment?"

"No!" said Joubert. "I wouldn't . . . I — never!"

Carmela gritted her teeth. Her voice was cold as ice. "Did you kill Kimber Breeze?" she demanded.

Joubert held up a hand as if to deflect her anger. "Absolutely not!" he cried. "I didn't even *know* the woman!"

"But you weren't afraid to capitalize on her death!" said Carmela. Really, this was the most preposterous prank she'd ever witnessed!

"Trust me, please," implored Joubert. "I only did it for business."

"Business!" Carmela spat out the word like it was a rotten hunk of fish. "That's the most ridiculous thing I ever heard!"

"I spent too much money amassing inventory," said Joubert. "And I'm not . . . no, the fact is I'm *horrible* at marketing."

Carmela paced his shop like an angry jungle cat. "Don't you have a Web site?"

Joubert shook his head. "No."

"Did you send out press releases?"

"Are those the same as invitations?"

"No," said Carmela. She tried to dial back her anger a bit. "What about reciprocal agreements with some of the local galleries and antique dealers? Handing out their business cards in exchange for handing out yours?"

Joubert put his head down. "I didn't think of that."

"You're stupid, aren't you?" said Carmela.

"I suppose so."

Carmela reined herself in before she really went off the deep end. She didn't like this crazy, screaming Carmela. This wasn't the rational, sane person she usually was.

Carmela held her hands out as if to placate him. "Okay. Enough. This postcard crap ends right here, right now. Okay?"

"Of course," said Joubert. "Whatever you say."

Carmela stared at a funeral urn for a long moment, then turned back to him. "I'm going to ask you one more time. Did you kill Kimber Breeze?"

This time Joubert's answer was a high-pitched wail. "No!"

CHAPTER 29

Carmela couldn't get through the door of Memory Mine fast enough. She slammed the door, locked it behind her, tossed her jacket and bag on the front counter, and headed for her office.

Where she collapsed in a heap.

What a crappy last couple of days. What a crappy week!

Kimber was dead, suspects lurked at every turn, and Babcock, her biggest ally, was spitting mad at her. Maybe so mad he never wanted to see her again.

Not good. Awful, in fact.

Carmela leaned forward and rested her forehead on her desk. Now what? Go out and try to have a fun Mardi Gras? Wave at the passing parades? Pretend that none of this had happened, that it wasn't eating at her gut like a batch of rotten microbes?

No can do.

Carmela, never one to retreat, was now

ready to throw in the towel. And the more she thought about it, the better it sounded. Yes, that was exactly what she'd do. Head back to Ava's place, cozy up with her dogs, and pull the leopard-print covers over her head. Try to sleep, try to dream, try to forget. Make like an ostrich for a while.

Her cell phone sounded, startling the crap out of her.

Carmela snatched it up. "What!"

"Jeez, Carmela, mellow out," said Shamus.

"Oh. It's you."

"Yeah, it's me," said Shamus. "And I've got some information for you."

"What is it? Something about Whit Geiger?"

"Actually," said Shamus, "it's the 411 on your foreclosure guy."

Carmela frowned and sat a little straighter in her chair. "Laforge? What about him?"

"First off, there's not going to be a foreclosure."

"You got Glory to change her mind?"

"Hardly," said Shamus. "The thing is, Billy Laforge is going to have plenty of money for his mortgage. Enough to pay off the whole shebang and still have a serious chunk left over."

"What are you talking about?" asked Carmela.

"As you know," said Shamus, suddenly sounding very proper and bankerish, "Crescent City Bank also has an insurance division."

"Yeah, yeah," said Carmela, wondering where this was leading, hoping he'd speed things along.

"So I did some checking, and it turns out we wrote all of KBEZ-TV's insurance policies," said Shamus. "Including key person insurance."

"Meaning?" said Carmela.

"Billy Laforge was listed as his sister's sole beneficiary," said Shamus. "So baby brother stands to inherit one million dollars in insurance money."

Carmela gasped out loud as Shamus's words echoed in her head. "Are you sure about this?"

"Yes, I'm sure," said Shamus, sounding peeved.

"Do the police know about this?"

"Mmm . . . doubtful."

"There you go," said Carmela, suddenly feeling energized. "There's the smoking gun!"

"Gun?" said Shamus, "I thought you said the guy's gun was stolen."

"Thank you, Shamus," said Carmela. "I mean it. Thank you so much and I'll . . . uh . . . talk to you later!" Carmela sprang up from her chair. "That's it!" she shouted, her voice echoing through her empty shop. She did a fist pump and thrust her arm high in the air. "There's the motive! Billy Laforge really did kill his sister!"

Carmela decided her next move had to be handled with extreme delicacy. After all, Babcock was still mad as a wet hornet!

But would he be quite as angry when she told him about the insurance money Billy was about to inherit? When she handed him the motive for a brutal murder on a silver platter? Probably not. Hopefully not.

Okay . . . so . . . make the call.

She grasped her cell phone and punched in Babcock's number.

There was a buzz of static, then a hollow sound, and Carmela thought maybe the call hadn't gone through. But then Babcock was on the line.

"Carmela? What?" His voice was tight with anger.

"I have to talk to you," said Carmela. She tried to sound cool and a little placating.

"Not much to talk about," snapped Babcock.

"I just now received some key information," said Carmela, "that seriously impacts your investigation."

"And I thought I made it quite clear that you were out of the investigation," said Babcock. His tone was pure arctic ice.

"Please," said Carmela, "hear me out."

A sigh. And then, "I'm listening."

"This is information I just got from Shamus," said Carmela. "But it's good information. Critical information about Billy Laforge."

"Go on."

"Here's the thing," said Carmela. "Billy's farm was being foreclosed on and he was desperate."

"Okay," said Babcock, a chill still coloring his voice.

"So he tried to borrow money from Kimber. When she turned him down, Billy figured out another way to get the money."

"Where are you going with this?" asked Babcock.

"The insurance money," said Carmela, her words tumbling out. "Billy was named beneficiary on Kimber Breeze's insurance policy."

"You're sure about this?" His voice thawed ever so slightly.

"Positive," said Carmela. "According to

Shamus, Crescent City Bank underwrote all the KBEZ-TV policies, particularly key person insurance."

"Son of a gun," Babcock said, softly. There was a long pause and then he said, "Billy did it. He offed his own sister."

"Yes, he did," said Carmela. She hesitated. "Plus, he kind of threatened me last night."

"He *what?*" Babcock's protective instincts suddenly asserted themselves.

"At Baby's party," said Carmela. "Billy turned up there, told me that he followed me. I don't know how he figured out that I was looking into things, but he did." She swallowed hard. "If someone hadn't come along, I think he meant to harm me!"

"Holy smokes," Babcock yelped. And then, more in control now, "I've got to grab Bobby Gallant and get out there right away!"

"I'm going with you!" said Carmela.

"No, you're not!"

"I have a right," said Carmela. "I helped figure this out."

Babcock groaned. "Carmela. Oh man . . ."

"I'm at Memory Mine," she told him. "I'll be waiting out front."

"Okay," Babcock said grudgingly, "a ride-along only. You have to stay in the car once we get there."

Carmela smiled to herself. "Absolutely, officer."

She quickly called Ava's phone. No answer. Ava would be worried, wondering if she was coming back.

So Carmela dialed Mumbo Gumbo's number and finally got hold of Quigg.

"It's me," said Carmela.

"Who's me?" said Quigg.

"You know darned well who this is," said Carmela.

"Carmela, sweetheart," said Quigg. "You ran out on me."

"Sorry," said Carmela. "I'm in the middle of something big right now."

"That's my girl."

"Just tell Ava . . . she's still there, right?"

"She's here. She's a little blitzed, but she's still here."

"Tell her I'm on my way to Billy Laforge's place, okay?"

"Hang on," said Quigg, "my TV people just showed up." Carmela heard a mumbled exchange and then Quigg was back on the line. "Okay, what'd you want me to tell Ava again?"

"That I'm going to see Billy Laforge," said Carmela.

"Got it," said Quigg. "Carmela. Going to see Billy Laforge. And what's the rest of the message?"

"That's it," said Carmela. "She'll know what I'm talking about. And thanks."

Carmela was sitting in the backseat of Babcock's car, all by herself, on a twisty road that led to Billy's cabin. Babcock had driven in a different way, a sneaky way. Gallant had called up MapQuest and Google Earth and they'd discovered a side road, really a trail, into the alligator farm.

"Be careful," Carmela had warned them, but Babcock and Gallant had jumped out of the car like paratroopers ready to storm the bastions. Now it was getting dark and Carmela had no idea what was happening.

Was Billy at his cabin? Or had he given them the slip? Had he gotten the drop on them? Or was he being led docilely back to the car in handcuffs?

Only fifteen or twenty minutes had gone by, but time hung heavy. Carmela gazed out at the landscape, saw nothing but bayou closing in. Tupelo trees, a few sickly looking oaks, lots of brackish water. Normally, she felt no fear in a bayou, had enjoyed spending time at Shamus's camp house in the Baritaria Bayou. But this was different. There were alligators around. Lots of them. True, they were ranched alligators confined to pens, but maybe there were some angry escapees? Could be.

Carmela was creeped out by that thought, enough so that when her cell phone shrilled, she jumped.

She flicked it on. *Babcock? Calling for help?* No, it was Ava.

"Where are you?" asked Ava. She sounded a little loopy, like she'd definitely drunk too much champagne. "Where'd you run off to?"

"Didn't Quigg give you my message?"

"No. But I was out in the street for a while watching the parades and he's been charging around here like a wild man." She let loose a high-pitched cackle. "Boozing and schmoozing."

"It's a long story," said Carmela. "I'm at Billy Laforge's place. With Babcock."

"You're what!" Ava cried. "You solved the murder?"

"Well . . . almost . . . I mean, I think . . ." said Carmela. "Babcock and Gallant are creeping through the swamp, on their way to apprehending him."

"Well, jeez Louise, Carmela!" said Ava. "That's just great. All your efforts really paid off!" She paused to take a breath. "Hey, I got something you'll get a kick out of! It's a photo I took earlier. You're not gonna believe this! I mean your eyes are gonna pop right out of your head!"

"What are you talking about?" said Carmela.

"Hold on," said Ava. "Okay, look at your phone. Did it come through yet?"

"No," said Carmela. "Wait a minute, it's coming now."

"You see it yet?" burbled Ava.

Carmela stared at the e-mailed photo Ava had just sent her. It was a photo of Ed Banister wearing the Canio costume!

"Dear Lord!" Carmela muttered, as an icy finger stabbed at her heart. "Is that who I think it is?"

"Pretty crazy, huh?" said Ava. "I thought you'd get a good chuckle out of that. You've been looking high and low for that silly costume and today it came sauntering into Mumbo Gumbo. Ain't that a wild coincidence? I wonder if Ed knows that . . ."

But Carmela had already clicked off. "Holy crap!" she screamed, her voice shrill and filled with panic. "The killer's not Laforge at all. It's Ed Banister!"

But, of course, nobody was around to hear her.

CHAPTER 30

Carmela crawled out of the car. The sky was growing darker by the minute. Thick, slate-gray clouds had tumbled in from the Gulf of Mexico and the scent of rain hung heavy in the air. Any minute now, the heavens would open wide and unleash a storm of biblical proportions, she just knew it.

But what to do? She knew Gallant had circled around one way and Babcock had circled the other way. They'd been planning to come at Billy's cabin from opposite directions.

She had to warn them, somehow stop them. She didn't want Babcock and Gallant involved in a needless and bizarre shootout. If Billy feared they were coming to haul him off to jail or foreclose on his farm, he might flip out and try to defend himself.

But which way to go?

Carmela stared at the narrow trail and decided to follow it. She took off at a slow jog as rain began to patter down. After a quarter of a mile, rain sliced down harder and she quickened her pace, even though she was getting soggier by the minute.

Still, she didn't seem to be making any progress. She fervently wished she'd taken a closer look at those maps Gallant had printed out. If she knew the general direction of Billy's cabin, maybe she could cut through the bayou?

She decided to risk it anyway.

Twenty feet in, past thickets of cane and more tupelo, soft mud gave way to a small creek. She slogged along the bank for a few minutes, slipping and sliding, wet branches slapping her face. The earth was sodden and spongy and she felt dampness seeping into her shoes.

Stopping in her tracks, wishing she'd worn more weatherproof footwear than her ballet flats, Carmela cocked her head and tried to listen. And just as a long, rolling thunderclap ended, she heard faint voices, off in the distance.

Gotta be them!

Carmela angled off in the direction the voices had come from and covered another fifty yards.

I must be getting close.

Wiping rain from her eyes, Carmela stared

through dense foliage. Way off in the distance, she thought she could see a patch of brown.

Billy's cabin?

She kept slogging as darkness closed in around her. Stopping again when she heard a high-pitched cry, Carmela decided that Babcock and Gallant must be ordering Billy to come out.

If she could just get a little closer, she could wave them off. Tell them they were after the wrong man and get them to stand down. Explain to them that the real killer was sauntering around the French Quarter in a white silk clown costume.

Ducking around a stand of wild camellias, Carmela was halted by a waist-high wire fence. Did she dare climb over it? Should she risk putting herself in danger?

She heard footsteps up ahead, someone running. *Babcock?* Had he gone back to the car? Finding it empty would drive him frantic with worry!

"Hey!" Carmela called out, trying to make herself heard above the slashing wind and rain. "I'm over here!"

She vaulted over the fence and plunged through dense foliage, moving as fast as she could. And just as she ducked around a fallen tree, she caught a burst of movement through the trees.

Was it Babcock?

"Over here!" she called out again. She dodged around a pine tree, then froze in her tracks.

Because the man who was creeping along wasn't Babcock at all. It was Ed Banister. Ed Banister carrying a gray snub-nosed gun!

"Carmela!" Banister suddenly called out. "I know you're there!"

Carmela flattened herself against a tree. *Now what?*

Now her mission was twice as urgent! She not only had to escape from Banister, she had to warn Babcock!

She spun wildly and flung herself behind a rough-barked oak. Panting heavily, she calculated that if she made a mad dash back to the little stream she could probably lose Banister. And still circle around and warn Babcock? Hopefully.

"Carmela," came Banister's singsong voice. "Come out, come out wherever you are."

Carmela pushed off hard, dodging left, then right, sprinting as fast as she dared. Behind her, she could hear Banister crashing through the trees, swatting branches and swearing at her.

If I can just . . .

Carmela ducked around an enormous moss-covered tree and ran directly into the arms of . . .

"Billy!" she shrieked, as she ran up hard against him.

Billy Laforge looped his arms around her and held her tight.

"Billy!" she babbled. "We've got to get out of here! Banister is . . ." She fought and twisted in Billy's arms, but he held her firm. "Billy!" Carmela cried, desperately trying to get through to him. "That's Ed Banister out there. He killed Kimber!"

Billy stared at Carmela, his dark eyes suddenly unreadable. She couldn't tell if he was rocked to the core or couldn't care less.

Then, with a rough jerk, he dragged her over to a slightly flatter area where high wet grass came up to their knees.

"I got her!" Billy called to Banister. "She's over here!"

"Billy, no!" Carmela pleaded, suddenly understanding that he meant to turn her over to Banister. "You're better than this!" She kicked at him, trying to drive a heel into his instep. But he gripped her tight.

"Kid!" Banister yelled, as he thundered toward them, "get out of the way!"

"Listen to me!" Carmela screamed, trying

to get through to Billy. "He strangled your sister!"

Banister crashed through the trees and out into the open. When he saw them, he stopped in his tracks. He was breathing heavily, face red as a tomato, eyes bright and menacing.

"Hey," Billy said to Banister. He lifted his chin and said, "You killed Kimber?"

Banister stared at him. "I'll kill *you* if I have to."

"Don't bother," Billy said in a harsh voice. "I'm on your side. Kimber was a worthless, self-promoting nobody." His face pulled into a sneer and a crazy light danced in his eyes.

"Billy, no!" cried Carmela. *What was he doing? Was he as crazy as Banister? As filled with hate?*

Billy dragged Carmela another couple of steps and stopped. He grabbed her wrist, twisted it sharply, and angled her behind him. "I wanna shake your hand, man," he said to Banister. "Can we do that? Can we shake hands?"

Banister snorted as he lowered his pistol. "Whatever," he said. He shook his head, took two steps forward, then suddenly stiffened, as if he'd just been shot through with a million watts of electrical current.

His mouth gaped open as he gasped in pain, his eyes rolled back in his head until only the whites showed, and the gun flew from his hand. Banister's face turned bright purple and he let loose a bloodcurdling scream!

"Gotcha, man!" cried an ecstatic Billy. "Gotcha good!"

Banister was bellowing like a stuck pig now. Bent over, wildly clawing and batting at his ankles and feet.

"Billy!" cried Carmela, trying to peer around him. "What did you *do*?"

Billy spat at Banister. "Too bad about that nasty leg trap," he rasped. "But, hey, dude killed my sister." Then his face crumpled into a look of supreme sadness as he turned to face Carmela. "Did he really?" he whispered. Billy's eyes brimmed with tears and his lower lip quivered.

"I'm afraid so," said Carmela. She put her arms around Billy and let him collapse against her. "I'm so sorry," Carmela crooned, as Billy's tears ran down his face and mingled with her own. "I'm so sorry."

CHAPTER 31

Banister sat on a stump in Billy's yard, handcuffed and moaning. Billy had pried a nasty-looking leg trap off Banister's foot, revealing an enormous bloody gash and what was undoubtedly a compound fracture.

Babcock was on his phone, giving hurried directions to the ambulance driver while Bobby Gallant talked quietly to Billy.

Which left Carmela free to drill Banister with questions.

"Did you call Billy and pretend to be the bank?" she asked.

"Yes," gasped Banister, twisting in pain.

"Then you came out here and stole his dog?" she asked.

Banister grimaced as he gave a resigned nod.

"Where's Billy's dog?" Carmela demanded.

Banister's lip curled. "Is that ambulance

coming? Because I'm about ready to die!"

"Answer the question!" Carmela snapped.

"The dog's safe," said Banister. "I dumped the mutt at the local humane society. I didn't hurt him or anything."

Carmela glanced toward Babcock and Gallant. "We've got to get that dog!"

"I'll make a call," said Gallant.

"How'd you know we were out here?" asked Carmela. "Did Ava say something to you?"

Banister gritted his teeth and shook his head. "I overheard."

Carmela thought for a minute. "When I was talking to Quigg. You were the TV people who came into Mumbo Gumbo when I was talking on the phone to Quigg."

Banister's shoulders ticked upward.

"There's still one thing I don't understand," said Carmela. "Why Kimber? She was your station's fluff reporter."

Banister shook his head angrily. "Stupid idiot fancied she was Woodward and Bernstein. Wanted to do *investigative* reporting."

A lightbulb clicked on in Carmela's brain. "What was the story?" she asked. "The story that would have led back to you?"

Banister just stared at her with hate in his flat rattlesnake eyes.

Carmela figured it wasn't a story about

Davis Durrell, so she said, "Was it Whit Geiger?"

Something registered in Banister's eyes and Carmela knew she'd scored a direct hit.

"That was it, wasn't it? You're involved with Geiger." Carmela took another shot. "In his real estate deal? If he went down, it would have led to you?"

"That jackhole swore it was legit," seethed Banister. "How was I to know his development deals were a complete fraud?"

"What was that?" asked Babcock, glancing over at them. "What did I just hear about real estate fraud?"

Banister snapped his mouth shut. "I'm not saying another word."

You know what?" said Carmela, "I think you've said enough."

Babcock sidled up to Carmela a few minutes later. "Are you okay?"

She nodded. "Pretty weird stuff, huh?" She was soaking wet and cold and felt like she was about ready to collapse.

Babcock nodded. "It always is. Weird, I mean."

Carmela gazed at him. "I'm sorry about that busted-up drug deal last night. I feel like a real fool. But . . . maybe you'll get another chance?"

"We already apprehended him," Babcock said in a mild tone.

"*What?*" This was news to her. "You arrested Durrell?"

Babcock nodded "We had the Coast Guard pick him up a mile or so downriver. Turns out Durrell was the linchpin for a whole drug-smuggling operation."

"When were you going to tell me this?" Carmela demanded. "That you already apprehended Durrell, I mean." She was furious and pleased at the same time. Even though Babcock had kept her frantic and at bay, Durrell had been arrested. She hadn't blown the deal completely. That certainly helped ease her guilty conscience.

Babcock put his arms around Carmela and pulled her close. "All would have been revealed when I was good and ready."

"Like . . . now?" She felt herself starting to relax.

"Works for me," said Babcock.

"Two cases wrapped up nice and neat," said Carmela.

Babcock blinked and shook his head. "Not really that neat."

"Oh jeez!" said Carmela, suddenly pulling away from him. "I gotta call Ava! She's going to be wondering what's going on. I hung up on her awfully fast."

She walked a few steps away from him and got Ava on the phone.

"What's that, *cher*?" asked Ava, as soon as she picked up. "You'll have to speak up, there's a full-fledged marching band going by."

"We got him!" screamed Carmela. "We got Banister!"

But Ava was confused. "What are you talking about?" she asked. "The message I got was that you were going to Billy Laforge's place. Isn't Billy under arrest?"

"We did go there," said Carmela. "But he isn't. It's a long, complicated story. But hey, that photo you sent me? It pretty much blew the case wide open. It turns out Banister was the killer!"

"Banister?" said Ava, sounding really confused now. "He's the killer? Holy dingbats, Carmela!"

"He came out here to, I don't know what, try to shut everybody up, I suppose. But Babcock got him," said Carmela, walking back toward Babcock. "We'll be driving back shortly, so I promise I'll explain everything in detail as soon as I see you."

"But what about . . . uh . . . your fight with . . . I mean, are you and Babcock okay now?" asked Ava.

Carmela dropped the phone to her chest

and smiled at Babcock. "Ava wants to know if we're okay. Are we?"

There was a slight pause.

"What'd he say? What'd he say?" Ava's voice crackled anxiously over the phone.

But Carmela couldn't answer her. She was too busy being kissed by Babcock.

SCRAPBOOK, STAMPING, AND CRAFT TIPS FROM LAURA CHILDS

Tear Bears

Create your own tear bears by assembling torn pieces of fuzzy paper, such as mulberry paper. When gently pulled and torn, the edges will be fuzzy just like a real bear. Start by making a pattern on white paper — a circle for your teddy bear head, a pear-shaped torso, oblongs for the arms and legs, and several small circles to use as ears, muzzle, and paws. Trace your pattern onto your paper and then gently tear. Now assemble your bear, playing around with various poses before you glue it. Be sure to draw in eyes and a smile, then use your tear bear to hug a photo or point to a piece of artwork.

Ask a Question

You don't always need a declarative headline or title for your scrapbook page. You can ask a question, then let your photos and artwork answer that question. Examples might be: *What little boy just started school? She did what at camp? Who's got ten fingers and ten toes? Where on earth are Mom and Dad? The dog ate what?*

Cigar Box Purses

Cigar box purses are the ultimate blank canvas. They can be found at your local craft store for just a few dollars, but you can decorate them to look like a million! Consider creating an evening bag with gold paint, velvet accents, and some beads and charms. Or a summer purse covered with floral paper and accented with silk flowers. Or you can use ephemera, such as old photos, bits of lace, and a scrap of handwritten letter. Carry on!

Scrapbook Place Mats

For a special birthday or holiday celebration, why not personalize your place mats by scrapping them? Combine photos, rubber stamp images, fun visuals, and a poem or meaningful quote. Simply create one, then make color photocopies. Or, if you're doing digital scrapbooking, simply print them out on larger paper.

Calling Cards

It's simple to create your own business cards or personal calling cards. Start by going to an office supply store and ordering a rubber stamp with your name, address, phone number, and e-mail address on it. They will have lots of different typefaces for you to choose from. Then buy a pack of blank cards, or cut pieces of card stock into the standard 2-by-3 1/2-inch size. Then personalize your cards — by gluing on bits of paper, using various rubber stamps, or swooshing on some ink or paint. Then simply stamp on your name and information. If you need more than a few dozen cards, create your master card and take it to a quick printer.

Exotic Papers as Table Runners

Some of the fabulous papers that are available to scrappers are far lovelier than a plain white tablecloth or gold table runner. Choose a raised damask paper and combine it with a pair of elegant candlesticks. Or an organic batik paper paired with a centerpiece of fruit and flowers. Even a tie-dyed or paisley paper makes for a spectacular table runner.

Puff Paint

Several varieties of puff paint are available, and they are really terrific! Use this paint to add dimension to your scrapbook pages, squiggle designs on ornaments, and even decorate T-shirts and tennis shoes.

FAVORITE NEW ORLEANS RECIPES

Bon Tiempe's Chicken Jambalaya
1 Tbsp. oil
1 large onion, diced
1 green bell pepper, diced
1/4 cup water
4 small chicken breasts
1 can (14.5 oz.) whole peeled tomatoes, chopped, juice reserved
Garlic powder to taste
Onion powder to taste
Chili powder to taste
1 cup instant rice, uncooked

Heat the oil in a skillet and sauté the onion and bell pepper for about 5 minutes. Pour in the water and add the chicken. Cook for 15 minutes. Add the chopped tomatoes, including the juice they came in, and the garlic powder, onion powder, and chili powder. Simmer for 5 minutes. Stir in the instant rice, cover the pan, and remove from the heat. Let stand for 5 minutes, then mix well and serve. Serves 2 to 3.

TANDY'S NO-BAKE
PEANUT BUTTER BARS

2 cups peanut butter, divided
1 1/2 sticks butter, softened
2 cups powdered sugar, divided
3 cups graham cracker crumbs
2 cups semisweet chocolate chips, divided

In the bowl of an electric mixer, beat 1 1/4 cups of the peanut butter with the butter until creamy. Gradually beat in 1 cup of the powdered sugar. Using a wooden spoon, work in the remaining 1 cup powdered sugar. Add the graham cracker crumbs and 1/2 cup of the chocolate chips and mix well. Press the mixture into a greased 9-by-13-inch baking pan. Now melt the remaining 3/4 cup peanut butter and the remaining 1 1/2 cups chocolate chips in a saucepan over low heat, stirring constantly until smooth and creamy. Spread this topping over the graham cracker crust in pan. Refrigerate for 1 hour, then cut into bars. Store in the refrigerator. Enjoy!

SHRIMP AND TOMATO STEW

1 lb. large shrimp, without shells
2 Tbsp. butter
1 tsp. dried oregano
1 tsp. fresh cilantro
1 tsp. garlic powder
1/2 cup heavy cream
2 cups stewed tomatoes
1/4 cup lemon juice
1/2 tsp. ground nutmeg
1 Tbsp. brown sugar
Salt and pepper to taste

In a large pan, sauté the shrimp in the butter along with the oregano, cilantro, and garlic powder until the shrimp are pink. Add the cream and cook for 5 minutes. Add the tomatoes, lemon juice, nutmeg, and brown sugar and simmer gently for an additional 15 minutes, letting the flavors meld. Add salt and pepper to taste and serve over hot rice.

STRAWBERRY PECAN MUFFINS

3 cups all-purpose flour
2 cups sugar
1 Tbsp. cinnamon
1 tsp. baking soda
1 tsp. salt
4 medium eggs, beaten

2 1/2 cups fresh strawberries, hulled and
  sliced
1 cup vegetable oil
1 1/2 cups chopped pecans

Preheat the oven to 400 degrees F. In a large
bowl, combine the flour, sugar, cinnamon,
baking soda, and salt. In another bowl,
combine the beaten eggs, strawberries, and
oil. Add the egg mixture to the flour mixture
and mix together. Gently fold in the
chopped pecans. Drop the batter into
greased muffin tins, filling each cup about
2/3 full. Bake for 15 minutes.

SALTY-SWEET KETTLE CORN

1/4 cup vegetable oil
1/2 cup popcorn kernels
1/3 cup granulated sugar
1 tsp. salt

Heat the oil in a large pot over medium-
high heat. Add the popcorn and sugar, giving it a quick stir, then cover immediately
with the lid. Once the popcorn begins popping, shake your pot every few seconds for
3 or 4 minutes, until the popping slows
down. Remove from the heat immediately
(before the sugar caramelizes and sticks!)
and pour into a large bowl. Sprinkle with
salt and serve immediately.

HONEY CRUNCH CHICKEN

1 cup crushed Pepperidge Farm Golden Butter Crackers
2 eggs, beaten
4 skinless, boneless chicken breast halves
1/4 cup butter, cut into pieces
1/4 cup honey

Preheat the oven to 375 degrees F. Place the cracker crumbs in a shallow dish and the eggs in a second shallow dish. Dip the chicken in the egg, then dredge in the cracker crumbs until well coated. Arrange the chicken in a baking dish. Place small pieces of butter on and around the chicken. Drizzle the honey on top of the chicken. Bake for 40 to 45 minutes. Serves 2 for dinner, 4 for lunch. Excellent atop a small green salad.

RED ROOSTER COCKTAIL

4 cups cranberry juice
2 cups orange juice concentrate
1 cup vodka

Mix the ingredients well, then put into the freezer until slushy. Pour out into your favorite stemmed goblets and serve with a lemon twist.

SWEET POTATO BISCUITS

2 cups cooked, mashed sweet potatoes
1 stick butter, melted
1 1/2 cups milk
4 cups self-rising flour
Pinch of baking soda
3 Tbsp. sugar

Preheat the oven to 400 degrees F. Mix the sweet potatoes, butter, and milk together. Stir in the flour, baking soda, and sugar. Combine the mixture and knead the dough a few times. Roll the dough out to about 1″ thick. Cut out biscuits using a 2″ biscuit cutter. Place the biscuits on a greased pan and bake for 16 to 18 minutes until golden brown. Serve warm with butter!

SPICY RED BEANS AND RICE

1 cup rice, uncooked
2 Tbsp. oil
1 lb. smoked sausage, sliced
1 can (14 1/2 oz.) stewed tomatoes
1 can (16 oz.) red kidney beans, drained and rinsed
1/4 tsp. cayenne pepper
Salt to taste

Cook the rice in 2 1/2 cups water. While rice is cooking, heat a skillet over medium heat, add the oil, then add the sausage.

Cook for 3 to 5 minutes, until lightly browned. Add the tomatoes, then add the kidney beans, cayenne pepper, and salt. Bring to a boil and simmer for 10 minutes. When the rice is almost done, drain it and stir it into the sauce. Cook for an additional 2 to 3 minutes until the rice is completely done. Serves 4.

CAJUN MEAT LOAF

1 1/2 lb. ground beef
1/2 lb. sweet pork sausage
1 cup cheddar cheese, cubed or shredded
2 eggs
1 medium onion, chopped
1/2 green bell pepper, chopped
1 cup milk
1 cup dried bread crumbs
1 tsp. salt
1/2 tsp. black pepper
1 tsp. celery salt
1/2 tsp. paprika

Preheat the oven to 350 degrees F. Combine all of the ingredients in a large bowl. Go ahead and use your hands to make sure everything is well mixed together. Line a large baking pan with aluminum foil and grease it. Now transfer the meat to the pan and form into a long, fat loaf, about 5 by

10 inches. Bake for 60 to 70 minutes. Serve hot. Also can be served cold as a great filling for sandwiches!

MARDI GRAS MEATBALLS

Meatballs
2 lb. ground beef
1/2 cup crushed crackers
1/2 cup grated Parmesan cheese
2 eggs
1/4 cup onion, finely chopped
2 Tbsp. Worcestershire sauce
1/4 tsp. pepper
1/2 tsp. garlic powder
1/3 cup ketchup

Sauce
2 cups ginger ale
1 1/2 cups barbecue sauce
1/4 tsp. salt

Mix all of the meatball ingredients together, then form into 1" balls. Now combine the ginger ale, barbecue sauce, and salt in a large skillet. Bring to a boil, then add the meatballs. Simmer uncovered, stirring occasionally, for about 45 minutes, or until the meatballs are fully cooked. Makes a great appetizer!

ABOUT THE AUTHOR

Laura Childs is the *New York Times* best-selling author of the Cackleberry Club, Tea Shop, and Scrapbooking mysteries. In her past life she was a Clio Award–winning advertising writer and CEO of her own marketing firm. She lives in Minnesota.